Em dived into him and wrapped her arms around him.

Nick squeezed his eyes shut and sighed as he hugged her back. He rested his cheek atop her head, loving the warmth and feel of her body pressed to his.

All of the tricks he'd relied on these past few years to ignore his attraction to his best friend no longer seemed to work. A part of him wished they could stay like this forever. He immediately thought of that last night they were together in Tulum. The night he'd almost kissed her. He hadn't done it because he'd realized the inherent risk of disrupting the dynamics of their friendship. It was a risk that he hadn't been willing to take. He'd made the same choice again last night. So now, he needed to be her friend and support Em the same way she'd always supported him.

"Thanks, Nick." Em finally pulled out of his embrace, creating a vacuum where her warmth and comforting scent had once been. "You have no idea how much this means to me."

"But I do know how much *you* mean to me." Nick shoved a hand into his pocket. "So whatever you need, just ask."

ALSO BY REESE RYAN

Second Chance on Cypress Lane
Return to Hummingbird Way

The soulmate project

REESE RYAN

FOREVER

New York Boston

Forever
Hachette Book Group
1290 Avenue of the Americas, New York, NY 10104
read-forever.com
@readforeverpub

First Edition: October 2024

Forever is an imprint of Grand Central Publishing. The Forever name and logo are registered trademarks of Hachette Book Group, Inc.

The publisher is not responsible for websites (or their content) that are not owned by the publisher.

The Hachette Speakers Bureau provides a wide range of authors for speaking events. To find out more, go to hachettespeakersbureau.com or email HachetteSpeakers@hbgusa.com.

Forever books may be purchased in bulk for business, educational, or promotional use. For information, please contact your local bookseller or the Hachette Book Group Special Markets Department at special.markets@hbgusa.com.

ISBNs: 978-1-5387-3450-6 (mass market), 978-1-5387-3451-3 (ebook)

Printed in the United States of America

BVGM

10 9 8 7 6 5 4 3 2

Dedicated to Tonie Jones.

You were such a phenomenal person. Funny, smart, adventurous, caring, and nurturing. You had so much weight on your shoulders. Yet you always bore it with love and grace. You were a loving daughter, sister, mother, grandmother, and friend. The world feels emptier without you in it.

I'm thankful for the knucklehead boy who brought us together when we were twelve. For the unforgettable trip we took together to New York. And for all the laughs and incredible memories. You were a better friend than I deserved. I love you, and I miss you. Rest well, sweet friend. Rest well.

Acknowledgments

Thank you to the Grand Central Forever Team for giving my Holly Grove Island series a home. Thank you to the readers who've read and loved this series. Your support means so much! And thank you, Sarah and Lesley, for your continued encouragement and support. I'm so fortunate to have writing partners like you in my corner.

The
soulmate
project

Chapter One

●─◆─●─◆─●

Emerie Roberts sank onto her beach blanket at Holly Grove Island's annual New Year's Eve Bonfire. The flames licked high, waving in the gentle breeze and casting their orange glow over the native islanders and a smattering of tourists gathered around the fire.

"What's with the face, sugar plum?" Sinclair Buchanan nudged Em's shoulder. Sin's East Carolina accent got a bit twangier with each celebratory drink. "You look like someone done kidnapped your dog and stole your man."

Em didn't have either, but she got the point of Sin's colorful statement.

She'd been mesmerized by bonfires from the first time she'd seen one. And there was something special about spending the day at the beach in the dead of the mild, coastal North Carolina winter. She got to hang out with her friends, family, and neighbors. They played games, and sometimes the town would show a movie. There were fun sing-alongs. Then there was all the delicious food. Everyone in town had their own special New Year's Eve Bonfire recipe, and they always brought enough to share.

As a teenager, she and her friends would spend the evening

stargazing, playing truth or dare, and imagining what their futures would be like. Her friends spent the evening talking about and flirting with the boys, but Em was a tomboy who was more interested in playing ball with the guys than kissing one.

The New Year's Eve Bonfire had always been the high-light of her year, but tonight, she couldn't muster her usual enthusiasm.

"I'm fine." Emerie forced a smile, hoping to dispel the growing concern on Sinclair's face. Her gaze drifted toward where her longtime best friend, Nicholas Washington, was chatting up some tourist.

Nick was an exec at the local resort and a talented drummer. He was smart, handsome, and Holly Grove Island's resident playboy. He seemed to have eyes for every pretty, single girl who'd graced the island—except for her. To Nick, she would always be one of the guys.

"So this is about our discussion on Christmas Eve." Sin lowered her voice, her gaze following Em's. "You still haven't told Nick how you really feel about him?"

"Shh!" Em hushed her friend, glancing around to see if anyone might've overheard.

"I'll take that as a no." Sin heaved a sigh. "You said you were going to talk to him."

"I said I'd *think* about talking to him," Em reminded her. "And for the past week, I haven't been able to think of much else."

"Listen here, Emerie Roberts..." Sin burrowed her red plastic cup in the sand, then held Em's hands in hers. "You are so sweet and kind. You go out of your way to take care of the people you love: family, friends, neighbors. I admire that about you, Em. But it's time you do something for yourself. So think about this and answer honestly... what is it that *you* want, sweet pea?"

The sting of tears pricking Em's eyes came on suddenly. She swallowed hard, refusing to let them fall.

She was the last unmarried member of her high school friend group. Something Em had become increasingly aware of with each engagement party, wedding, baby shower, and christening.

Em leveled her gaze with Sin's—who patiently awaited her response. She held up the other woman's hand, her engagement ring sparkling in the moonlight.

"I want what you and Rett have." Em nodded toward her cousin, who was Sin's fiancé. "And what Dex and Dakota have." She indicated her oldest brother and his wife, who was Sin's best friend. It was something she'd been afraid to admit, even to herself. But a part of her was glad she had Sin to confide in. Sinclair wasn't just a friend. Em regarded her and Dakota as older sisters. "I'm the only person on this island who isn't moving forward with their life. I'm stuck in this holding pattern, spinning my wheels."

"That isn't true." Sin squeezed Em's hand, her voice filled with compassion. "You've come a long way, too. You made a major career change and started your own business. And your clientele is growing."

"True." Em had worked in accounting at a factory off-island where she'd dreaded every single minute of her day inside her windowless office. Two years ago, she'd started picking up freelance graphic design jobs—utilizing the discipline she'd minored in and truly had a passion for. Six months ago, the business had grown enough that she'd quit her job and become a full-time entrepreneur.

"You took a calculated risk with your career. And you're much happier now because you had the courage to go after what you wanted."

"True," Em said again.

Her brows furrowed as Nick flashed the effortless smile that no single woman in his orbit could seem to resist. Miss Ohio or Michigan, or wherever it was he'd said she was from, giggled and tossed her blond box braids over one shoulder.

"So tell Nick how you feel about him," Sin urged. "Yes, the conversation will be uncomfortable. And I understand that the possibility of things changing between you two is probably terrifying. But bottling up your feelings for Nick isn't healthy, hon."

"What if I tell Nick, and he doesn't feel the way I do?" She'd posed the same question to Sin a week ago. Unsurprisingly, Sin's response hadn't changed.

"Then at least you'll know, and you can move on. Besides, as my granny always said, 'Closed mouths don't get fed.' So put on your big-girl panties and tell that man how you feel. *Now.* Or you will always regret not doing it."

Em inhaled deeply. Sin was right. What if Miss Midwest was the woman who finally persuaded Nick Washington to settle down? She would be devastated that she hadn't been brave enough to shoot her shot.

"I can't win if I'm not in the race, right?" Em mumbled more to herself than Sin.

"Damn straight." Sin raised her red cup, then took a sip.

"Okay. I'll talk to Nick. *Tonight.*"

"Thattagirl!" Sinclair hugged her tight.

Em leaned into it, needing the reassurance.

"Everything okay?" Rett ambled over.

Her cousin was cool and laid-back. The perfect complement to Sin's fiery, high-energy personality. One of the many reasons they were so perfect for each other.

"Everything is fine. Em and I were just having a little girl talk." Sin extended her free hand. "Help a girl up?"

Rett pulled Sin to her feet and into his arms. She rewarded him with a tender kiss.

"I love you two, but you're annoyingly adorable," Em grumbled, and they both laughed.

"Sorry?" Rett shrugged.

"You're blocking my view of the bonfire with your PDA; go enjoy your soon-to-be-wedded bliss on your own beach blanket," Em teased.

Rett grinned. "Love you, kid."

"Love you, too, cuz." Em grinned as they walked away, hand in hand.

Rett and Sin had been mortal enemies with secret crushes on each other back when their best friends—Dexter and Dakota—had dated in high school. While helping to plan the couple's wedding earlier that year, they'd gotten to truly know each other, and they'd fallen in love.

Em was at the Christmas Eve party last week when Rett proposed to Sin and gifted her with a fur baby—an adorable black-and-white Havapoo puppy named Stella. She was happy for them. Still, she couldn't help wishing that her happy ending was at least on the horizon.

Em folded her arms and placed them atop her knees as she stared into the bonfire, replaying her conversation with Sinclair.

What if I tell Nick and he doesn't feel the way I do?

Then at least you'll know. And you can move on.

But moving on seemed more frightening than holding on to her unrequited feelings for Nick—an agony to which she'd become accustomed.

"Hey, Em, what's wrong?" Nick settled onto the blanket beside her, his dark eyes narrowing with concern. He draped an arm over her shoulders, as he had so many times before, oblivious to his effect on her.

Her temperature rose as the warmth of his skin penetrated hers through their light jackets. Her heart beat faster as she inhaled Nick's familiar, subtle citrus and cedarwood scent. His wide shoulders and broad chest shielded Em from the chilly breeze blowing off the Atlantic Ocean.

"You're not yourself tonight. You're usually hoisting the cornhole trophy by now, but I haven't seen you pick up a beanbag once. You weren't even into the sing-along, which you love. And I'm pretty sure you've only had one plate tonight, so something is *definitely* wrong."

"Who are you, my mother?" Em groused, her eyes squeezing shut involuntarily as she settled against her best friend, her skin on fire and her pulse racing. "Maybe I'm just tired. Did you consider that?"

Em opened her eyes, turning to look at him. *Big mistake.*

Bathed in the soft moonlight and the glow of the raging fire, the man looked like a freaking god with his cocoa-brown skin; soulful, dark eyes that managed to be both warm and mysterious; and a half smile that always hinted at mischief or some tightly held secret. All he lacked was a thunderbolt or maybe the Tesseract, if Thor and Loki weren't using them.

"C'mon, Em." Nick's dark eyes glinted. His voice was a low, sensual whisper that sent a shiver down her spine and created a shudder in a place she was trying *really* hard not to think about right now. "I know when something's up with you. Might as well spill it because you know I'll figure it out."

True.

From their meeting as kids, he seemed to understand her in a way no one else did. Even when she'd been reluctant to express how she was feeling about something, Nick had always been so perceptive. He'd been there through everything from mean girls teasing her because she was a tomboy to her first crush and every relationship that had crashed and burned since. He'd been there through the rough patches in her parents' marriage and their eventual divorce.

So how was it that Nick managed to know her so well, yet seemed clueless about her falling for him?

She'd realized that she was attracted to her best friend during their vacation together in Mexico five years ago. But she'd moved back to Holly Grove Island, and he'd lived in Los Angeles at the time. It had seemed best to ignore her perplexing new feelings for Nick.

But they were now in their thirties, living in the same city for the first time since college. They spent most of their free time hanging out together. So it was getting harder to ignore the romantic feelings she'd developed for her childhood friend.

Nothing about Nick's demeanor suggested he felt the same.

"C'mon, Em. Whatever it is...you can tell me." Nick leaned in, his face inches from hers. His warm breath, carrying a hint of whiskey and some sort of pie, mingled with the cool, crisp sea air, creating steam. "If someone upset you, point him out. You know I've got you."

A pained smile curved Emerie's lips. She and Nick had met when Dexter and Dakota brought them along on their date to see an animated children's film. She was Dex's little sister. Nick was Dakota's next-door neighbor, whom she looked after when his parents were away on business. They became friends instantly, and despite Em already having three older brothers, Nick assumed the role of her protector.

They'd attended college on opposite coasts. Yet, Nick had been ready to hop on a plane or drive across the country anytime she needed him. She was a grown woman fully capable of taking care of herself. Yet, Nick's sense of protectiveness hadn't waned.

"It's not like that." Em stared into the fire. "So don't go breaking out the boxing gloves, Baby Creed."

"But it is *something*." Nick didn't address the *Creed* movie reference, which he always found irritating.

Was it her fault Nick looked like Michael B. Jordan's long-lost cousin?

"So what's going on with you tonight? The bonfire is your favorite event of the year."

Em drew in a deep breath, her eyes squeezing shut. Her heart pounded as Sin's words echoed in her head.

Then at least you'll know.

"No one has done anything to upset me, Nick." Em wrapped her arms around her knees. "It's just…" The sound of rushing blood filled her ears, dampening the sound of the swirling wind and the waves crashing against the shore of Holly Grove Island Beach. "I like someone, and I'm not sure how they feel about me."

"You're wondering if you should say something first." Nick rubbed his whiskered chin and nodded knowingly.

"Something like that." Em waved and smiled at Marcus and Elliot: two locals heading back inside Blaze of Glory.

"But it's neither of those guys, right?" Nick tipped his chin by way of greeting but didn't smile at either of them. "Because Marcus is a dick and Elliot is a mama's boy."

"You're terrible, Nick."

He'd always been able to make her laugh when she was uneasy about something. From a bad case of nerves before the fifth-grade spelling bee to a near-meltdown before a big client presentation two weeks ago, Nick could always get her to relax and reset.

"Maybe, but I didn't hear you say I was wrong about

them." Nick stretched out on Em's blanket. "So please tell me it's neither of those knuckleheads."

"It isn't."

"Okay. But it is *someone*." Nick propped himself up, one elbow on the blanket, as he glanced up at her. "Is it Derrick? Or Paul down at the garage? Wait…" He bolted upright and frowned. "You realize Blaze is *way* too old for you, right?"

"No, he isn't. He's like forty-five."

"And you're thirty-one," Nick noted. "Don't get me wrong, Blaze is a great guy. He'd give you the shirt off his back. But—"

"It's not Blaze or Derrick or Paul, all right?" Em huffed. She turned to face her friend, her heart thudding in her chest and her hands trembling. "It's *you*, all right?"

"*Me*?" Nick's eyes went wide, and he poked a thumb to his chest as he whispered the word. He stared at her as if he was awaiting the punchline of a poorly delivered joke. When she didn't respond, Nick rubbed his forehead and cleared his throat. "Oh."

Not the response I was hoping for.

This confession of love was an absolute disaster. She should say something, but she wasn't quite sure what. It was too early to claim it'd been an April Fools' joke.

The few torturous seconds in which neither of them spoke felt like millennia. Heat spread through Em's chest and filled her cheeks. Her breathing was quick and shallow.

Was this what a panic attack was like?

It felt like a whale had washed ashore and rolled onto her chest. She focused on the sounds of the waves hitting the shore, the laughter of their friends and neighbors, and the crackling of the fire as it consumed the wood.

She'd *finally* admitted her feelings for Nick. There was no turning back. She'd been surprised by her initial attraction to her best friend. Maybe Nick needed to sort through his feelings for her, too.

"Yes, *you*, Nick." Emerie forced her eyes to meet his and struggled to keep her lips from quivering and her hands from shaking. "You really haven't ever thought of me that way?"

Nick winced, his brows furrowing.

Em knew her friend well, too. The apology in his expression was a clear negative response.

Her stomach twisted in knots, and her cheeks stung with embarrassment.

"Em, you're my best friend. You know how much you mean to me. That I would do anything for you. But..."

"But you're not into me like that." Em whispered the words beneath her breath, saying them more to herself than to him. She swallowed hard and nodded. "I get it."

"You're beautiful, fun, amazing. Any guy would be lucky to have you." Nick squeezed her arm.

"Any guy but you, right?" Em blinked back the tears that burned her eyes. She sniffled. "Roger that."

"There are a lot of things I do well, Em. Being in a serious relationship isn't one of them. The friendship we have...We can't risk losing that. *I* can't risk losing *you*." Nick pointed at himself, then at her. "You're the smart, sensible one, Em. So deep down, you know what I'm saying is true." He nudged her shoulder.

The temperature seemed at least ten degrees colder. Em shivered in response to the sudden chill deep in her bones.

Don't freak out. Just play it cool.

"You're right. Of course." She forced a smile. "It was the alcohol talking. Let's just pretend this conversation never happened."

"That's probably best," Nick agreed.

His phone vibrated, as it so often did with text messages or phone calls. It seemed like the perfect cue for her to take her leave. Em climbed to her feet and dusted the sand off the back of her jeans. "I'm gonna head inside, chat up Blaze, and get another drink. Can I get you anything?"

"I'm good. Thanks," Nick said.

Em headed toward Blaze of Glory, eager to end the painfully awkward conversation that would forever make things weird between them.

"Em!"

She stopped, then turned around.

Nick was standing. His handsome features were marred with worry. "We're good, right?"

"That whole weird, awkward conversation never really happened, right?" Em shrugged. "So why wouldn't we be?"

"Right." Nick tilted his head. "And you won't do anything...impulsive tonight?"

"A sensible girl like me?" Em asked incredulously. "Don't worry, I'll be fine. You should go find Miss Ohio. I'm pretty sure she's looking for you."

Em hurried toward the bar. She needed a strong drink, the comfort of sinfully decadent carbs, and to forget what had just happened between her and Nick.

Why on earth had she listened to Sinclair?

Chapter Two

Nick stood on the beach watching his friend—who was in full flight mode—scramble across the beach like that perfect ass of hers was on fire.

Nick cursed under his breath, their conversation replaying in his head as he considered the dozen ways he could've better handled the painfully awkward situation.

He'd botched things with Em, and he wasn't sure how to fix it. Em was upset and embarrassed, and he hated that he'd been the one to hurt her.

Nick's first impulse was to go after Em and assure her this was no big deal and it wouldn't affect their friendship. But that would be thoughtless, not to mention absolute bullshit.

If overthinking was a sport, his best friend would be an Olympic gold medalist. There was no way Emerie Roberts had admitted to having feelings for him without thinking through the consequences more times than she could count. Therefore, her confession was a big fucking deal. And they both knew it.

It had taken guts for Em to make that admission.

It would be disingenuous of him to pretend it hadn't

already changed the dynamic between them. But Em was his closest friend. They'd find a way to work through it. Because they'd always been honest with each other.

So why had he lied to Em, saying he'd never thought of them together?

Nick squeezed his eyes shut and tried to calmly think through the best way to handle this. He felt like shit for hurting Em and for lying to her for the first time in his memory.

Of course he was attracted to Em. There was something incredibly sexy about the woman, despite the fact that she went out of her way to *not* look sexy in a traditional sense.

Em lived in either shorts or a series of comfy leggings— all of them black or a bold print with a black background. She wore the things until they damn near disintegrated. The inner thighs were threadbare, and the fabric over the knees was thin. On a "special occasion," like tonight, she'd wear a pair of jeans. A well-worn T-shirt and a pair of Converses completed her look. The majority of her fashion budget was spent on kicks. Em was a first-class sneaker head.

Still, anything Emerie wore clung to her toned, athletic body, highlighting each of its assets. Lean, strong arms and shoulders. Firm, perky breasts that weren't especially small or particularly large. Just the perfect mouthful. Strong, toned thighs. A firm, curvy ass honed over two decades of track, tennis, and beach volleyball. And she was infinitely confident in her body regardless of what she was wearing.

When Nick moved back home, he'd quickly learned to employ a series of Jedi mind tricks to avoid thinking of Em in a sexual way. Because despite his physical attraction to her, there were too many variables at play.

What if she was less adventurous in bed than he was? What if one or both of them got bored with the relationship?

What if they were simply better as friends? What would happen to their friendship then?

So despite the fact that he'd imagined taking his friend to bed more than he'd care to admit, gambling with their friendship would be too big a risk. One that could destroy the relationship that was most important to him.

Instead, Nick forced himself to look past the incredibly enticing wrapper and focus on the core of who Em was and all the reasons she was and would always be his best friend. As long as he didn't fuck things up. And there was no quicker way to torpedo a perfectly good friendship than by trying to add love into the mix. He should know; he'd tried it twice.

He'd dated a friend in college, and it had ended badly. They made great friends but terrible lovers. There was the sexual incompatibility, the sudden clinginess, and the jealousy of his friends—male and female. When he suggested they go back to being friends, she'd been devastated, and he'd felt like a jerk. Needless to say, the friendship hadn't survived.

Years later, he was the drummer for the house band at a club in LA. His friendship with the lead vocalist progressed into a romantic relationship, and he'd fallen hard for the woman who was ten years older. She got her dream gig with an emerging rock band and abruptly ended the relationship before moving to New York. Nick had been gutted. He'd honestly never known heartbreak like that.

He'd promised himself that he would never date another close friend. He was supposed to be older and wiser now. So he wouldn't repeat the same mistake. He couldn't afford to this time. His friendship with Em and their circle of friends—which included much of her family—meant the world to him.

They'd met when he was struggling with his parents being busy and away so much. He'd been grumpy and with-drawn. Sometimes, he'd acted out, getting in trouble in school. And he'd been determined not to enjoy the theater outing Dakota had taken him on. But then his surrogate big sister had introduced him to Emerie Roberts.

There had been something so sweet and compassionate about her—even as a little girl. He'd practically scowled at her when they'd been introduced. But while they were stand-ing in the concession line, Em had given him the biggest smile and hugged him tight, taking him by surprise. Before he could pull out of the hug, she'd whispered that she'd be sad, too, if she ever had to leave all her friends and family behind.

There was something cathartic...almost enchanting... about that hug. He felt seen—his pain acknowledged in a way that wasn't condescending. The suffocating anger and resentment he'd held on to for so long had slowly dissi-pated...like a deflated balloon. He could breathe again for the first time since they'd moved to the island.

When she'd finally released him from the hug, Em had said she was sorry he'd lost all his friends back home, but that she'd like to be his friend. Still stunned, he'd accepted her offer. They'd been best friends ever since.

Nick rubbed his forehead and sighed.

Em needed some time and space. He couldn't bear the thought of her at the bar, crying in her beer while she chat-ted up some random tourist. But he definitely wasn't the person she'd want to see right now.

"Hey, Nick. Have you seen, Em?" Kassandra Montgom-ery asked. The shy, sweet program director of Holly Grove Island's aquarium and arboretum approached. Her sing-song voice always made it sound like she was apologizing for one thing or another.

Kassie was Em's closest female friend. The two women had known each other since middle school but became close while Nick was living in LA.

He'd once teased Kass about trying to steal his best friend, and the woman had actually apologized. Maybe humor wasn't Kass's strong suit, but she'd been a good friend to Em, and she was the perfect person for this situation. If he asked Sinclair or Dakota to check on Em, they'd ply him with forty questions about what he'd done to upset her.

"Em just headed inside the bar. She's a bit...upset," he said. "Would you mind going to check on her?"

"Oh no!" Kassie pushed her glasses up her nose. "I mean...yes, of course, I'll check on Em. I'll go look for her now."

"Thank you." Nick breathed a sigh of relief as he gazed toward Blaze of Glory. Several people were seated at the tables on the restaurant's back deck or going in or out of the place. Em wasn't among them.

"Wait...why can't *you* check on Em?" Kass folded her arms. "What did you do?"

Nick groaned quietly and lowered his head. "I didn't do anything...*exactly*. But I'm probably not the person she wants to see right now. Could you just do me a solid and check on Em?"

"Of course." Kassie gave him a suspicious stare.

"Great. Could you text me and let me know that she's okay? *Please*?" Nick cleared his throat, realizing that his voice had taken on a pleading tone.

Kassie pulled out her phone and added a new contact before handing it to him. "Fine. Type your number in there. I'll let you know when I've found her and if she's okay. I won't provide any details beyond that unless Em asks me to."

Sweet little Kassie wasn't a pushover after all. Good for her.

"Thanks, Kass. I appreciate this." Nick typed his number and name into Kassie's phone, then handed it back to her.

"I'm doing this for Em." Kassie shoved her phone into her back pocket. "But you're welcome." She headed toward Blaze of Glory. "I'll text you when I've found our girl."

Nick shoved a hand through his short curls and sighed. He wanted to believe that one day soon what happened tonight would feel like the distant past, and they'd joke about it over a beer while watching a game.

But the growing uneasiness in the pit of his stomach indicated otherwise.

———

Em sat at a wobbly table in a dark corner of the bar and wolfed down a mound of fries drowned in cheese, bacon, pulled pork, and jalapeños. She grabbed the table just as a couple was leaving to join the bonfire. She'd hardly eaten tonight, and now she was making up for it.

"Emerie! Nick sent me in here to check on you. Are you all right?" Kassie stood over her table, her dark hair pulled back into a low ponytail.

"I thought you said you weren't in the mood to go out tonight," Em mumbled through a mouthful of fries.

"I thought about what you said." Kassie shrugged, plopping onto the seat across from Em. "You're right. I need to get out more and live a little. Even my parents went out tonight. They're at that pricey New Year's Eve party hosted by the resort. But you didn't answer my question. What did Nick say to send you face-first into a tower of fries, and how badly do I need to hurt him?"

They both laughed. Sweet, mild-mannered Kassie Montgomery wouldn't hurt a fly. But Emerie appreciated the support. Em's laughter gave way to tears. She brushed them from her cheeks, which were stinging with the heat of embarrassment.

"Oh, sweetie." Kassie placed a gentle hand on Em's arm. "Seriously, hon, what's wrong?"

"Not really in the mood to talk about it." Em stuffed a few more fries in her mouth.

"Prefer to eat your feelings instead?" Kassie raised an eyebrow and stole a few fries from Em's plate. "Hmm... feelings are delicious."

Em's mouth curved in a half smile at her friend's attempt to cheer her up. She huffed, wiping her hands on a napkin. "I should just go home."

"Before the countdown begins in"—Kassie looked down at her fitness wearable—"twenty minutes?" Kassie looked alarmed. "You look forward to the countdown every year."

Em considered her friend's words. She hadn't missed a New Year's Eve countdown on Holly Grove Island Beach since she was a kid. Was she really going to break her streak because she was behaving like a temperamental child who hadn't gotten what she wanted?

"You're right. I can't leave before midnight." Em sniffled, then forced a smile. "I'm being silly about this."

God bless her sweet friend. Kassie didn't ask what *this* was—even though the question burned behind her big, brown, soulful eyes.

"Can I get you two anything else?" Blaze, the owner of Blaze of Glory, asked as he loaded plates from another table onto a tray. The older man was handsome with his freckles and the head of coppery-red hair that had earned him the nickname Blaze.

"Two Long Island iced teas, please?" Em said before Kassie could say no thanks.

"Sure thing, Cupcake." Blaze winked, then made his way through the crowd.

He'd been calling her that since she was about fourteen and had accidentally walked directly into him one day when he was in town on leave from the Marines. She'd been holding one of the most delicious cupcakes she'd ever eaten, and it got smashed all over his fatigues.

Blaze had been calling her Cupcake ever since. More so whenever they'd found themselves in competition. Like when they ended up on opposing teams at one town event or another.

"I need to text Nick." Kass pulled her cell phone from her back pocket.

"Why?" Panic gripped Em's chest.

"He's the one who sent me looking for you." Kassie typed out a message. "I'll let him know you're okay ..." She glanced up from her phone. "Unless there's something else you'd prefer that I say."

"No. That's good." Why had it sent her into a panic thinking there might be something between her friend and Nick? He clearly didn't have feelings for her. "I just didn't realize that you and Nick had each other's cell numbers."

"Relax, *bestie*." Kassie could barely hide her amusement. "Nick and I exchanged numbers just now so I could let him know you're okay. Once I send the message, I'll delete his number, if you'd like."

"No. I don't ... I mean ... why would I care?"

"Maybe because you're *clearly* in love with the man," Kassie said.

"Shh!" Em shushed one of her friends for the second time that night. "Can we please not broadcast it to the entire town?"

Gossip rolled through Holly Grove Island quicker than a forest fire could consume a stand of trees during a drought. Em preferred being a consumer of town gossip to being the subject of it. The last thing she needed was for Nick's rejection to become the first headline of the new year.

"Here you go, Cupcake. Two Long Island iced teas." Blaze set them on the table and waved Em off when she reached for her credit card. "This round is on the house."

He tapped the table and gave her what she was pretty sure was a look of pity.

Emerie glared at her friend.

"Sorry." Kassie sipped her Long Island iced tea. "But at least we scored free drinks."

"Well, there is that." Em sipped her drink, too. Blaze had been generous with the vodka, rum, gin, and tequila. So maybe the humiliation of him knowing she had a thing for her best friend was a fair trade-off.

"Is that what this is about? Did you finally tell Nick how you feel about him?"

"Seriously, did everyone in town know except for Nick?" Em asked.

Kassie shrugged and sipped more of her drink, then nibbled on a few fries.

"It's a quarter till midnight, folks!" Blaze barked, tapping his watch. "Last call before we close the bar down until after the fireworks."

Blaze could be a grumpy smart-ass, but he was good to his employees. Every year, he closed the bar down during the countdown and fireworks so his staff could enjoy the town traditions, too.

"C'mon. We don't want to miss the fireworks." Emerie stood, slipping her arm through Kassie's when her friend stood, too.

They made their way toward the bonfire. "We'll talk about my disastrous night over brunch tomorrow."

"Another chance to eat and drink our feelings?" Kassie teased. "I'm here for it."

"Perfect."

"Emerie! Kassie!" Em's cousin Isabel—Garrett's younger sister—hugged each of them excitedly. "The countdown is starting soon."

"Then we should get out there before it begins." Em widened her smile, hoping Izzy wouldn't notice her red-rimmed eyes.

The three of them laughed and chatted, warming themselves around the bonfire. They joined everyone in counting down to the new year, then celebrated with hugs and a sip of their drinks.

Em's gaze was drawn to where Dexter, Dakota, Rett, and Sinclair stood. The high school friends—one couple married with a young daughter, the other engaged—were among the many couples who greeted the new year by sharing a kiss. Both couples had gotten their well-deserved happy endings, and Em was thrilled for them.

So why did her joy for them evoke a deep, gnawing sadness for herself?

Maybe because she was heading into another new year with no prospect of finding the kind of bliss Dex and Rett had.

It wasn't that she felt incomplete without a partner. But watching her friends and family find happiness in relationships and start families made Em realize she wanted that, too. And she wanted it with Nick.

Em glanced over to where her lifelong best friend stood. Nick stared in her direction, his eyes filled with concern. His mouth curved in a soft smile, and he mouthed the words "Happy New Year."

"Happy New..." Before Em could finish the words, Miss Ohio stepped in front of Nick and kissed him as she presumably wished him a Happy New Year.

Em's face was hot, and her heart ached. She shifted her gaze to where Sin and Rett stood together. Rett's arms were wrapped around Sin's waist from behind as he nuzzled her neck and Sin giggled, looking happier than Emerie had ever seen her.

Maybe taking Sin's advice to talk to Nick had backfired. But her admonition to get it together and go for what she wanted was solid advice.

Em wanted love and meaningful companionship. A soulmate. Someone she could plan a life and start a family with. If Nick wasn't her soulmate, she would find the man who was.

The perfect guy wouldn't just land in her lap. She had to be proactive about finding him and about creating the life she wanted for herself.

Emerie stared at the raging bonfire and made a promise to herself. This time next year, she'd be standing here with the man she could see having a future with.

That was the objective. Now she needed a plan to make it happen.

Chapter Three

Emerie took her first bite of the crisp, fluffy Belgian waffles with warm peach syrup at The Foxhole's annual New Year's Day brunch. She murmured with pleasure, then nibbled on a strip of delicious, perfectly crisp bacon. The combination was so good, Em was pretty sure she was humming.

"I'm glad that you're feeling much better today." Kassie grinned, then shoveled a forkful of pancakes drenched in homemade blueberry syrup into her mouth.

"Me, too." Em smiled broadly before slicing into her fried egg.

Last night had been devastating. And though today had started out rough, she'd gone to bed in the wee hours of the morning with clarity and an actionable plan. Her chest felt lighter, and she was clearer about her goals for her personal life than she'd ever been.

"I was worried about you at the bonfire last night," Kass admitted, a pained frown on her beautiful face. "So was Nick."

Em's shoulders stiffened at the mention of her best friend's name. She dropped her fork onto her plate with a loud clang that drew the attention of nearby diners.

She cleared her throat, picked up her fork, and resumed eating. "I appreciate your concern. But I'm fine now."

"Fine enough to talk about what happened last night?" Kassie stabbed a sausage link.

Emerie sighed quietly. She looked forward to sharing her exciting new life plan with her friend. But first, she needed to level with Kassie about what had prompted it.

"Last night, I told Nick I like him as more than a friend." Em shoveled more waffles into her mouth.

"You've always insisted that you and Nick were just friends. When did that change?"

"You mean when did I actually fall for my best friend, or when did I stop lying to myself about it?" Em asked.

"Both." Kassie's kind smile eased the tension that knotted Emerie's shoulders.

"You've been spending too much time around me. You're a lot more direct now."

"Thank you." Kassie batted her eyelashes and grinned. She pointed at Em with her fork. "Now stop stalling. When did you first realize that you'd fallen for Nick?"

"When we vacationed together in Tulum a few years before he returned to town." Em shoved food around her plate with her fork.

"That was when he'd broken up with his girlfriend or something and had already paid for the trip, right?"

Em nodded. "It was an incredible trip. We explored the Mayan ruins, then laid out on the sand at Playa Ruinas, this beautiful beach at the foot of the cliff where El Castillo—the largest of the ruins—is perched. We swam in the crystal-clear, aquamarine waters of the Caribbean Sea. Nick taught me the basics of surfing. We explored the town and had some amazing meals at the best little hole-in-the-wall restaurants recommended by locals."

"Sounds enchanting and very romantic," Kassie said.

"It was." A smile spread across Em's face as she recalled their time in Mexico. It had been her first and only trip out of the country.

"At night, we'd share this king-size bed in the room he'd booked. We'd lie awake all night talking and laughing. I looked over at him at like two in the morning the last night we were there and...I just knew things had changed for me. That I didn't just see Nick as a friend."

Em squeezed her eyes shut briefly, and it felt like she was back in Tulum on that humid night, the windows open and the wind rustling the curtains.

"There was a moment when I thought Nick was going to kiss me...but then he didn't." Em shrugged.

"Why didn't you kiss him?" Kassie asked.

It was a question she'd asked herself many times.

How different might their lives have been if she'd found the courage to kiss Nick that night in Tulum?

"He'd just broken up with his girlfriend. We were literally on the vacation he'd planned to surprise her with." Em nibbled on a piece of bacon. "The timing was terrible. Besides, Nick was living out west then, and I was here on the island. Neither of us is the long-distance type."

"But Nick's been back for a while now. Why haven't you said anything since his return?"

"Nick hasn't been in many serious relationships. But I'm pretty sure he was in love with Aliza. When she suddenly ended things, he was heartbroken. Since then, he seems determined not to let anyone in. I've been hurt before, too. So I figured that Nick needed to process things in his own way before he'd be ready to get serious with anyone again."

"Is that the only thing that kept you from speaking up?" Kassie asked the question as if she already knew the answer.

Em frowned. She both loved and hated that her friends knew her so well.

"I'm the polar opposite of the glamorous, runway-worthy women Nick dates." Em sipped her mimosa.

"You're a toned, athletic, sporty girl. But you are *not* the opposite of glamorous." Kassie jabbed her fork in Em's direction, indignant on her behalf. "Why are you comparing yourself to those women anyway? Nick clearly adores you."

"I know he does." Em's chest ached all over again. "But he's never looked at me the way he looks at them." She sniffled, determined not to shed another tear over Nick Washington. "I buried my feelings because I didn't want to risk what happened last night."

"What did happen last night?" Kassie's voice was soft.

Em's stomach knotted as she recounted the details of her failed confession. When she was done, she ordered another round of mimosas.

"I'm sorry, Em." Kassie squeezed her wrist. "But I'm also really proud of you. It was brave of you to confess your feelings to Nick."

"Thanks." Em dabbed the corners of her eyes with a napkin. "But I wish I hadn't. Then things wouldn't be weird between us now."

"Is that why you've been ignoring his calls?" Kassie nodded to Em's phone, which was buzzing with another call from Nick.

He'd called once last night and twice that morning. She wasn't ignoring his calls because she was angry at him. Last night had been humiliating. She wasn't ready to face her friend yet. Not even via a phone call.

"Nick was really worried about you," Kassie said. "I know you wish things had turned out differently. But last night was tough for him, too."

Em glanced up from her mimosa and frowned. She'd been so consumed with her own disappointment and misery, she hadn't considered how the conversation might've impacted Nick.

"I hadn't thought about that." She set her glass down and folded her arms on the table. "But he seemed to recover quickly enough with Miss Ohio."

"As I recall, *she* kissed him," Kassie noted. "But that didn't stop him from stealing glances at you the rest of the evening or texting me to ask that I make sure you got home okay."

"That isn't helping me *not* be in love with Nick."

Nick's protective nature was one of the many things she adored about him.

"Right. Sorry." Kassie sipped her mimosa. "So what happens now? I realize that things are awkward right now, but you can't ignore Nick forever."

"I know." Em stared at the phone she'd ignored moments earlier. "We'll work through it. We always do." She tried to sound more confident than she felt. "But instead of pining over Nick, I'm making a concerted effort to get over him."

"I applaud your determination to move on rather than dwelling on it." Kassie set down her glass and folded her arms on the table, too. "But it's okay to give yourself the time and space to feel however you feel. And to mourn the loss of the dream you've been holding on to."

"Being with Nick was the *who* of my dream," Em said. "But the *what*…being in a loving, committed relationship with someone who adores me as much as I do them and eventually starting a family together…I can still have that."

"Of course you can." Kassie squeezed her wrist again. "One day, the perfect guy will come along."

"Or…instead of waiting for him to find me, what if I make the effort to find him?"

"You're going to search for this perfect guy?" Kassie's eyes widened. "How? Please tell me you're not planning to put up a billboard ad."

"Maybe that'll be step eight…if it comes to that." Em burst into laughter when her friend's jaw dropped. "I'm joking, Kass. Relax. I won't do anything outrageous. But I've wasted so much time hoping and waiting for someone else to take action. It's the exact opposite of how I'd behave on the tennis court or in my business. I need to be as proactive about my love life as I am in all other aspects of my life."

"I understand wanting to feel more empowered." Kassie frowned, likely lamenting her own love life, which she referred to as nonexistent. "But if you're not really over Nick—"

"What choice do I have?" Em shrugged. "It's like that movie *He's Just Not That Into You.* Sometimes, you just need to cut your losses and move on."

Em didn't miss the irony of referencing a movie she and Nick had watched together many times to explain why she needed to move on from her feelings for him.

At this point, her life felt more and more like a cosmic joke.

"Agreed, and I fully support this plan. But there's no need to rush it."

"Actually, there is." Em smiled, and her brunch companion regarded her warily. "Because by the time New Year's Eve rolls around again, I plan to be at that bonfire with the man of my dreams."

"You're putting a timetable on this?" Kassie looked increasingly worried about her friend's state of mind. "And you don't think this is a rash response to Nick's rejection?"

Em couldn't blame Kassie for her reaction. If it was the other way around, she would be worried, too. But this wasn't an impulsive decision. It was a logical, well-thought-out plan that Em had stayed up most of the night carefully designing.

She'd spent three hours online reading articles written by romance gurus and listening to their YouTube chats. She'd taken notes from what she'd considered to be the most feasible advice. Then she'd spent another hour devising the perfect seven-step plan.

"Last night was…devastating," Em admitted. "But it was also enlightening and freeing."

This seemed to pique Kassie's interest. "Freeing? How?"

"Now I can let go of my misplaced fantasies about a future with Nick. Instead, I'll take action based on my reality," Emerie said. "I spent my twenties believing the right guy would eventually come along. Then I spent the past few years believing Nick was that guy. But I was wrong. I'm thirty-one. So if I want to have children before I'm forty, I can't passively meander through my life anymore. We're on this earth for a finite amount of time," Emerie noted. "I can't afford to waste any more of it. It's time I take control of my life." Em's shoulders sank a little in response to the quizzical expression on her friend's face. "You think I'm losing it."

"Not at all." Kassie smiled encouragingly. "I admire you for going after what you want. And I'd like to help."

"Good. Because I could use the support." Em was grateful for Kassie's reassurance. All night, she'd been vacillating between whether her mission to find Mr. Right was epically brave or pathetically sad.

"So let's hear about this…"

"Seven-step plan." Emerie pulled a notebook from her

designer backpack. The bag had been a concession to her mother. An upgrade from the sling backpack she used to tote her things around in, if she bothered with a bag at all.

"All right. Let's hear about this Soulmate Project of yours." Kassie dug into the glazed fruit tart that looked so perfect Em had almost questioned if it was real.

"The Soulmate Project! I love that." Em pulled out a pen and scribbled the name across the top of her notes. "We're definitely using that. See, you're being helpful already."

Em slid her apple coffee cake in front of her and dug in.

Her phone rang again. Nick's handsome face filled the screen. She'd taken that photo when they'd celebrated Nick's thirty-third birthday at his friend's place in the Hamptons.

She held back a whimper.

Why couldn't Nick be "the one"?

Kassie nibbled on a bite of her fruit tart. Her eyes silently pleaded with Emerie to take Nick's call.

"Fine." Em huffed, answering the phone. "Hey, Nick. Sorry I didn't answer your call earlier. Kassie and I are at brunch at The Foxhole."

Kassie scrunched her eyebrows in response to her half-true excuse for dodging Nick's calls. Em chose to ignore her friend's judgy glare.

"Well, we both know how much you enjoy a good brunch," Nick teased, his chuckle uneasy. "I was just calling because we haven't spoken since last night. I wanted to make sure that we're good. I'm sorry if I upset you."

"You were honest with me, and I appreciate that, as always." As devastating as Nick's rejection had been, at least she knew where things stood with them now. "I like knowing I can always count on you to tell me the truth. Even when it's not what I want to hear."

There was a long pause on Nick's end of the line. Had she dropped his call?

"I'm glad you feel that way, Em," Nick said finally. "Our friendship means everything to me. I don't want this to make things awkward between us. Because as far as I'm concerned, nothing has changed."

Emerie grimaced.

Nick's words—intended to comfort her—had the opposite effect. They slammed the lid on any lingering hope she had that he might rethink his decision.

Em forced a smile and infused her voice with all the cheerfulness she could conjure up. "Great. See you at Rett and Sin's place for dinner?"

"Right. I forgot. See you there."

Em ended the call, a smile plastered on her face for Kassie's sake. Yet, her heart ached, and her stomach twisted in knots, knowing the person she would eventually build a life with wouldn't be Nicholas Washington.

But Kassie wouldn't allow her to descend into a pity party. "So when does Project Soulmate go into effect?"

"No time like the present." Em tipped her chin.

"Perfect. As your partner in crime, you should read me in on all the details. But first . . ." Kassie lifted her glass. "To the Soulmate Project. May you find all the happiness you deserve and more."

Em smiled, grateful for her friend's unwavering support. She blinked back tears and clinked her glass to Kassie's. "To the Soulmate Project."

Chapter Four

─ •─■─• ─

Nick arrived at Rett and Sin's place and slapped palms with his friend. He was greeted by the savory aromas of collard greens, cornbread, and black-eyed peas: the traditional, Southern good-luck trio eaten on New Year's Day. Most of the feast had been prepared by Sinclair and Rett's grandmother. Mama Mae had originally owned the lovely little cottage that Rett and Sin called home.

They'd made the space their own, expanding the first and second floors of the cottage. The kitchen was double the size of what the original footprint had been when he, Em, and Dexter had helped Rett demo the place before renovations began. The updated cottage was the perfect space for the couple since Sinclair loved to cook and she and Rett frequently entertained.

Nick shrugged off his black, wool coat, and Rett relieved him of it.

"I'll throw this on the bed in our room," Rett said. "There's beer in the wine fridge and a bottle each of white and red wine floating around here somewhere. Or feel free to help yourself to something from the bar." He gestured to an antique bar cart set up in the great room.

"Thanks, Rett," Nick said. "Congrats again on the engagement. I'm *really* happy for you and Sin."

"Thanks. Me, too." Rett beamed, folding Nick's coat over his arm. They both glanced in the direction of Sinclair, who was holding their goddaughter, Olivia, and singing to her, much to the infant's delight.

"It's wild," Rett said. "A year ago, I couldn't possibly have imagined that I'd be engaged or that I'd even want to settle down. I sure as hell wouldn't have dreamed I'd be doing it with Sinclair. But despite years of trying to convince myself otherwise, Sin has always been the one for me. I'm incredibly lucky that she feels the same."

When Rett turned back toward him, love and pure joy lit his face. The man sincerely meant every glowing word he'd uttered about his fiancée.

Nick felt a twinge of envy.

He didn't have anything against marriage and family. He just hadn't had any real reason to consider either. But neither had Rett before returning home and teaming up with Sinclair to plan their mutual best friends' wedding.

"Make yourself at home. I'll be right back," Rett said.

Did Rett know about Em's confession at the bonfire last night? Was that why he was talking about settling down and finding "the one"?

Perhaps. Or maybe Nick had been so consumed with the conversation that everything made him relive it.

"Nick, hey." Emerie handed him a beer and offered a tentative smile. "Glad you made it."

"Hey, Em. It's good to see you. How are you?" he asked after an awkward pause.

"Yep, not weird at all," Em deadpanned.

They both laughed nervously.

"Look, about last night..." Nick began.

"Water under the bridge." Em waved a hand. Her smile broadened, and it alleviated the tension in Nick's chest. "We honestly don't need to discuss it again. Like... *ever*. In fact, I'd really appreciate it if we didn't."

"Like I said, it never happened." He nudged Em's shoulder, then sipped his beer. "How was brunch with Kassie?"

"Phenomenal. The Foxhole outdid themselves this year. I wasn't sure I'd be able to eat again so soon. But everything smells so good. Now I'm starving again."

"Well, my brunch buddy ditched me today." Nick chuckled. "I had to survive off of whatever I could find in my fridge."

"My bad." Em scrunched her nose, her expression apologetic. "That was kind of petty of me."

Even if he could muster the nerve to be angry with Em for ditching their brunch plans, those big brown eyes and that adorable smile made it impossible for him to stay mad.

"You can make it up to me by treating next time we play cornhole at Blaze of Glory. Not whipping my ass so badly would also be a nice change," Nick teased.

"Yes, to treating you. In your dreams, pal, to taking it easy on you. If you want my crown, you'll have to take it. And I'd love to see you try." Em grinned.

That was his best friend. Kicking ass, taking names, and talking shit the entire time.

Nick heaved a quiet sigh of relief. He'd been worried for nothing. Everything between them was just fine.

———

After dinner, Nick grabbed another beer, then cruised the dessert bar laid out with delectable, made-from-scratch creations. There was Sinclair's banana pudding and peach cobbler and Mama Mae's sweet tea cake and red velvet cake.

Nick wasn't sure where to begin. He only knew that he was happy to be starting off the new year with the people he cared about.

Em especially.

He was relieved to see Em laughing and smiling, surrounded by her family and friends. After last night, he honestly wasn't sure things would ever be the same between them. The loss of their friendship was a devastating prospect that had kept him up most of the night—especially when Em wouldn't answer his calls.

He'd lain in bed, tortured by that pained expression on Em's face playing on a loop in his brain. He'd only seen Em that upset once before: when her parents divorced after she graduated from college. Otherwise, Em had always been a warrior who could handle anything.

Growing up with three older brothers, Em was as tough as nails. She participated in all kinds of sports: basketball, street hockey, softball, rock climbing, and rugby—which was too rough, even for him. She'd been battered and bruised, had sustained cuts, sprains, and the occasional broken bone. But the pain on her face at the bonfire rivaled any physical pain he'd seen her endure.

Seeing Em so broken had cut him to the core. And knowing that he'd been the one who'd caused her that pain was like a kick to his front teeth. Seeing how she'd bounced back today only proved that he'd made the right call.

Nick would always be Em's ride-or-die road dawg. But he was also a relationship disaster. Which was why he'd given up on relationships years ago.

He'd returned to Holly Grove Island where he could be near friends and family while living his best fuckboy life—mostly hooking up with tourists who would be on the island for a couple weeks at most. Always making it clear he had no interest in a relationship. So how had he missed that his best friend had developed romantic feelings for him?

"I realize that you have a lot of options, but the rest of us are ready to dig in." Em bumped his shoulder, shaking him from his daze.

"Right. Sorry." Nick grabbed a slice of Mama Mae's sweet tea cake.

Em set a dish of peach cobbler and a slice of red velvet cake on a larger plate. She and Kassie followed him to the additional seating in the great room. Card tables were set up in the dining area.

The night was going well, and everything between him and Emerie felt normal with barely a hint of the awkwardness they'd experienced when he'd first arrived. But when Em stood up and said she wanted to tell everyone something, there was a tightening in Nick's gut and a fluttering in his chest. It felt like a subtle shift in the very fabric of the universe, signaling that his life was about to drastically change.

———

Emerie stood in front of her friends and family. Their happy, expectant, and slightly inebriated faces smiled back at her. Her heart thumped hard against her rib cage like a basketball thudding on the asphalt courts she and Nick still played on sometimes. Her mouth felt like it was filled with sand, and her stomach was tied in knots.

Em felt a sudden sense of panic. She opened her mouth, but no words came out.

Maybe telling everyone about the plan is a bad idea.

Puzzled looks started to appear on everyone's faces. Em looked at Kass, who offered a warm smile and an encouraging nod. She held up one finger and mouthed the words "Step One."

Sinclair's grandmother's words echoed in Em's head. *Closed mouths don't get fed.*

Emerie released a strangled breath, then stood taller.

"Before we go on to the fun and games tonight, there's something I want to share with all of you..." Em took a deep breath, then amped up the wattage on her smile. "Over the past two years, I've watched my brother and cousin reconnect with their soulmates and fall in love. I'm incredibly happy for them, and I'm so grateful for my niece Olivia. But it's made me realize that kind of love is what's missing in my life." Em was surprised by the rise of emotions that made her eyes sting. "I'm ready to step into the next phase of my life. A husband. A family. So I've devised a seven-point plan to connect with my soulmate by this time next year."

"Good for you, sweetheart!" Mama Mae whooped.

"That's wonderful, baby." Em's mother, Marilyn, beamed as she bounced little Olivia on her knee.

"I love when a woman knows what she wants and is determined to go for it. Girl, you already know I'm on board." Sin nodded approvingly and cast a not-so-subtle side-eye in Nick's direction.

Dexter and Dakota exchanged worried glances, but neither of them spoke.

Kassie beamed like a proud mother at a ballet recital.

The bronze skin of Nick's cheeks and forehead was flushed—something she probably hadn't seen since Nick was in middle school. His eyes were wide, his mouth hung open, and he looked stunned.

Em hated to be petty, but she couldn't help deriving a tiny sense of satisfaction from Nick's reaction.

Her smile deepened and some of her earlier nervousness faded in the wake of the encouragement she was receiving from most of the women in the room.

"I'm thrilled that you're so clear on what you want for your life, Em. And it's beautiful that seeing how happy we all are has inspired you." There was a cautious tone in Rett's voice. He wrapped an arm around Sin who was seated beside him on one of the sofas. "But you're only thirty—"

"Thirty-one," Em corrected her cousin. She folded her arms and cocked a hip, preparing herself for whatever Rett had to say.

"Okay...The point is that you're still young, and you have your entire life ahead of you. Why the rush?"

"Did you not just hear the woman say she wants to have children?" Sinclair nudged Rett with her shoulder.

"There's that." Em gestured toward Sinclair. "But also, it's what I want at this stage in my life."

Rett glanced over at Nick, who still looked shell-shocked by her announcement. Rett stood and wrapped Em in a hug.

"If this is what you want, you know Sin and I will support you," he said.

Em sank into her cousin's hug, her shoulders sagging with relief. "Thank you, Rett."

"So tell us about this seven-step plan. I can't wait to hear it," Em's mother said.

Em tucked her hair behind her ear and grinned, excited to share the plan she'd devised.

"Step One is putting my intentions out into the universe, which I just did. I want the people closest to me to know my plan and to be a part of it."

"I love that." Mama Mae smiled proudly. "What's Step Two?"

"A makeover," Em said. "Not because I'm unhappy with who I am, but because I realize that my sense of style is still very much fourteen-year-old tomboy and could use a refresh." Em turned in a circle, modeling her favorite pair of athletic leggings and an oversize T-shirt that had seen better days.

"Need a volunteer style consultant?" Sin rubbed the ears of her sleepy Havapoo, Stella, who was nuzzled in her lap. She kissed the top of the puppy's head. "I'm always up for an excuse to go shopping."

Everyone in the room laughed, including Rett.

"You're hired." Em flashed a grateful smile because neither she nor Kassie could be trusted for fashion advice. "That brings us to Step Three…" A shudder ran down her spine. "Joining a few dating sites."

There were cheers, some commiserating moans, and a few people tossing out recommended sites.

Em glanced at Kassie who was typing the names of the suggested sites into her phone. At brunch earlier, she'd volunteered to help Em set up her dating profiles.

"On it," Kass said.

Em ticked off the remaining four points: focus on self-improvement and self-care; focus on personal ambitions outside of romance; try something outside of her comfort zone; and travel more.

"That's a brilliant plan, Emerie." Mama Mae squeezed her hand. "It's well-thought-out and focuses mainly on self-improvement so that you attract the kind of person you truly deserve. Don't you think, Nick?"

The level of tension in the room amped up the moment Mama Mae called Nick's name. As if everyone was holding their collective breath and expecting Nick to object.

Nick's eyes widened, and Em was pretty sure he was

sweating. He shifted in his seat, his complexion looking a little green.

He cleared his throat and nodded. "Yes, ma'am. Seems like a very well-thought-out plan."

Sin, Mama Mae, Em's mother, and a few other older women in the room responded to Nick's comment with a disbelieving side-eye or a *humph*.

Em could barely hold back a snicker as Nick shifted in his seat under the women's collective stare.

"Well, this is exciting, Emerie," Mama Mae said with a shimmy of her shoulders. "We'll do everything we can to help you find the right man." She leaned in and whispered in Em's ear. "Once you do, I'll give you a stash of love potion tea. That stuff is too powerful to be using on any old body."

The older woman whose clothing bore the scent of all of the delicious foods she'd been cooking and baking all day pulled back and winked at her. "Good luck, baby. But I have a feeling you're not going to need it."

Em smiled broadly, a sense of pride filling her chest at Mama Mae's approval.

She'd always adored Rett's grandmother. She was in her eighties, wise, no-nonsense, and as sweet as could be. Any remaining doubts Em had about her plan disappeared.

The only people in the room who didn't seem fully on board were her brother, her sister-in-law, and Nick.

She could understand their concern. Making a plan to find the love of her life and announcing it to everyone she cared about wasn't really Em's style. But if she wanted different results, it was time to do things differently. Besides, it was her life—not theirs.

One thing she knew for sure: Dex, Dakota, and Nick loved her and only wanted the best for her. Eventually, they'd come around.

Chapter Five

Nick tried to go about the rest of the evening as if his heart hadn't stopped when Em made her big announcement. Once he'd recovered enough to breathe naturally, he'd pressed his lips into a smile and gone on as if everything was okay. When Em—who nearly always partnered with him for games like bid whist and Pictionary—said Kass had called dibs on being her partner for the night, Nick tried to quell the panic growing inside him.

"You good?" Dexter asked when he sank onto the seat beside him.

"Yeah, I'm good." Nick smoothed down the front of his sweater. "Why wouldn't I be?"

"You've been a little off since my sister made her big announcement." Dex looked at him as if the answer should be evident. "You two are best friends, but you clearly didn't see this coming. Did something happen between you two?"

"Em's a grown woman. She doesn't run everything past me." Nick tried not to sound as irritated by the question as he was.

Dexter narrowed his gaze, a sign that he wasn't

oblivious to the fact that Nick had dodged answering his direct question.

"Well, now that she's put it out there, what do you think of this idea? Because I feel like she's putting too much pressure on herself. I don't want Em to get hurt."

"I couldn't agree more." Nick lowered his voice as he glanced around the room. "As her older brother, you should be the one to tell her that."

"As her older brother, she'll think I'm trying to run her life and tell her what to do," Dex noted. "Seems like a conversation her best friend should have with her. Unless there's some reason you can't talk to Em about this."

Nick pinched the bridge of his nose and inhaled deeply. "Em and I are good. I'll talk to her."

"Thanks. Keep me posted." Dex seemed relieved. "Oh, and by the way, great job on the marketing support you've been giving the New York office while they're searching for a replacement VP. Our CEO loved the marketing campaign you proposed for the property in Virginia. You still interested in moving up in the organization, even if it means relocation?"

Nick glanced over at Em who was animated and practically glowing as she talked to Mama Mae about her Soulmate Project. He sighed quietly, then forced a smile. "Yes, sir."

"Good. Because Jeff asked if you were open to relocation. I'd hate to lose you, but I understand." Dexter offered a pained smile. "I'll email Jeff first thing in the morning and let him know. He's pulling together a team to discuss the plan further. Looks like you'll be making a trip to New York soon." Dexter clapped a hand on Nick's shoulder. Then he joined his wife on the other side of the room.

Nick rubbed the back of his neck and heaved a sigh. Two

days ago, he would've been thrilled about the news that he'd impressed the CEO of their resort management company. And he'd have been especially excited about the possibility of moving to New York, where he could pick up gigs as a session drummer—something he'd done when he'd lived in LA. He'd hoped to talk Em into moving to New York with him. But given what had happened over the past twenty-four hours, that was no longer a possibility.

Moving to New York with his best friend would've been an adventure. But after Em had admitted that she had feelings for him and he hadn't reciprocated...asking her to be his platonic roommate in a city where she didn't know anyone would make him a selfish asshole of epic proportions.

But he was jumping the gun. The CEO asking if he'd relocate was very different from actually being offered a job. Right now, he had much bigger concerns. Because he could just imagine how this conversation with Em was going to go.

Even if Dex hadn't asked him to speak to Em, Nick would've. They'd always been straight with each other, and they never avoided calling each other out on something if they believed the other person was making a mistake. Having tough, honest conversations was what friends did.

Why should this be any different?

Nick went to the dessert buffet for coffee and a piece of red velvet cake. Kassie was there picking up a piece, too. He tried not to be insulted that Em had consulted her about this Soulmate Project but hadn't mentioned it to him at all.

He and Emerie had always been open about everything going on in their lives—including their love lives. The gory details? No. But the basics? *Yes.* So despite their insistence that everything was fine between them, Em was definitely acting brand-new.

"Hey, Kass…this plan of Em's. What do you think about it?" Nick tried to sound casual as he filled a mug with decaf coffee.

"I was a little concerned at first," Kassie admitted. "It seemed like a knee-jerk reaction to…*you know.*"

"But now you don't think it is?" Nick added cream and sugar to his coffee.

"Her argument was convincing." Kassie cut the moist cake with her fork and popped a bite into her mouth.

"Which was?"

"That's a conversation you need to have with Em." Kassie sighed quietly. "You two have been friends forever. You're not into her. Okay, fine. But you can't fault her for wanting what she wants. I mean, c'mon, Nick, you had to have seen this day coming. You couldn't have possibly believed she'd be content to be your sidekick forever."

Nick was momentarily stunned by Kassie's direct words. It was the lengthiest conversation the two of them had ever had. Kassie was normally shy and all smiles. But today, she was pointed and unapologetic. She cared about Em as much as he did, and she was staking her ground and trying to protect her friend. He admired that.

Besides, Kassie wasn't wrong. It wasn't that he'd never considered that Em would one day get seriously involved with someone. It was just that he'd tried not to think about it. And since they both had a shitty track record with relationships, he'd only had to tolerate whomever she might've been dating for a few months, tops.

"You should talk to Em, Nick." Kassie's tone was compassionate. But then she gave him a stern face and pointed a finger at him. "Just remember, you can't straddle the line on this. If you really care about her, and you're not 'the one,' don't get in the way of her finding the man who is.

That is what she wants, and she deserves to be happy. You don't get to have your cake and eat it, too, Nick. You need to choose."

Kassie walked away before he could respond. It was just as well. There wasn't much he could say, because she was right. Still, he couldn't let this go without talking to Em about it himself. He'd promised her brother he would. And it was what a true friend would do.

Nick stayed at the party until Em declared that she was leaving. He offered to walk her to her car. Em hesitated before saying, "Sure." It was unlike her. They'd always treasured the time they got to spend together—even the tiniest moments, like a seemingly inconsequential walk to the car.

They walked together in silence with their take-home bags as they left Rett and Sin's cottage. Since she didn't bring it up, he said, "So about this Soulmate Project… when exactly did you put this plan together? Before or after you admitted to having feelings for me?"

He hadn't intended to come off sounding like a jilted lover. His mouth had gone rogue.

"*After.*" Em stopped and turned toward him, her arms folded as she stared up at him defiantly. "In the wee hours of the morning when I couldn't sleep, if you must know."

Had she been unable to sleep because of his rejection? Because he hadn't been able to sleep because of the guilt he harbored for hurting her.

"And you don't think this plan is directly related to the fact that things didn't go as you'd hoped last night?"

Em chuckled bitterly. She turned and walked toward her car again.

"I can appreciate why you'd think that. But let me clear things up for you, Nick. This isn't some elaborate plan designed to make you jealous in the hopes that you'll change your mind. You said you don't have feelings for me, and I accept that."

Nick frowned, biting back the truth. That he was attracted to Em. He could feel the heat emanating from her soft skin on this chilly night. Was intoxicated by the scent of the perfume she was wearing. The scent of citrus and flora made him think of the incredible vacation they'd taken together in Tulum. And how he hadn't wanted their time there to end. But they were best friends. Adding love and sex to the mix would jeopardize their friendship.

"Surely, you must see why the timing seems . . . *curious*." Nick fell in step beside her.

" 'Don't call me Shirley.' " There was a glimmer of amusement in Em's eyes as she employed the quote from *Airplane!*—a 1980 screwball comedy that parodied disaster films. He'd introduced her to the film because it was a favorite of his dad's.

Normally, the quote would send them both into a fit of laughter. But this was no laughing matter—at least not to him.

"Last night, you declared your interest in starting a relationship *with me*." Nick slapped a hand to his chest while trying to keep his voice even and appeal to Em's sense of logic. "Now, less than twenty-four hours later, you've devised a plan to find the love of your life."

Em unlocked her car, put her things in the backseat, then shut the door before turning to him again. "Here's the thing, Nick. I *do* have feelings for you. And for a long time, I believed that you were my soulmate. That you would be my happily ever after. That someday, we'd have kids, and a house, and two dogs. Because I dream of that life, and I want it with you. But now I know I was mistaken—maybe even delusional—for fantasizing about having a happily ever after with you. It doesn't mean I don't still want those things. It simply means I can't have them with you. So I need to find out who I'm meant to have that life with."

Nick's heart squeezed in his chest, and his lungs constricted. The thought of Em starting a life with someone else caused him physical duress. But he couldn't fault her for wanting what she wanted. He just wasn't capable of giving her that life.

"I realize this is new territory for us and that it's uncomfortable. But this is important to me, Nick. I know we haven't really ever talked about it, but I want a fairy-tale romance. To be with someone who loves and adores me the way Dex loves Dakota. And I want kids of my own someday, but it feels like my window is closing."

"I'm not saying you shouldn't want those things," Nick said. "I'm just suggesting that maybe you shouldn't force them."

"I won't wait around anymore hoping that Prince Charming will come along one day and sweep me off of my feet. I can't afford to lose more time. Besides, I've always gone after what I've wanted. So as scary as it may be, I *need* to do that right now. And I need you to support me in this, just like I have always supported you."

Em's words were like a punch to the gut. She had been there through thick and thin, anytime he needed her advice or support. They'd been there for each other in more ways than he could count, but...

"You have always been the person who talks me down off a cliff. You gas me up when I need a boost of confidence. Maybe I was being a little petty by not telling you about my plan ahead of time. But I knew you'd react like this."

"I care about you, and I just want what's best for you."

"Then be the friend I need right now and trust that *I*

know what's best for me." Em poked a finger to his chest. "I'm going to do this, Nick. And it's exciting, but it's also terrifying. Kassie is great, and I'm glad to have her in my corner. But you're my best friend. We've always been there for each other. *Always.* Is your support on this really too much to ask?" Her voice broke, and her dark eyes were suddenly filled with tears.

Shit.

Nick had convinced himself that he wanted to put a halt to Em's little project because, like her brother, he wanted to keep her from getting hurt. He wanted to spare her any additional rejection and keep her safe in the bubble of their friends and family. But he was being selfish. Trying to maintain the status quo because it was more comfortable than the unknown of introducing a new person to their world who might not understand or accept their friendship.

Nick rubbed his bearded chin and sighed, Kassie's words echoing in his head.

You can't have your cake and eat it, too. You need to choose.

"You're right, Em. I was wrong to doubt your motivation and your judgment. If this is what you want, then I'm on board, too. All right?"

Em dived into him and wrapped her arms around him.

Nick squeezed his eyes shut and sighed as he hugged her back. He rested his cheek atop her head, loving the warmth and feel of her body pressed to his.

All of the tricks he'd relied on these past few years to ignore his attraction to his best friend no longer seemed to work. A part of him wished they could stay like this forever. He immediately thought of that last night they were together in Tulum. The night he'd almost kissed her. He hadn't done it because he'd realized the inherent risk of disrupting the dynamics of their friendship. It was a risk that he hadn't been willing to take. He'd made the same choice again last night. So now, he needed to be her friend and support Em the same way she'd always supported him.

"Thanks, Nick." Em finally pulled out of his embrace, creating a vacuum where her warmth and comforting scent had once been. "You have no idea how much this means to me."

"But I do know how much *you* mean to me." Nick shoved a hand into his pocket. "So whatever you need, just ask."

"Actually, I was thinking—" Em sighed quietly when Nick's phone buzzed in his coat pocket. "Never mind. You should get that, Romeo."

"Whoever it is, I'll call them back later," he said.

"It's not important. Nothing worth keeping your adoring fans waiting. Answer the call. We can talk later." Em pressed a soft kiss to his cheek—something he couldn't recall her doing before. Then she wished him good night, got into her car, and drove off.

Nick stood frozen in place as he watched Em drive away, not bothering to check his phone. He reminded himself that supporting his best friend's quest for love was the right thing to do. So why was the little voice in the back of his head wondering if he was making the biggest mistake of his life?

Chapter Six

—•◦•—

It'd been a jam-packed day filled with shopping, glamour, and pampering—three things Emerie Roberts had typically avoided. But she'd enjoyed it more than she'd expected.

When Em admitted that she felt a little self-conscious about the makeover, Sin suggested they make it a spa weekend for the girls. Dexter had been generous enough to provide a deluxe suite at the Holly Grove Island Resort for the weekend and discounts at the spa. He'd also offered to take care of Olivia while Dakota spent time with the girls.

Em stood in front of the mirror of the suite and sifted her fingers through her hair, still unaccustomed to her new look. She honestly couldn't believe how different a haircut and a little makeup made her look and feel.

Emerie had played a variety of sports since middle school: volleyball, basketball, tennis, even rugby. She'd pulled her shoulder-length hair into a sleek ponytail for most of her life. But now, her hair had been cut into a layered, angled, chin-length bob that complemented her bone structure and made her feel like a movie star. She'd barely recognized herself once the stylist and makeup artist were done.

Emerie, Sinclair, Dakota, Kassie, and Izzy spent the afternoon getting pampered and having their hair and nails done, too. Afterward, a photographer Dakota often referred her marketing consultant clients to took professional headshots of each of them and Rett—since Sin wanted new photos for her and Rett's real estate website.

Em had always been content with who she was. Her style was basic—functional and comfortable rather than fashionable and elegant. But Sinclair showed her that she could have both comfort *and* elegance; functionality *and* fashion.

She'd traded her worn, comfortable leggings for dress pants that had the fit of yoga pants. She'd traded her tried-and-true Chucks for simple, elegant, foldable ballet flats. And she'd let the girls talk her into purchasing two pairs of platform heels that were comfortable and provided more stability than the stilettos Sin had tried to talk her into.

To replace her favorite, comfy men's T-shirts, she'd purchased an array of scoop neck, V-neck, and off-the-shoulder T-shirts that were just as soft and comfortable while also being flirty, sexy, or a little edgy.

"See? It's still you. Just with some added drama and glamour." Sin stood behind Em in the mirror, her hands on her shoulders. "I think you look stunning. What do you think?"

Em smiled, pleased with her reflection. "I love the new look. But I don't know if I'll be able to maintain all this…" She indicated the hair and makeup.

The makeup artist had called it a *no-makeup look*, but it had taken at least ten products to achieve the look the woman kept calling "simple."

"Isn't Step Four of your plan self-improvement and self-care?" Sin asked.

Kassie had posted all seven steps of the plan on a large

sheet of paper currently stuck to the wall. The question was rhetorical, but she nodded anyway.

"And that's why you have all those products for your new hair and skin routines. Plus, I recorded the entire thing while Anntonia walked you through the steps. I'll send you the video. And after you've done it a few times, it'll feel as natural as brushing your teeth."

Em hoped so. Because the instructions for applying foundation, highlighter, blush, and at least five other products had sounded a lot like algebra. Her eyes had glazed over the moment the woman started talking about contour. But Sin's confidence in Em boosted her belief that she could replicate the look.

"Thank you, Sin and Dakota, for arranging all of this." Em smiled at the two women she loved like sisters, then turned to Kassie and Izzy. "I know how busy you both are, so thank you for doing this with me."

"Anything for you...and discounted salon services." Isabel burst into laughter, and so did everyone else. "You know I'm kidding, Em. You've always been there when I've needed you. Spending the weekend shopping with you and being pampered is the least I can do." Izzy hugged her, then stood in front of the list of steps for the Soulmate Project.

"Maybe there's something else I can do to help." Izzy flashed a mischievous smile.

Em knew that look. It usually meant trouble.

"We've covered every element of personal care *except* for sexual health." Izzy didn't blink when every woman in the room stared at her. Poor Kassie's cheeks were the shade of pomegranates.

"If you're talking about condoms..." Em started.

"Condoms are a given." Izzy waved a hand dismissively. "I'm talking about a top-of-the-line vibrator."

"Isn't the point of this for Em to find an actual human being who'll replace her current battery-operated boyfriend?" Sinclair cocked a hip, the twang of her accent intensifying.

"But she's single now, and self-pleasure is an important part of sexual health," Izzy said. "Besides, the better we know our own bodies, the more easily we can guide a partner to ensure that we both leave the experience satisfied. And even in a long-term, committed relationship, toys and role-playing can add a little spice to the equation. Keep things from getting stale."

"And just when did you become the Afro-Latina Dr. Ruth?" Sin looked equal parts surprised and impressed.

"Who's Dr. Ruth?" Izzy asked.

Sin and Dakota laughed.

"Dr. Ruth Westheimer. A badass sex therapist who talked openly about sex when everyone else still considered it taboo," Dakota said finally.

"Oh. Cool." Izzy scrolled through her phone, apparently looking her up.

"And when did you become so *knowledgeable* about the subject?" Sinclair prodded her future sister-in-law.

"I'm twenty-one, Sin. You didn't *actually* think I was still a virgin, did you?" Izzy flashed a devilish grin. "But to answer your question, there was a point when I considered switching my major to psychology because I was thinking of specializing in sex therapy."

"Your mom is a nurse, so she probably could've handled it. But your dad..." Em whistled, just imagining the man's reaction to his baby girl becoming a sex therapist. "Uncle Hector would've had a heart attack."

"I know." Izzy sighed. "Dad cried at my quinceañera, at my high school graduation..." She counted on her fingers.

"Your dad is a sweetheart." Sin smiled. "Just a big ol' teddy bear who loves his family and his baby girl something fierce."

"Count yourself lucky." Kassie's voice, filled with sadness, drew their attention. She shifted her gaze from the room of women to her hands folded in her lap. "I mean... my stepdad is great. My mom and I are lucky to have him in our lives. But my dad... He walked out when I was a kid, and I haven't heard a peep from him since. So you should be grateful that your dad loves you so much. I'd rather have a clingy, emotional father than an absent one who doesn't care anything about me."

Izzy sank onto the sofa on one side of Kass and Em sat beside her on the other, both of them giving her a hug.

"I'm fine, really." Kassie sniffled and offered a shy smile. "Maybe I should've minded my own business, but I just thought you should know there are worse things than having a dad who loves you and isn't afraid to let the world know that."

"You're right, Kass. Thank you for the reminder." Izzy squeezed her arm. "Now we only have the room for one more night. I, for one, plan to enjoy it. Another round of Long Island iced teas?"

Everyone but Dakota—who was still breastfeeding—responded with a resounding yes.

"We should watch a movie tonight," Em suggested.

"We will. *After* we complete the mission." Kassie tapped a few keys on her computer, which she'd connected to the television in the suite's living room. She cast her screen to the TV so everyone could see it.

Em's dating profile, complete with photos Sin had taken on her iPhone, popped up on the television screen.

"You look stunning, Emerie." Dakota smiled, and everyone else in the room agreed.

"Now it's time to find our gorgeous girl a soulmate." Sinclair squeezed onto the sofa beside Izzy as Kassie pulled up a search screen.

"As much as I'd love to hang out with you ladies all night, this mama is exhausted." Dakota stood and slipped on her coat and gloves. "Besides, I miss my baby girl. If I head home now, I'll be there in time to feed her. But I'll meet you all in the morning for brunch."

Dakota said her goodbyes, then Em walked her to the door.

"Has Nick seen your new look?" Dakota lowered her voice so only Em could hear her.

"No." Em shook her head, tucking her hair behind her ear. She couldn't explain why her cheeks felt warm at just the mention of Nick's name. "I figured I'd spring it on him the next time I see him. Not that he would care," she added quickly. "He probably won't even notice the difference."

"Nick will *definitely* notice." Dakota gave her a knowing smile. "And he'll be blown away. Maybe as shocked as he was when you announced your search for the love of your life. There was a moment when I was sure the boy had stopped breathing."

Em glanced back to make sure the other women weren't listening. She lowered her voice to a whisper. "I told Nick how I feel about him at the bonfire. He doesn't feel the same."

"I'm sorry, sweetheart." Dakota's pained expression made Em's heart ache.

It'd been nearly two weeks since Nick's rejection at the bonfire. Em refused to get emotional again. But whenever she did, she reminded herself that she was over it and moving on.

"Well, his reaction at the dinner makes it hard to believe that he doesn't have feelings for you, too." Dakota fitted her knitted beanie firmly on her head and lifted her bag onto her shoulder. "How've things been between you two since then?"

There was a hint of concern in her sister-in-law's voice.

"We're... good." Em shrugged. "We grabbed dinner at Blaze's the other night. Everything was fine."

Maybe *fine* was overstating it. But things between them were definitely *okay*, if a bit weird. Whenever Em brought up her plans with the girls for the weekend, Nick had changed the subject. When he couldn't, he did the adult equivalent of sticking his fingers in his ears so he couldn't hear: He picked up his phone and started scrolling.

Something in her sister-in-law's expression made Em doubt she was buying her *everything's fine, there's nothing to see here* story.

"I need to get home and feed your niece. Love you, babe. See you in the morning."

"Love you, too." Em hugged her sister-in-law. "Kiss Olivia for me and thank Dexter again for arranging this weekend."

Em returned to the room. She sipped her Long Island iced tea and settled onto the chaise near the window, one leg folded beneath her.

But as the other three women debated the pros and cons of the men who popped up in Kassie's search, Em couldn't help wondering what Nick would think of her new look.

Chapter Seven

●—◦—●—◦—●

Nick chalked his cue, leaned over the billiard table at Blaze's, and positioned his pool stick. It was an incredibly easy shot. One he could make in his sleep. He just needed to sink the eight-ball in the corner pocket. Then he'd win his third consecutive game tonight.

He focused and slowly drew back his stick. But before he could make contact with the ball, he heard one of his earlier opponents greeting Emerie.

"*Dayum*, Em! Is that really you?" Marcus gawked, a hand cupped over his big mouth.

Nick completely botched the shot, much to his current opponent Doug's relief.

But Nick was too busy trying to catch a glimpse of Em to pay attention to Doug talking shit. Besides, the man still had four balls on the table.

Marcus was grinning like a wolf. His hooded gaze raked down the body of the woman standing in front of him.

"Em?" Nick whispered her name beneath his breath. He could hardly believe the woman whose partial profile he'd caught a glimpse of was his best friend. But he barely had time to take in Emerie's new look because his attention immediately returned to Marcus who was staring at Em like she was a prime rib and he hadn't eaten in a month of Sundays. Two other men, who seemed just as mesmerized by Em's new look, had joined the conversation.

Nick gripped his pool stick tight, his jaw clenching as he watched the men fawning over his best friend. A few women joined the conversation.

Nick gritted his teeth and tried not to entertain his sudden urge to land a punch squarely on Marcus's misshapen jaw and tell him to leave Em the hell alone.

Marcus had never considered Em as anything more than one of the guys. So why was he acting as if she was a completely different person now?

Then again, why was he? Or more specifically, why had he been struggling to look at Em as just a friend since she'd admitted at the bonfire that she had feelings for him?

Doug's celebratory shout brought Nick's attention back to their game of billiards.

"You ran the table?" Nick eyed the empty pool table, then looked up at Doug again.

Shit.

"Double or nothing?" Nick asked, his attention still split as he watched people fawning over Emerie.

"Given how distracted you are right now, I'm tempted to take you up on that offer." Doug chuckled. "But I think the safer bet would be to collect." The older man wiggled his fingers, his palm open.

Nick pulled a twenty-dollar bill from his wallet, glad they only made small, friendly bets at Blaze of Glory—one of Blaze's rules. He stuffed the crinkled bill in Doug's palm, then returned his attention to the crowd surrounding his friend.

It was Wednesday night. Four days since Em's big makeover with the girls on Saturday. But she'd been adamant about not sending pics or video conferencing since then. She'd wanted him to see her big transformation in person.

She was finally there for their weekly night out, and he was still waiting to get the full effect of the makeover because his view was blocked by the locals crowded around her.

He should've chosen The Foxhole instead. Wednesdays were a lot slower there.

Nick got the attention of Glory—Blaze's mother and half of the bar's namesake.

"I'll take that table now, please, Glo," Nick said. "And another beer for me and a cherry lemonade for Em."

"Yes, sir. Just grab your regular table, and I'll bring 'em over." Glo nodded toward his and Em's preferred table over by the deck.

The big windows offered a lovely view of the Atlantic Ocean—even on a winter's night. And the mounted televisions permitted them to watch whatever games were on.

Glo wiped down a table that had just been vacated. "That bestie of yours is a showstopper tonight. She's got everyone talking, and she's turning quite a few heads."

Nick's hands involuntarily curled into fists at his side. He forced a smile that barely stirred the corners of his mouth. "The new look seems to be a hit all right."

Nick glanced over toward the commotion. He could still only see the back of Em's head and the peacock-blue peacoat she was wearing. Yet, he couldn't pull his gaze from the fraction of Em that he could see.

"Looks like our girl got tired of waiting for her bestie to get a clue."

Nick snapped his attention to the older woman who was well-known for her unsolicited bits of wisdom that were always on point.

Was he the only person in town who hadn't realized that Em was into him like that?

"I . . . I mean we're just . . ." Nick stammered, unable to think of what he could say that the woman wouldn't call bullshit on—and rightly so.

He snapped his mouth shut again and sighed quietly.

"Em and I have never been involved romantically," Nick finally managed. "That's how we've been able to maintain our friendship all these years."

The older woman clucked her tongue, her eyes narrowed as she shook her head in what he was pretty sure was a silent "Bless your poor, pitiful heart."

"Well, doesn't matter how perfect I think you two would be together or that Em probably believes you would be, too. If she isn't the one you want, she just isn't. I just hope that A: you won't come to regret that choice someday and B: you won't be a hater and cockblocker to every other guy who sees what a jewel our girl is."

A sixty-five-year-old woman had just accused him of being a cockblocker. He definitely needed to work on his nonchalant expression if he was going to support his best friend in this Soulmate Project of hers. Because he'd promised her that he would.

"No, of course not. I love Em . . . as my best friend," Nick added quickly. "I want her to be happy. If this is what makes her happy, I'll support her. And I *do* realize what an amazing person Em is—that's why I value our friendship so much. But I wouldn't be doing my job—as her best friend—if I didn't try to protect her from someone who is wrong for her or who doesn't have her best interests at heart." Nick stood taller, his shoulders pulled back and his gaze resolute as he met Glo's stare.

"Then make sure any objections you make are about

what's best for Em, not about trying to keep her in a box so you won't lose your faithful sidekick." Glo poked a fingernail polished in her signature black into his chest.

Nick nodded. "Yes, ma'am."

Glory rolled her eyes and walked away, tossing over her shoulder, "Be back with your drinks in a sec."

Nick held back a tiny smirk. Glory hated being called ma'am, Ms. Glory, or any of the other niceties common to most Southern folk. She rode into work most days on a big, loud Harley-Davidson motorcycle wearing an old-school, black motorcycle helmet with a gray rose etched on it and a small visor. Glory had her fair share of tattoos, and her preferred style was tattered jeans, T-shirts with smart-ass sayings, and anything bearing a skull and crossbones—like the gleaming silver ring on her right hand. Glory Blaisdell definitely wasn't your typical grandmother. So her accusing him of being a cockblocker was pretty much on brand.

Or maybe she's just... right.

"No." Nick shook the thought from his head and moved toward his usual table. "That's not true."

"What's not true?"

Nick turned around, startled by Em standing behind him.

Had she heard his conversation with Glory?

"Em? Oh my God." Nick scanned the woman standing in front of him. The slicked-back ponytail was gone. An angled, chin-length haircut showed off Em's gorgeous face and amazing cheekbones. Her simple makeup highlighted her expressive eyes and full, sensual lips.

Why had he never noticed that her lower lip was just a tad bit fuller? Or how her dark eyes glinted in the light?

"*Dayum*," he said finally.

He wanted to say something profound and encouraging.

But his capacity for language had abandoned him the moment he'd caught a glimpse of Emerie Roberts's fine ass putting everyone in that bar on notice that she wasn't one of the boys. She was a showstoppingly gorgeous woman.

"Okay. I'm not sure if that's good or bad." Em flashed a shy smile and raked her short, manicured nails through her layered hair so it wouldn't cover her eye.

"Are you kidding me?" Nick rubbed his chin and shook his head, still hardly able to believe it was his best friend who'd spent most of her adult life in T-shirts, leggings, and Chucks. "Em, you look fucking amazing." Nick's neck and cheeks suddenly felt hot. "Here, let me take your coat."

Nick helped her out of the blue peacoat and tried not to gasp. Em wore a baby-blue off-the-shoulder sweater that looked like angora or cashmere. A navy, wool skirt hit her mid-thigh and was the perfect complement to her black, knee-high riding boots. The sweater and skirt highlighted the subtle curves of her toned, athletic body. And she smelled like some heavenly combination of flowers and citrus. It took everything he had not to lean in and press his nose to her neck to get a deeper whiff.

"Thank you for the compliment and for taking my coat. But you didn't need to do that." Em folded her coat over her arm. "We're not on a date. I don't expect you to treat me differently because I'm wearing a skirt and a little makeup."

Em slipped into her side of the booth, placing her neatly folded coat on the bench beside her.

"Right." Nick slid into the seat across from her. He picked up his menu, but he found himself staring at Em over the top of it.

"Oh my God, stop it." Em put her menu down and tucked her hair behind her ear. "You're making me self-conscious.

I realize that I look different—better, even. But y'all are acting like my old look was a complete dumpster fire."

"Well, I wouldn't go straight to dumpster fire," Nick teased, and they both laughed. It seemed to ease the tension for both of them.

They'd chatted on the phone several times since that night at the bonfire. They'd even seen each other a couple of times. But things hadn't felt the same. And he missed his best friend. Nick was determined to put any lingering uneasiness behind them tonight so they could go back to the way things were before the bonfire debacle.

"Okay, yes, Sinclair did make me throw away a lot of my old clothes," Em admitted. "It was like being in my own private episode of *What Not to Wear*, and Sin was doing her best to channel both Clinton and Stacy."

"I can definitely envision that." Nick laughed, thinking of the weekend they'd hung out on her couch, her sprained ankle propped on pillows, and watched a marathon of the old reality makeover show—a longtime favorite of Em's.

Her mother had threatened to move in and take care of Em while she recovered from a sprained ankle and sprained wrist sustained during an awkward fall while playing volleyball, but Nick had offered to keep her supplied with snacks, baked goods, and sudoku puzzles instead. He'd watched the first episode of *What Not to Wear* as a concession to his injured friend. By the fifth episode, he had been fully invested, providing commentary and critiquing the outfits and hair and makeup choices. In the end, he'd had to begrudgingly admit he enjoyed the show.

"Well, whatever Sin did . . . you look amazing."

Glory brought their drinks over, and Nick thanked her.

"Thanks, Glory," Em said. "But I'd love a mojito tonight."

"Excellent choice." Glory nodded approvingly as she reached for the glass of lemonade.

Em clamped a hand around the glass and dragged it closer. "No need for this to go to waste. I'll take the mojito with dinner. And I think we're probably ready to order now. You know what you want, right, Nick? *Nick*?" Em called his name again, snapping him out of his temporary daze.

"*You*, apparently," Glory whispered so only Nick could hear.

He glared at the older woman who was amused by his silent mortification.

"Sorry, I didn't hear you." Em shifted her gaze between him and Glory, a puzzled look on her gorgeous face.

"I was just saying that maybe Nick still needs a little time to figure things out." Glory broadened her smile as she turned to Em. "He seems a little unsure about what he wants."

Nick hadn't realized that he'd been staring at Em the entire time, still mesmerized by how incredible his friend looked. Now that Em and Glory were staring at him expectantly, his cheeks and forehead were hot, and the erratic beat of his heart sounded like the crash of cymbals inside his head. For a moment, he was convinced both women could hear it.

"But the menu is pretty much the same every week," Em noted. "You either get a steak or a burger. Besides, haven't you been here like an hour playing pool?"

Emerie looked genuinely confused about his current struggles. But so was he.

Nick wasn't himself tonight. In fact, he hadn't been since his conversation with Em on the beach. But seeing her tonight...He hadn't been this far off his game since he'd had a crush on Marsha Simpson in middle school.

"I…uh…" Nick tugged on his collar which suddenly felt way too tight. "I guess I'm not sure what I'm in the mood for tonight." Glory made a quiet *humph*, her thinly-drawn-on eyebrow spiked as one side of her mouth curved in a smirk. "I'll give you two some more time. But if you're looking for a recommendation, tonight's special is the lasagna. I think you'd appreciate the layers and unexpected complexity of the dish, Nick."

"That sounds good, Glo. Thanks. I'll have that." Nick handed his menu to her, then sipped his beer to soothe his suddenly parched throat.

"I'll have the lasagna, too." Em handed Glory her menu. "And can we have an order of potato skins and fried oysters to start?"

"Oysters, huh?" Glory winked at Em, then headed for the kitchen. "Right away, hon."

Today, of all days, Em would be in the mood for oysters.

Nick was already trying his damnedest to keep it together and act like this was any other Wednesday night he and Em hung out. To pretend he wasn't completely captivated by her new look and more attracted to his best friend than ever. And now she wanted to add an aphrodisiac to the mix.

Was she *trying* to torture him?

"Nick." Em waved a hand.

"Sorry, what?" Nick cleared his throat. "I zoned out for a minute. I just…you look…amazing, Em. Sorry if I keep staring. It just seems so weird, you know?"

"Why? Because I look like someone else?" There was a hint of sadness in Em's voice, and her gaze didn't quite meet his.

"No, not at all." Nick leaned forward and lowered his voice, placing a hand on hers. "That's the thing that makes it so wild. You look very much like yourself. It's just *you* with a whole lot of sparkle and glitter, if that makes sense."

The corners of Em's sensual mouth curved in a soft smile and her dark brown eyes twinkled. She gently tugged her hand from beneath his and sipped a little of her lemonade. "This is all new and weird for me, too," she admitted.

"Because of all of the attention from everyone at the bar?"

"Yeah. That." Em stirred her straw in her lemonade. "But what's weirder is…we've been friends for two decades, and you've never complimented me the way you have tonight."

"That's not true." Nick leaned back against the booth, hurt by Em's accusation. "I compliment you all the time."

"No…you say things like, 'Cool shoes,' or 'That's a badass jacket, Em.'" She imitated the deep tone and relaxed cadence of his voice. "But you've never said that *I* look good." A slight frown furrowed her brows, her gaze still on her drink.

"I told you how good you looked when we were in Dexter and Dakota's wedding," Nick countered, searching his brain for additional examples of him complimenting Em— not just her taste in footwear and jackets.

He was coming up woefully short.

"Right. But you didn't say, 'Hey, Em, you look really amazing tonight.' It was a group thing. We were taking photos and you said, 'You *ladies* look stunning,'" she reminded him.

Shit. She was right.

He worked hard to ignore the fact that Em was an incredibly attractive woman. Which meant he sucked as her best friend. Because, as her friend, wasn't it his job to hype her up and tell her how good she looked?

"It's not a big deal. It's not like I need my ego stroked."

Right now, he wanted to stroke a hell of a lot more than just her ego. Her hair, her skin, her full glossy lips, her...

"Like I said...it's just *strange* hearing you say it now." Em's dark eyes met his. "I realize I knocked our friendship off balance when I said what I did the other night. But we agreed to act like it never happened. So all I'm saying is... let's not make it weird, okay?" Em tipped her head toward the TV screen on an opposite wall. "Who are you picking in the basketball game tonight? Cavs or the Celtics?"

"The Celtics, of course. They're at home and none of their key players are injured."

"I think it's the Cavs' night," she countered. "They've got a lot more to prove."

"Speaking of having something to prove...That marketing campaign I developed for the Virginia property our company is planning...our CEO was impressed with it."

"Of course he was." Em grinned, genuinely happy for him. "Way to kill it, friend." She gave him a high five. "Are they going to let you run point on the plan?"

"I don't know about that." Nick shrugged. "But Jeff has asked me to sit in on a few meetings to discuss it. I'll be flying to New York later this week."

"Oh." Em frowned, then suddenly forced a smile. "I mean...that's exciting, right?"

"It is." Nick's voice was flat. His smile was as unconvincing as hers. "If I want to take on a larger role in the company, this is exactly the kind of opportunity I need. It's a chance to impress the CEO and the rest of the executive team."

"And I know you will." Em's sad smile made his heart ache. She raised her glass of cherry lemonade and clinked it against his bottle of beer. "To making our wishes come true."

"Cheers." Nick sipped his beer. But it felt like their world had been turned upside down. He wanted the best for Em. But if they both got the thing they wanted, it would slowly pull them apart. Nick wished things could go back to how they were before New Year's Eve. Before everything changed between them in an instant. Knowing they never would.

Chapter Eight

—•—•—

Emerie widened her painted-on smile and thanked an older couple who were longtime residents of the island for their compliments on her new look. Then she and Nick wished them a good night.

Em enjoyed being the belle of the ball as much as any girl. But she couldn't help feeling a little resentful and seriously judged about her look prior to the makeover.

So maybe ponytail-and-leggings-casual-chic wasn't exactly her best look. But the way everyone had been fawning over her tonight made her wonder what people had been thinking of the well-loved, uber-comfortable attire she'd been wearing. Since those old clothes were now in a landfill somewhere, that pretty much answered her question.

Still, she was the same person now as she had been before her makeover. Em couldn't help feeling a little conflicted about the effusive praise of her new look. Then there was the matter of Nick being invited to join a team based out of his company's New York office. She was proud of and happy for her friend, of course. But she couldn't help worrying what all of the changes happening would mean for their friendship.

She loved having Nick back home on the island. But they'd maintained their friendship while living worlds apart before. So it wasn't just the prospect of Nick relocating that made her uneasy. It was because things felt *different* this time.

"Everything okay?" Nick nudged her foot beneath the table with his own. Concern filled his dark eyes. "I thought you'd be happy about all of the compliments you've been getting. Wasn't that the point of this?" He indicated her new look with a tilt of his bearded chin.

Was it all in her head, or did Nick look particularly handsome tonight? And was that a new cologne? Because the man smelled incredible.

"No, it wasn't the point," Em said. "I mean...yes, of course, I want to attract the right guy. But I'm not looking for someone who is so shallow that they can't see past my favorite leggings and T-shirt. And I certainly didn't expect my new look to garner so much attention." She gestured around the bar. "Mabel Jenson wears a different color wig every week. She literally had a fake parrot on the shoulder of her dress the other day. People barely batted an eye."

"Because Mabel wearing the unexpected is expected. But I'm pretty sure everyone around here thought you were allergic to makeup and skirts." Nick chuckled. "Face it, kid. You're a knockout, and everyone in town is blown away by your new look. Guess you're just gonna have to find a way to live with it." He ate the last of his lasagna and shoved aside his plate.

"Let's hope the novelty wears off soon." Em set aside her plate, too. The lasagna had been delicious, but the servings at Blaze of Glory were huge. She'd take the rest to go and have it for lunch the next day.

"So you made the big declaration and got the big make-over. What's next? Are Sin and your mom setting you up on blind dates?" Nick sipped his beer.

"Izzy and Kassie set up dating profiles for me."

Nick coughed and sputtered, his eyes wide.

"Nick, are you all—"

"I'm fine." He held a hand up to stop her from springing out of her seat. Nick cleared his throat and set his beer down roughly. He loosened the collar of his shirt and frowned. "You're hooking up with guys on dating apps?"

"Not all of us have dating prospects falling into our laps," Em said in a loud whisper, shifting her attention to the server who approached them.

"Would you like a to-go container?" the woman asked Em. Yet, her gaze and broad smile were directed at Nick.

"That'd be great. Thank you." Em forced a smile and told herself she was not at all jealous of the woman who was just Nick's type. Stunningly gorgeous without even trying and built like a 1950s pinup model.

"Anything else I can get you?" the server asked suggestively, her dark brown eyes flickering.

"Another beer would be great." Nick employed his polite smile, which was only half a watt dimmer than the charming, panty-dissolving grin he usually flashed when he was flirting. "Thanks…Taneeka." He peered at her chest, ostensibly to read her name tag since she was new to the bar.

The woman's smile broadened, and she tucked her wavy, dark hair behind one ear. "Be back in a flash."

"And I'd love another mojito. Thanks!" Em called to the woman's back.

Taneeka froze momentarily, then turned back to them with an apologetic smile. "Sorry. I'll be back with your mojito, too."

"See what I mean?" Em sipped the last of her watered-down drink. "Waiting for the right guy to fall from the sky isn't an option for me. So I need to be proactive."

It seemed best not to state the obvious: that she'd wasted the past few years wishing and hoping that Nick would realize that *he* was the one she wanted. Bringing it up would only make things even weirder between them, and neither of them needed that. The goal was to eventually get things back to normal—aside from the part where she'd been secretly pining for Nick for years. That was a habit she was definitely trying to kick. And she would...*eventually*.

But staring into those dreamy dark eyes of Nick's now, with electricity flowing up her leg from where Nick's foot still rested against hers beneath the table...Getting over her unrequited feelings for her best friend felt like a monumental task.

"I thought you shared the plan with your friends and family because you wanted us to recommend *vetted* prospects. And so you wouldn't have to connect with random weirdos from the internet." Nick was anxious and in full protective mode.

"If you suggest that I join a knitting circle or the church choir, I swear—"

"We both know you couldn't knit if your life depended on it, and you sound like a wounded animal when you sing," Nick teased.

He wasn't wrong.

"If anything, I'd tell you to join an auto repair workshop or a badminton league."

"I already know how to do basic car repairs, and you know how much I hate badminton," Em groused. "You're not being very helpful, Nick. And you promised you would help. Besides, who isn't on dating apps these days?"

"That's my point." Nick leaned back and folded his arms. "The randos on those sites could be psycho creeps, potential stalkers, or already married." Nick ticked each item off on his long fingers.

"I appreciate your concern. And I love that you care about me and have always looked after me." Em placed a hand on his. "But I'm committed to doing this. What I could really use right now is a wingman, not a pessimist."

Nick huffed quietly, like a pouting toddler. Neither of them spoke for a few moments. Finally, he responded. "If this is really what you want—"

"It is."

"Then I'll find a way to be helpful. I promise."

"Here are your..." Taneeka halted, disconcerted by the sight of Em's hand on Nick's. Her smile dimmed as she set down their drinks.

Em pulled her hand from Nick's and thanked the woman.

"Glory will be back from her break shortly. Let me know if you need anything else." Taneeka offered a sad smile and turned to walk away.

"Actually, Taneeka, my friend Nick and I were just wondering if you were new to the island. We know most of the folks here, but I don't recall meeting you before."

"Nick's your friend?" Taneeka's eyes lit up. "I mean... yes, I'm new to the island. I'm from Jersey, but I went to school in Raleigh and moved here about a month ago. I'm in the elementary education master's program over in Elizabeth City."

"A future teacher...that's awesome." Em broadened her smile. "Well, welcome to Holly Grove Island, Taneeka. I hope you'll love it here as much as we do."

"Thank you both." Taneeka shifted her gaze to Nick, her eyes lingering on him for a moment before she finally turned to leave.

"Now *that's* what a good wing person does." Em flashed a self-satisfied grin. "I deliver the alley-oop and set you up for the easy slam dunk. If you fumble this one, that's totally on you, bruh." She pointed a finger.

"Except I didn't actually ask you to set me up with Taneeka," Nick noted with a raised eyebrow. He sipped his beer. "Or are we just setting each other up with random folks now? Because I'm pretty sure I could get you a date with Marcus over there. He's been staring at your ass since the moment you walked in. Except, of course, when he's busy staring at your chest."

Em glanced down at the baby-blue, off-the-shoulder, cashmere sweater she was wearing. Who knew she could be cute, sexy, elegant, *and* comfy? And yes, in this demi push-up bra, her size 32B bust looked spectacular, if she did say so herself.

"I'm fishing for the right guy. Going out with Marcus would be the equivalent of catching an old boot instead of a catfish, then trying to take it home and make a meal out of it." Em set her drink down. She folded her arms on the table and gave her sneering friend her best stink eye. "Also, you're fired. Please don't make any more dating recommendations. Thanks." Em stood with her drink and glanced over at the two billiard tables, one of which was just opening up. "A couple of games of pool before we end the night?"

"Wait...you're going to bend over the table and make shots...in that?" Nick asked. "I mean..."

"Oh my God. You are a complete hypocrite, Nick Washington. How many times have I seen you helping some woman with her shot whose skirt was maybe half as long as mine?"

Nick cringed as he lumbered to his feet. "You're right. I'm sorry. You know I'm not that guy." He shook his head, then grabbed his beer. "I'm just...not used to you looking like that. Besides, you don't have the most graceful pool stance." He smirked. "Didn't you actually put your leg up on the table once rather than just using the damn bridge cue?"

Okay, maybe that was true. Her mother had practically had a conniption telling her how unladylike she'd looked with one leg propped on the table like that. But it didn't mean she was letting Nick off the hook.

"I'll keep both feet on the ground. Promise." She held up her free hand, then collected the bag with her boxed meal, her purse, and the expensive new coat she adored. "Now come on before someone else claims the table."

———

Nick joined her at the billiard table and racked the balls. "So back to this Soulmate Project... There's the declaration, the makeover, the dating sites..." It caused him physical discomfort every time he thought of his friend going out with dating site randos. "What else?"

"Dakota and I are meeting tomorrow to come up with rebranding and marketing strategies for my graphic design business."

Nick stopped what he was doing and stared at his friend, his mouth hanging open as she compared two pool cues obliviously.

She finally selected her stick and turned to face him. "What? Did you want this one?"

"Nothing's wrong." Nick grabbed a pool stick. "Go ahead and break."

"Then why are you wearing that funky-ass scowl?" Em moved to the head of the pool table as she assessed him.

"I'm surprised you went to Dakota for help. You do realize that I'm the marketing VP at the resort, right?" he asked incredulously. "I've offered to assist you with a marketing plan for your business. But whenever I bring it up, you always say—"

"That I have more clients than I can handle," Em finished his sentence. "I know, and I did feel that way. But now I realize that I've been thinking small when it comes to relationships and my business. I shouldn't make choices based on fear of the unfamiliar."

Em's explanation hit him in the chest like a bowling ball launched out of a cannon. He was definitely in his feelings, which wasn't like him.

She broke, sending the balls tumbling against the rails. A five dropped in the side pocket. "I've got low balls." Em chalked her cue stick, then went for the four-ball.

"So you're saying that when you were interested in me *just two weeks ago*"—he held up two fingers for emphasis—"it was because you were *thinking small* and I just happened to be around?" Nick gripped the cue stick tightly, his mouth twisted, and his jaw tense.

Em frowned, looking confused. She lowered her voice to a whisper, likely hoping he'd do the same. "What the hell is going on with you tonight, Nick? You're being super weird."

"I'm not being weird. I'm simply asking a question and trying to get clarification." He crossed his arms.

"Are you seriously offended right now?" Em sifted her fingers through her hair, and it was the sexiest thing he'd ever seen. Which was disturbing on a variety of levels when he'd declared that he *wasn't* into her like that. "Please tell me you're joking."

"So…what…I don't get to have feelings?" Nick sounded whiny, even to himself. But also…he was genuinely offended by the implication of her statement, and he needed clarification.

"Of course you do. And I'm not trying to hurt your

feelings." Em squeezed her eyes shut momentarily and pinched the bridge of her nose. She released a quiet breath before returning her attention to him. "I developed feelings for you because you're an incredible person and an even better friend, and I adore you. *Period*. Not because you just happened to be around. Maybe what I should've said is that I dismissed the possibility of a relationship with someone else because I preferred the comfort and familiarity of being with someone who already makes me happy. As opposed to risking the jack-in-the-box reality of dating. Does that make sense?" Em placed a gentle hand on his bicep. The tension there seemed to ease immediately.

"Yes. I get it." Nick rubbed his bearded chin, then sighed. "You're right. I am being weird about this, and I'm sorry. Things have felt off between us since…" His voice trailed off.

"I know, and I'm sorry. I just hope I haven't wrecked things between us."

Her voice broke slightly, and Nick felt awful.

"I know things are off between us right now, Em. But it's always been me and you…through hell and high water, we've always had each other's backs. We'll work our way through this. And don't ever apologize for admitting how you feel. I'm glad you got it off your chest. We dealt with it; now we can both move forward."

"So…we're cool?"

"Of course we are." Nick set his pool cue against the billiard table, then opened his arms. "Bring it in here, kid."

Em leaned her stick against the table, then stepped into his arms. He hugged her tight, her warmth penetrating his skin, and her sweet scent tickling his nostrils. It felt good holding her in his arms like this. He honestly didn't want to let her go.

———

"You two actually plan on playing pool or are you going to just hug it out all night?"

Marcus. Of course.

"I was just about to take my shot actually, smart-ass." Em pulled out of Nick's hold, though he seemed reluctant to let her go. She picked up her stick and got back into position to take her shot.

She hit the four-ball at just the right angle, putting a little English on it. The ball spun off into the corner pocket, and she moved around the table in search of her next shot.

"You two an item now?" Marcus probably thought he was being stealthy. Unfortunately, his indoor voice was more like a down-the-hall-and-'round-the-corner voice.

"Em and I are just friends. You know that." Nick seemed agitated by the question while trying very hard to appear nonchalant about it.

"Then you don't mind if I…"

"Em's a grown-ass woman with a mind of her own," Nick said.

Why did it bother her so much that Nick didn't care whether Marcus asked her out?

Em sucked in a deep breath, then tried to sink the yellow one-ball in the same corner pocket. It hit the side rail and hovered near the edge but didn't drop in.

She cursed under her breath and stepped aside so Nick could take his shot.

"Hey, Em, I'm going bowling with some friends on Friday. I thought maybe you'd like to come." Marcus was suddenly beside her, and she wondered if he'd left any of the cologne in the bottle. The cloying scent nearly made her cough.

She snuck a glance at Nick. He didn't react to Marcus's question.

But what had she expected him to do? Slam his pool cue on the table, declare that she was his woman, and insist Marcus back off?

Then again, maybe Nick hadn't reacted because he expected her to turn Marcus down.

"I haven't been bowling in a while," she said. "Sounds fun."

"Really?" Marcus asked.

"Really?" Nick chimed in, now giving them his full attention.

"*Really.*" Em broadened her smile. "Oh, and if I were you, I'd go for the eleven." She pointed to the ball hovering in a corner pocket.

Nick cleared his throat, his cheeks and forehead flushed and his brows furrowed. "Thanks," he said sarcastically before stalking over to the ball.

"You're seriously going to go out with me?" Marcus asked.

Em tugged him farther away from the pool table, her back to Nick. She leaned in close to Marcus and lowered her voice. "Yes, I'll go out with you. But only if we go Dutch and you understand that under no circumstances whatsoever will I be sleeping with you."

"On our first date?" Marcus asked hopefully.

"*Ever.*" Em poked a finger to his chest.

"Aww, come on, Em…"

"Those are my terms, Marcus. I respect that it's probably not the way you saw this going. Which is why I won't take it personally if you turn down my offer."

The man frowned.

"Look, we've known each other forever. And until I walked in here dressed like this, you barely even realized I had breasts. You certainly didn't have any hope of seeing them. So let's just chalk this up to temporary insanity and go bowling together...*as friends*. Might be fun. What do you say?"

"Fine. But can we at least call it a date? I made a bet with Lester that I'd be the first guy here to take you out."

"Fine. Whatever. It's a date. But I am not riding in your car. It's a trash dumpster on wheels. We'll meet at the bowling alley."

"Deal." Marcus grinned. "You're a good friend, Em."

"I know." Em smirked, and Marcus laughed. "Hey, if I ask you a question, do you promise to answer it honestly?"

"Shit. This can't be good," Marcus muttered, dragging a hand down his face. He sighed. "Go ahead. I promise to be straight with you."

Em drew in a deep breath, her brows furrowing. "Why haven't you asked me out before?"

"Classic Em. Straight for the jugular." Marcus chuckled as he rubbed his chin. He sighed quietly. "The truth? You're strong, athletic, mechanically inclined. I stopped to help you that one time when you had a flat tire. All you'd let me do was hold the flashlight." He shrugged. "Didn't much seem like you needed anyone."

Translation: You were too dude-like.

"So you're one of those guys who desperately needs to be needed." *Also known as an insecure jerk.* "Good to know."

Any man who thought that way wasn't the type of man she wanted. Still, it hurt her pride a little that she'd been summarily disregarded because she was independent and self-sufficient.

"Anything else?"

"The fact that you could probably beat my ass was kind of a factor, too." Marcus leaned in closer, his voice lowered.

Em was pretty sure he was only half joking. She folded her arms and stared up at him. "You planning to do anything that would require me to beat your ass?"

"No, of course not. You know I'm not that kind of guy. I'd never put my hand on a woman," Marcus stammered, his face red.

"Good. Then you don't have anything to worry about." Em poked Marcus in the gut playfully, and they both dissolved into laughter. "Now that that's settled, can I please get back to my game?"

"Sure thing, Em. See you at the bowling alley at seven on Friday night. And don't keep a brother waiting, all right?" Marcus leaned down and kissed her cheek, then said his good nights.

When she returned to the billiard table, Nick looked like he was fit to be tied. He'd missed the shot he should've been able to make in a dark room while the high school band played "Cuff It" by Beyoncé. He was waiting for her impatiently.

Mission accomplished.

"Guess that shot must've been a little trickier than we thought." Em picked up her stick again and assessed the current configuration of the balls.

She'd go for the green six-ball this time instead.

"So you're really going out with Marcus after the conversation we had about him earlier?" Nick asked disbelievingly.

"Yep." Em lined up her shot.

"So how's that boot tasting?" he asked.

Em made her shot. The white cue ball smacked the green six-ball and sent it rolling across the table and into one of the corner pockets. Em stood and smiled. "I'll let you know."

She was pretty sure she could see every vein in her friend's forehead and that there was smoke coming out of his ears.

And yes, maybe she was a petty bitch for enjoying Nick's obvious discomfort with her seeing Marcus. But she was loving every single minute of it.

Chapter Nine

●━━●━━●

Hey, Nick, what's going on with you?" Quinton Carson—the pianist of their band, the Holly Grove Island Players—asked after they'd finished rehearsing. "You've been off all night. We're performing at this wedding in three days."

"Sorry." Nick huffed, annoyed with himself. He'd never been this distracted during a performance or practice.

The band was more of a hobby than a career for the five band members, but still, they'd always taken their obligation to it and each other seriously.

When Nick looked up, all four of his fellow band members were staring at him with concern. In addition to Nick and Quinton, the group consisted of their bassist, Jay Montgomery, Rich Vargas on tenor sax, and Em's brother Dexter on alto sax.

Jay and Rich looked just as confused by the fact that he'd been unable to focus all night. But Dexter's frown held more pity than irritation.

"Give him a break, fellas." Dex removed the black and gold saxophone strapped around his neck and placed it into its case. "Nick's got a lot going on with this big project he's taken on at work. You know he'll come through on Saturday night. He always does. You just worry about keeping pace with the rest of us on that last piece, Q. Feels like you're a step behind."

"I'll keep working on it," Quinton groused, closing the piano lid.

Nick gave Dex a subtle nod of thanks for covering for him as he collected his things.

Jay and Rich took Quinton up on his invitation to stay for beers, but Dexter was eager to get back home to spend some time with Dakota and Olivia.

Nick wished Dex a good night as they walked out to their cars, parked in Quinton's circular drive. But Dex halted Nick with a hand on his shoulder.

"I know I told the guys they shouldn't worry, but is everything all right?"

"It's like you said…this project I'm doing for the New York office, in addition to my own job, is an adjustment, but nothing I can't handle," Nick assured his friend who was also his boss.

"And this has nothing to do with this soulmate search of Em's?"

Nick's spine stiffened at the mention of his best friend's quest for the perfect man.

"If that's what Em wants, it's what I want for her, too." Nick tried to force a smile, but it felt more like a scowl. "I'm just not used to her shutting me out like this."

"My tomboy little sis is in her soft life girlie era, and I love that for her," Dex said. "Besides, Dakota, Sin, Kassie, and Izzy are a better source of advice about navigating the dating world from her perspective."

"I know." Nick frowned. "But I can give her the inside scoop on what a guy is thinking and what his cryptic messages actually mean. I might not be enthusiastic about this project, but I want to help."

"Then you should remind her that you want her to be happy...even though that means she'll end up with someone else."

Nick didn't need to turn his head. He could feel the heat of Dex's stare.

"So you know that..."

"She admitted that she's into you, and you turned her down? Yeah. It's a small town, man." Dex shrugged. "So I have to ask...are you sure that what you're feeling isn't regret or jealousy now that you aren't the center of her world?"

How in the hell was he supposed to answer that question?

He hadn't even been completely honest with himself about his feelings for Emerie.

"I regret hurting Em," Nick said carefully. "And maybe I am a little worried that if she finds this perfect guy she's looking for..." Nick's voice faltered, and his throat tightened.

"That she won't have room in her life for you anymore?" Dex sighed quietly when Nick didn't respond. "You two have been best friends forever. I can only imagine how you must be feeling. But you had to know that at some point Em was gonna fall for *someone*. And if you don't feel that way about her—"

"I know." The reality of Dexter's words felt like a weight on Nick's chest.

"You might have chosen to spend the rest of your life as Peter Pan. But just remember...eventually, Wendy decides that she'd rather grow up. The question is...are you going to step up as her best friend and support her efforts, despite your hurt feelings, or is this friendship only about what's in it for you?"

Nick's attention snapped to his friend. His gut knotted. "Shit. I sound like that selfish, asshole friend who needs to be the center of attention all the time."

"I didn't say that." Dexter held up his open palms. "You've been a great friend to Em. I've rested easier many nights because I knew that if my brothers and I couldn't be there, you'd have Em's back. Even my dad, who *hated* the idea of you being his baby girl's best friend, has come to like and trust you. All I'm asking is that you continue to be the man we all believe you to be. That means either you want to be the only man in Em's life or you're willing to set your ego aside and be the friend she needs as she searches for the man who wants to be."

"I get it, boss." Nick drew in a deep breath, not committing to which option he would take. "I won't let Em down."

"Didn't expect you would." Dex clapped a hand on Nick's shoulder. "Now I'm going home to the two women who mean the world to me—my wife and daughter. Good night."

As Nick watched Dexter drive off, his friend's words echoed in his head.

He'd chosen to prioritize his friendship with Em by not getting involved romantically. And though he'd agreed to help Emerie find her soulmate, his commitment to the project had been half-hearted at best. Em had always been there for him, and he'd do anything for her. So he needed to prove it by being the friend she deserved. Even if helping Em find the man who would steal her heart would break his.

Nick pulled out his phone and dialed Em, asking if he could drop by for a few minutes. Hearing her voice always made him smile.

As he drove toward Em's condo, his heart thumped, and his pulse raced. He told himself it was because he was eager to spend some time with his best friend. But a little voice at the back of his head called him out as a liar who was afraid to face the truth: that he wanted more than just friendship with Em.

It didn't seem wise to admit his feelings to Emerie. But at the very least, he should be honest with himself. He needed to remind himself of why he'd chosen not to pursue a relationship with Em. Of why he was sacrificing the chance to be the man who got to lay beside her each night. He was protecting her heart and their friendship—at all costs. Two things he could *not* afford to fuck up, as he had before. Otherwise, he'd spend the next few months in absolute misery.

Em opened the door just enough to peek her head out. Her half smile lit something in Nick's chest. He was immediately struck by how pretty Em was. Not that he hadn't known and appreciated that all along. But lately, he couldn't relegate that knowledge to the back of his brain as a basic, known fact—like gravity or the capitals of each state. No, it was determined to sit front and center and disrupt his thoughts.

"You look nice." Em scanned his tan wool coat, beige sweater, black jeans, and black leather boots. A black, wool scarf was draped around his neck because it was particularly chilly. "I thought tonight was just band practice. Why do you look like you're going on a date?"

"I can't look nice just because?" He shrugged.

"You can, and you do." Em's grin widened. "It's just so unfair that you can look this good effortlessly. Meanwhile, now that I'm trying to put some actual effort into my look, it takes me forever to get ready whenever I leave the house. I'm exhausted before I make it to the car."

"Well, you've knocked it out of the park with your new look. Besides, if it makes you feel good and gets you closer to your goal, I'd certainly say you're worth the extra time and effort." Nick couldn't help smiling.

"You're right. I *am* worth it. I'll remind myself of that the next time I'm struggling to recall the order of application for the ten products required for my 'no-makeup look.'" She used air quotes, then laughed. The sound warmed his chest. "Thanks, Nick. You always know what to say. But I didn't expect to hear from you tonight. I've already gone into full pajama mode. C'mon in."

Em opened the door and stepped aside to let him in.

"I didn't expect to call, but…" Nick froze as he slowly scanned the length of Em's body. She wore a fitted, long-sleeve, V-neck, pink Henley shirt and boy shorts. Her pajamas were more body-conscious than anything Nick had seen her in before. The deep V-neck revealed the dark brown skin of her chest, and the short shorts exposed a lot more thigh than he was accustomed to seeing except for when they were on the beach. The sleep set was playful and sexy, highlighting all the things he loved about Em's body. She wore a long, cable-knit sweater over it with matching thigh-high socks.

Fuck.

Em looked incredibly sexy in that little getup. It was stretching his determination to see her as just a friend to its absolute limit.

Nick realized he was standing there with his mouth hanging open. He swallowed hard, thankful his coat was shielding his body's reaction to her. "Uh…that's…new."

Nick had seen his best friend's entire collection of sleepwear: T-shirts and baggy shorts too battered to wear in public. But he'd never seen her in anything that highlighted her numerous assets the way this outfit did.

"Yeah, Sin was brutal. She made me ditch the old stuff and buy actual pajamas and loungewear. She said I should buy something that makes me feel sexy and that I'd actually want someone else to see me in. I resisted at first, but this set is like one of my *favorite* things I've purchased for this new makeover. It's warm, cozy, and super comfortable." Em placed a hand on her belly, glancing down at her legs. "I didn't know how I'd feel about these shorts being so short, but these thigh-high, cable-knit socks are *everything*."

"I *definitely* agree with that." Nick loosened the scarf around his neck because Em had the place toasty on a chilly winter night. Though that wouldn't account for the racing of his pulse. He cleared his throat. "I mean, I'm glad you're investing in yourself. You look good...and happy," he added. "What are you up to tonight?"

"I was watching TV." Em gestured toward the sofa. "You want anything? Hot chocolate? A soda? Maybe a beer? I think I have a few bottles of that import you like in the back of the fridge. And my mom made ham. You can make a ham sandwich, if you're hungry."

Em was rambling—something she did when she was nervous. They were just hanging out at her place, as they had a hundred times before. So why did tonight feel... *different*?

"Quinton's wife made tacos. I'm good. Thanks." Nick slapped a hand to his stomach, and Em's gaze dropped there. She nibbled on her lower lip before shifting her gaze back to his.

"You said you needed to talk to me about something?" Em sank on the opposite end of the sofa and turned toward him, as if she needed the space. She sat cross-legged and hugged one of the oversize pillows to her chest. It was her preferred way to sit on the couch. But today, he couldn't help noticing the gleaming brown skin on her toned thighs. "Is this about your project for the New York office?"

"No. It's not about work." Nick tried to pull it together and focus on why he'd come here. "It's about this dating quest you're on."

"We've talked about this already, Nick." Em huffed. "I said I'd be cautious."

"That's not what I was going to say." Nick held up a hand. "I came to say I want to help."

"You already said so." Em frowned suspiciously.

"But you didn't actually believe me," Nick noted. "Or you wouldn't be shutting me out."

"Shutting you out? How? We spoke earlier today."

"But we talk less. Hang out less…"

"You're a busy corporate exec, and I'm an entrepreneur trying to grow my business. There are only so many hours in the day, Nicky," Em reminded him.

"I know." Nick leaned forward; his hands folded between his open legs. He hated sounding clingy, but the sudden distance between them wasn't all in his head. "But things have definitely been different between us since New Year's Eve."

"I know, but eventually, it'll be like it never happened." Em dropped her gaze from his as she repeated the words that neither of them believed, no matter how much they wanted them to be true.

Nick could only hope that the more they said it, the truer it would become.

"You're overthinking it," Em said: an admonition he usually gave to her. And he was nearly always right.

"What if this is like that crack in your windshield you kept ignoring? Eventually, it spread until you had to replace the entire windshield." Nick turned toward her, draping an arm over the back of the sofa. The thought of losing their friendship was shattering. "I don't want that to happen to us, Em."

"It won't." Her frown deepened. She placed a warm hand on his arm, propped on the back of the couch. "Because we won't let that happen."

"That's why I'm here," Nick said. "I know you've been hesitant to talk to me about how things are going with your Soulmate Project. But I don't want you to feel that way. I *want* you to be happy, Em. So I'm completely on board, and I want to help."

"I appreciate that, Nicky." Em hugged her pillow again. "But let's face it, you can't help me select the right bra for my body type or teach me how to apply my makeup so I don't end up looking like a circus clown."

He had a myriad of opinions on the bra issue, but it seemed best not to mention that.

"Point taken." Nick grinned and Em giggled. It eased the tension that had settled between them since that night on the beach. "Maybe I'm not the right person to school you on how to apply winged eyeliner or wear stilettos without breaking an ankle. But I can give you valuable insight into the male mind." Nick tapped his temple with two fingers. "Consider me your male mind strategist slash bullshit detector."

"Now that is the kind of valuable intel I could use." Em nodded thoughtfully. "I guess it would be nice to have an informant on my side." A slow grin teased the edges of Em's full lips. But then her expression sobered. "I know that we've always talked about everything, but we're usually pretty surface-level about relationship stuff. We avoid talking in depth about our feelings and we never, ever kiss and tell."

"That's an unwritten rule we are *definitely* keeping." Nick was willing to make sacrifices for the sake of their friendship, but he wasn't a masochist. He didn't need to hear the details of Em being with someone else.

"Deal." Em extended her hand, and Nick shook it, trying not to think of how soft and warm her skin felt or how reluctant he was to let her hand go. "So let's talk. Ask me anything you want to know."

"All right." Nick clapped his hands together and regarded his friend. "Let's start with your date with Marcus. You two went out over a week ago. But whenever I bring up your date, you dodge the question."

"I wasn't—" Emerie halted mid-sentence when Nick raised an eyebrow. "Okay, fine. I was dodging your questions," she admitted with the most adorable pout. "It wasn't so much a date as two people who've known each other forever hanging out with a group of his friends. And, if I'm being honest, our night out wasn't bad." Em went to the kitchen and turned on the teakettle. "You sure you don't want some hot chocolate?"

"If you're making some already . . . sure." Nick followed her to the kitchen and parked on a stool. When Em didn't volunteer any additional information, Nick pressed further. "So when you say that it wasn't bad, do you mean that—"

"I mean that when Marcus isn't feeling the pressure of trying to impress the guys at Blaze's, he's actually a decent human being and a lot of fun. I had a good time with him and a few of his friends. He was comfortable with them. So he didn't feel the need to put on a pretense. When Marcus is just being himself with all the other nonsense stripped away, he's a fun guy. Also, I discovered I don't hate bowling as much as I thought. I just needed someone to teach me."

"Marcus is a solid bowler," Nick acknowledged.

"Maybe that's what made him so comfortable. We were on his turf playing a sport at which he excels. Apparently, his pride is still a bit hurt from the time I wiped the floor with him one-on-one in basketball."

Nick laughed. "The man is a bit sensitive."

"Sure you don't want that sandwich?" Em opened the refrigerator.

"Your mom does make a good ham." Why had Em made the quick conversation pivot? With Em, there was always a reason. "Okay. You talked me into it."

"Good. Because I *really* want another one, but it felt rude to eat it in front of you if you're not eating." Em washed her hands, then rummaged in the refrigerator for the makings of ham sandwiches.

Nick's eyes were immediately drawn to Em's curvy bottom beneath that cable-knit cardigan as she searched her refrigerator shelves.

"I know there are pickles in here somewhere." Em shoved things around. "Nick, could you toast the bread?"

"Could I…uh…sure. Of course," Nick stammered. He cleared his throat, feeling guilty for shamelessly ogling his best friend's ass. "Let me wash my hands."

Em gathered the items from the fridge and set them on the counter. "Are you okay? You look a little"—she gestured to her own face—"flushed."

"I'm…fine." Nick shifted his gaze from hers, then grabbed a paper towel to dry his hands. Em wasn't the only one who could change the subject when things got sticky. He returned the conversation to their original topic. "I was pretty shocked when you agreed to go out with Marcus. I'm even more stunned to hear that you enjoyed your night with him." Nick tossed the paper towel. "I guess that means you plan on going out with him again."

He'd meant it as a statement, but the inflection in his voice indicated it was a question.

"I already did." Em didn't acknowledge the wide-eyed astonishment on his face but did offer further explanation. "Marcus's friend was having brunch at her house the next day, and she insisted that I come. You know how I feel about fluffy pancakes and crisp bacon, so..."

"And they say food is the way to a *man's* heart." Nick shook his head as he placed slices of sourdough bread into the little toaster oven on the counter. "If someone wanted to kidnap you, I swear all they'd have to do is leave a trail of pancakes and bacon leading into the back of the kidnapper's van. You'd walk right in, sit down, and make yourself a plate."

"Hey! It was damn good bacon. The kind with the peppered edges. And it was cooked to absolute crispy perfection." Em made the chef's kiss gesture. "If his friend wasn't already spoken for, I would've considered asking her to marry me." She grinned.

"Enough about the bacon." Nick was only half teasing. "Is there going to be a third date with Marcus?"

"Probably not. I mean we might hang out and go bowling or something. The man bowls a 220. You know how competitive I am. If I'm gonna bowl, I wanna learn from the best."

"Fair." Nick acknowledged this with the nod of his head.

"But that same competitiveness is the reason I could never be interested in a man like Marcus. He'd be uncomfortable in situations where I excel and he doesn't. He's intimidated by my abilities and independence. I don't need a guy like that in my life. I want someone who will champion my accomplishments whether they're in business or in sports. But…" Em frowned, her words trailing off as she turned away from him. "Never mind."

"Hey." Nick put his hands on her shoulders, forcing Em to face him again. "I'm proud of you for realizing that you shouldn't settle for someone who wants you to play small to make themselves feel bigger. You deserve more than that, Em. Even if that considerably reduces the dating pool."

"I know, but thanks for saying that. It's nice to hear." Em nodded toward the toaster oven that had just dinged.

"So what's next?" He used wooden tongs to remove the slices of bread from the oven and set them on plates.

"Kassie's cousin is coming to town for a visit, and since I've been hesitant to accept any dates from the apps, I let her talk me into setting us up."

"Oh." Nick frowned immediately, then mentally chastised himself for it. He made the effort to neutralize his expression. "When?"

"He'll be here in a few days." Em took the plates from Nick. "Hand me a butter knife?"

"So soon, huh?" Nick handed her the utensil. "Have you considered that if things don't work out, it might affect your friendship with Kass?"

"No. Why would I?" Em frowned, glancing up from smearing stadium mustard onto all four pieces of bread. "Sure, Kassie hopes things will work out with me and Dillon. But she's not going to throw a tantrum and stop being my friend if we don't hit it off."

"Okay," Nick said. Again, more of a question than a statement.

"And this is you being helpful?" Em was irritated as she spread a thin layer of mayo on each slice of bread.

"Does being helpful mean I can't also be honest with my best friend?"

"Make your own damn sandwich." Em shoved the plate toward him and started constructing her sandwich, piled high with ham, Swiss cheese, and dill pickle slices.

"C'mon, Em." Nick stood beside her and assembled his sandwich. "We always keep it one hundred with each other, even when that means saying something that's hard for the other person to hear. You said you want us to go back to the way things were. That's what I'm trying to do here."

"No, what you're being is contradictory. First you tell me I should rely on my connections to find someone my family or friends can vouch for. I do that, and now you're getting me all worried that I'm going to break Kassie's heart if I don't like her cousin."

"When you put it that way—"

"Exactly! Make up your damn mind, man. I have enough jitters and concerns about this. You're supposed to be my hype man, Nick. Not create more doubt. I've got that part covered already, thanks." Em was pissed, and he couldn't blame her.

"Okay, you're right. I'm sorry. I'm still working out all the bugs with this thing," Nick admitted as he constructed his sandwich. "I'll keep working on that. But I've dated a friend's cousin, and let's just say we're not friends any-more." Nick shrugged.

"I hate it when you go and make a valid point while I'm trying to be mad at you." Em expressed her supreme dis-pleasure with an exaggerated groan. "Fine. I'll talk to Kass before my date with Dillon. But if she says she'll be cool about it, even if I don't like her cousin, I trust her word. Just like I trust yours."

Nick couldn't help feeling guilty. Not that he'd done anything that made him untrustworthy. But he wasn't being one hundred percent honest with Em about his feelings for her, either.

"Great. And since I'm here anyway and apparently having a second dinner, how about we watch a movie, your pick?"

"Even if I feel like watching *Brown Sugar* again?" Em propped a fist on her cocked hip.

"I just happen to be in the mood for a lil' Taye Diggs and Sanaa Lathan." Nick grinned. "I'll even make you an amaretto sour." He nodded toward the bottle of Disaronno on the little tray where she kept her alcohol. "Deal?"

"Okay, fine. But you know the rules. That constantly buzzing phone of yours—"

"I'm turning it off right now." Nick took out his phone and turned it off.

"Okay, fine. Whatever." She agreed with a dramatic eye roll.

"You know you love me." Nick chuckled, pulling her into his arms for a hug.

He hadn't meant it *that* way, and he was sure Em realized that. But as she settled into his arms, her lush curves pressed against him and her arms wrapped around him, he couldn't help wondering if maybe he did. And if the person he wasn't being honest with was himself.

Chapter Ten

• • •

Agreeing to spend the evening watching a romantic comedy about two longtime best friends falling for each other probably wasn't the smartest move Nick had ever made. But he'd missed Em and had been desperate to spend some time with her.

Still, as he'd watched the movie—a favorite of Em's for as long as he could remember—what had happened between them on the beach on New Year's Eve loomed over them like a five-ton elephant squeezing his ass into the small space between them on Em's sofa.

Nick could practically see the accusatory question on Em's face.

Why can't we be like Dre and Sid?

Nick groaned internally. The answer was simple. Because Dre and Sid weren't real.

Sometimes he wished he could be as much of an optimist as his best friend was. She believed that both lasting love and eternal friendship were possible for them because she'd seen it in countless romantic comedies and read about it in books. But Nick couldn't help thinking that if there had ever been a follow up to *Brown Sugar*, it would've been a drama about the reality of Dre and Sid discovering that they couldn't truly be both best friends and life partners. That they'd lost the friendship to the relationship and maybe even that was on rocky ground as they tried to maintain it through the demands of intensely stressful, high-level jobs that required lots of travel while also trying to start a family. Because that would be the reality of the movie's neatly packaged, tearjerker of a happy ending that currently had his best friend in a chokehold.

Nick glanced over at Em during the final scene, in which Dre appears at the radio station where Sid is being interviewed and declares, "I don't wanna be your friend no more."

Em was sniffling and gliding a finger beneath one eye, then the other. She usually did a better job of hiding the inevitable tears the scene always evoked. He usually played along, pretending he didn't notice and offering to grab them both a beer. But this time, he couldn't.

"You might be a killer at the billiard table and on the basketball court, but you're as soft and squishy as a marshmallow on the inside." Nick draped an arm around Em's shoulder and tugged her closer.

"True. But that's why you love me," she countered, scooting closer. She lay her head on his shoulder and wiped away tears. "And yes, I know it's just a movie. But I can't help being happy for Sid and Dre because they finally figured it out. The ending gets me every time."

Nick leaned his head against hers. "And maybe it's hitting a little harder now that you've decided you want a happy ending of your own?"

"Maybe." Em sniffled. "I don't want crustless cucumber sandwiches at my bridal shower or anything," she said, referring to a scene in the movie, and it made them both laugh. "But I do want my happily ever after. And like Sid, I'm tired of waiting for it."

"I know." Nick frowned, his chest tightening. He was glad Em couldn't see his expression. "And you will get your happy ending. The right guy will come along eventually. Just don't be fooled into taking the bait from the wrong guy or you'll miss out on your Hip-Hop."

Em nodded her silent agreement, the two of them huddled together.

Being here for Em like this felt perfect. Like everything he'd ever wanted.

But he couldn't help thinking about the words uttered by Taye Diggs's character.

I don't wanna be your friend no more.

Every woman he knew swooned at that moment in the movie, thinking it was romantic that Dre had come to the realization that he wanted to be Sid's lover, not just her friend. But Nick had always taken those words literally. To him, it was Dre's admission that they couldn't have both—so he was choosing romance over their friendship. Something Nick wasn't prepared to do.

His friendship with Em had outlasted many of their friends' parents' marriages.

A little fun between the sheets wasn't hard to find. A friendship like theirs was precious and rare. So he wouldn't risk it.

"Thanks for watching *Brown Sugar* with me again. But I've got an early morning meeting with a client. I should probably get some sleep." Em sat up, wiping tears from her damp eyes.

Nick stared at Em a moment. His gaze dropped from her watery brown eyes to her full lips, and he couldn't help wondering about the taste and feel of them. His heart thudded in his chest, and his throat suddenly felt dry.

"You're sure you're okay?" Em studied him with concern. "You were in a daze for a second there."

"Yeah. I'm fine. I'm just glad we got a chance to hang out tonight and catch up." Nick stood suddenly. "I'll put away the dishes."

He grabbed their plates and glasses and headed toward the kitchen.

"You don't need to do that." Em followed him. "I can take care of the dishes."

"You gave me the last of your mom's ham. Taking care of the dishes is the least I can do." Nick rinsed their plates. The moment he glanced at the refrigerator, he froze, struck by the memory of how perfect Em's ass had looked as she'd bent over to rummage inside the fridge.

He was hard and had to readjust his stance remembering how incredible she'd looked.

"We're playing at a wedding at the resort this weekend," Nick said. "You could be our emcee. The gig doesn't pay, but we can compensate you with overpriced wedding cuisine. I know how much you love cocktail shrimp."

"Sounds fun." Em pulled her sweater around her tightly. "But that's when I have my date with Dillon."

"Oh. Right." It felt like Nick's chest was being crushed by a boa constrictor. "Next time, then."

"Next time," she echoed. "Now stop stalling. We both need to get into bed... separately, of course." Em sifted her fingers through her soft curls, and he wanted to do the same, but he shoved a hand in his pocket instead.

"I can't just hop into bed anymore. There's a whole routine to this." She indicated her hair and face. "First, I have to wrap my hair up in a scarf, which is a lot trickier than I thought. The makeup has to come off and there's an entire skin care routine that has like five steps."

"Shit. Look at you. You've officially become high maintenance," Nick teased. "Guess you'll be traveling a lot heavier on our next vacation. Speaking of which..." He turned to her, an idea suddenly churning in his head. "Traveling more is a part of your Soulmate Project, right?"

"Yes, but I haven't gotten that far on the list," she admitted.

"I've got a couple of work trips coming up. The first one is to San Antonio in a few weeks. You should come with me."

"But you'll be working," Em said.

"Not the entire time. And when I am working, it'll give you a chance to work on client projects or explore the city a little on your own. What do you say?"

"Are you sure you want me tagging along? This sounds like the perfect out-of-town hook up situation for you. We're both a little too old for leaving a sock on the doorknob."

"I know, smart-ass." Nick grinned. "I'm not interested in hooking up with anyone."

"How will you know until you get there?" Em folded her arms.

"Because I'd rather spend that time hanging out with my best friend and helping you check the next few items off your list."

Em silently assessed him, her eyes narrowing. "Text me the dates, and I'll let you know."

Nick maintained a neutral expression. But inside, he was doing a happy dance. Time with Em was harder to come by now. He relished the chance to have her all to himself for a few days. "Will do."

He headed into the living room and collected his coat, slipping it on.

"Now I need to think about Step Six: doing something outside of my comfort zone," Em said. "There's a new dance studio in town, and I'd really like to take lessons."

"Why? You dance just fine. Your Wobble is a little wobbly, and you get lost every single time in that Tamia line dance. But I'd give you a solid eight and a half for the creativity you bring to your Electric Slide," Nick teased.

"That's line dancing. There are patterns to follow, and I can handle that. As can every eighty-year-old grandmother out there. Except that Tamia one. That one is hard." Em pointed a finger.

Nick wanted to mention that eighty-something Mama Mae managed that dance just fine, but there was a good chance his friend would toss him out on his ass...deservedly so.

"But dancing as a couple—like we did for Dexter and Dakota's wedding—is a completely different ballpark," Em continued. "I looked like an uncoordinated loon out there on the dance floor."

Nick snorted because while he wouldn't have described Em's dancing so harshly, she wasn't exactly wrong. But he did his best to hold back a laugh when Em gave him the evil eye.

"See what I mean?" Em pointed an accusatory finger at him, and Nick dissolved into laughter. "Rett and Sin's wedding will be here before we know it. I do *not* want to be the weakest link in the bridal party this time. I'd like to look like I know what I'm doing out there. I just don't want to take the classes alone."

"If you're doing this in hopes of finding someone, wouldn't it make more sense to take the class by yourself?"

"Probably. But I'm nervous about taking the class solo. There's a reason Will Smith had Jazzy Jeff, Chuck D had Flavor Flav, and Biggie had . . . never mind," Em said.

"So you plan to go into the class with your own hype man, like you're a 1990s rapper?" Nick asked incredulously.

Who is this woman right now? And why do I find her so incredibly hot—aside from the booty shorts, thigh-high socks, and her impeccable taste in hip-hop?

"When you put it that way, it makes me sound either delusional or a bit full of myself." Em grinned. "The point is that it's nice to have company and someone who thinks you're awesome, even when you move like an uncoordinated duck." She shrugged, shoving his shoulder when he chuckled. "I've been trying to talk Kassie into taking the class with me, but the girl has two left feet. The idea of taking dance classes made her break into a cold sweat."

"Then I'll do it," Nick said, surprising himself.

"You're volunteering to take a dance class with me? In addition to work, and this extra project, and playing with the band?" Em counted each of Nick's responsibilities off on her fingers.

"This is important to you, right?"

"Yes." The laughter was gone from her voice.

"Then it's important to me, too," Nick said plainly. "Sign us up, and I'll send you the money for my class registration. I probably won't be able to attend every class. But hopefully by the time I miss one, you'll be feeling more comfortable."

"Thank you, Nick." The relief on his friend's face made the juggling of his schedule that he'd have to do these next few weeks seem worth it. "Wait, you almost forgot this." Em grabbed the wool scarf she gifted him the previous

Christmas from the sofa and tied it around his neck. "*There.*
Now you're ready to face the elements."

Nick stared at Em, studying her gorgeous face as she
gazed up at him gratefully.

Em had wished him good night like this many times
before. So why did everything about tonight feel so different? And why couldn't he stop staring at her mouth, wanting to cover those pouty lips with his own?

Because that night had changed everything. And those
body-hugging jammies and thigh-high, cable-knit socks
weren't helping. He honestly might never get the vision of
Em in that outfit out of his brain.

"If you need anything, remember I'm just a phone call
away." Nick buttoned his jacket.

"Thanks, but I'll be fine. I promise to avoid trails of pancakes leading to kidnappers' vans. Nor will I spend my evening crying lonely-girl tears into a bottle of gin."

"Of course not. You're a rum girl. You'd make yourself a
pitcher of mojitos instead." Nick winked.

"Sometimes, I hate that you know me so well." Em
pressed a quick kiss to his cheek. "Text me to let me know
you made it home, and don't argue with me." Em jabbed a
finger in his direction. "I'm already stressed about wrapping my hair right. I don't need to be worrying about
whether you made it home safely, too."

"Yes, ma'am." Nick saluted.

"Smart-ass." Em shook her head. "Good night."

Nick wished her a good night, then headed back to his car.

Spending time with Em was always the lift that he
needed. The thing that made him feel like his life was back
in balance—no matter what else might be going on.

He wanted his friend to be happy. But it broke him to
think that someday soon it would be someone else who

would put that smile on Em's face and be her shoulder to cry on. He only hoped that someone would be confident enough in their relationship to respect his friendship with Em rather than being envious of it.

Was that too much to ask?

Chapter Eleven

* ● *

Emerie sat in the booth at Casa de Lupita and snuck a peek at her compact mirror. She raked her fingers through her bangs, trying to create the perfect sideswept effect. The kind of look that said "I'm the girl you want" without being too obvious about it. Also, she wanted to make sure that her lipstick was still on her lips—not overshooting her mouth or staining her teeth.

So far, so good.

Em slipped the compact back into her purse and picked up her napkin.

"You must be Kassie's friend, Emerie." A tall, handsome man wearing a gray blazer; a black sweater; black, casual pants; and horn-rimmed glasses stood over her. "I'm her cousin, Dillon. It's a pleasure to meet you." He extended his hand.

"Dillon, hi." Em stood and shook his hand. Hopefully, her broad smile belied the jittery nerves that knotted her stomach and made her heart thump in her chest. Despite being several weeks into her soulmate quest, this was her first bona fide date, and it showed.

It didn't help that Dillon was giving off sexy professor vibes.

But Dillon's sweet, nervous smile made Emerie feel more at ease. It was possible that he was even more nervous about their date than she was.

"It's a pleasure to finally meet you," Em said. "Kassie has always had such glowing things to say about you. Your work as an educator has inspired her so much in her work at the arboretum."

"That's great to hear," Dillon said. "And we have you to thank for helping my cousin break out of her shell. She was super shy as a kid, but she's opened up a lot since you became friends."

Emerie smiled so wide, her cheeks hurt. She was thrilled that her friend had come into her own over the years. Kassie was sweet, funny, and brilliant, and so giving and compassionate. But she'd been painfully shy early on—making it difficult for people to get to know her.

"I'm just lucky to have her as a friend," Em said honestly. She gestured to the other side of the booth. "Please, have a seat."

"Thank you." Dillon hung his coat on the hook beside hers.

They both took their seats. Dillon adjusted the collar of his sweater while Em fiddled with the pashmina tied around her neck. They seemed equally nervous about their date.

Though they hadn't met, Em felt like she knew him a little because of how proudly Kassie and her mother had spoken of him. But she was eager to learn more about the handsome professor.

"So...Dillon. Tell me about yourself." Em folded her hands on the table and flashed him a bright smile and the subtlest flutter of the eyelashes she hoped she hadn't applied crookedly.

"I'm the thirty-seven-year-old son of two schoolteachers. I began my career in Silicon Valley, burned bright, then burned out. I shifted gears and became an IT professor instead."

"Your parents must be proud that you followed in their footsteps."

"They are." Dillon was far more handsome than the photos stored on Kassie's phone would've led her to believe. Then again, photography was *not* one of her friend's gifts. Kassie took the worst cell phone photos known to man.

Dillon's deep gray eyes, reminiscent of the sky swirling over a stormy sea, had the slightest hint of blue. His eyes glimmered in the light of the festive, handwoven basket lights hanging overhead.

Handsome? Check. *Doesn't go on and on about himself?* Check.

"Which college do you teach at?" Em took a sip of her water.

"UNC Wilmington."

"My best friend's parents are both professors there, too." Em set her water glass down excitedly, splashing a little water on the tablecloth. "Doctors Timothy and Evelyn Washington. Maybe you know them?"

"I know *of* them, sure. They're kind of a big deal around campus." Dillon sipped his water, too. "You're friends with their daughter?"

"They don't have a daughter," Em said. "I've been best friends with their son, Nick, since we were kids."

"Oh, I see." Dillon's smile dimmed the tiniest bit. He picked up his menu and scanned it. "A lifetime friendship like that is pretty special," Dillon noted. "I'm still good friends with my college roommate and several of my fraternity brothers. But nothing that goes back quite that far.

Most of the kids I went to elementary school with were too busy teasing me for my oversize glasses and obsession with books to start up a friendship." There was still a hint of pain in his voice.

"Kids can be cruel," Em said. "I was a tomboy, so I got teased a lot. I also landed my fair share of punches when they did."

Dillon laughed, and Em did, too.

"I guess that's another reason Nicky and I got along so well. He was kind of new to the area. His parents moved here after his grandmother died and left them her house a stone's throw from the beach. He needed a friend, and I needed an ally."

"How'd you two meet?"

An involuntary smile spread across Em's face whenever she thought of the kismet of the meeting that would forever change her and Nick's lives.

"The Washingtons were busy professors and researchers. Their next-door neighbors often babysat Nick. Their youngest daughter, Dakota, who is now my sister-in-law, was dating my brother, Dexter. They took the two of us to the town showing of one *Toy Story* movie or another. We hit it off, and we've been best friends ever since."

"Wow. That's…great." Dillon lowered his menu and offered Emerie a polite smile, then shifted the topic. "I know that you have an older brother, that you and Kassie are good friends and that she adores you, and that you have a longtime best friend. Oh, and I know that you grew up as a tomboy. But that was clearly a very long time ago," Dillon added.

"Not as long ago as you might think," Em muttered.

"High school?"

She shook her head.

"College?" Dillon leaned forward with one eyebrow raised.

"About a month ago." Em picked up her menu. "And believe me, no one is happier about the transformation than my mother."

Dillon looked shocked for a moment, then his expression shifted to a grin. His chuckle turned into a full belly laugh and Emerie couldn't help laughing, too.

"Well, I would've pegged you as the high school cheerleader and homecoming queen. Because, if you don't mind me saying so, you look absolutely stunning tonight."

"I don't mind at all." Em swept her bangs to the side, her cheeks heating as she glanced down at the little black dress Kassie had recommended she wear. Thanks to Sin, she now had several LBDs. "And thank you for saying so. You look quite handsome tonight, too."

"What, this old thing?" Dillon tugged on the lapels of his jacket. "Totally kidding. I'm still in my awkward tech nerd phase. There's a good chance I might never grow out of it. So tonight's designer couture is courtesy of my mother and sister who took me on a shopping trip specifically for this date. They didn't want me to embarrass them."

"Well, they did an amazing job. But now I feel the pressure to ensure that you leave this restaurant feeling like the date was worth the time and money you invested in it."

"Then let me put your mind at ease. It already is," Dillon assured her, revealing a deep dimple in his right cheek. "Now I have the feeling that the proprietors of this lovely establishment are eager for us to order."

Dillon gave a subtle nod in the direction of Ms. Lupita—the owner of Casa de Lupita—and her daughter, Sofia. When Em glanced over at them, they both pretended to be cleaning the counter.

Ms. Lupita and Sofia had undoubtedly heard about Em's dating project and were invested in how her evening turned out. But she didn't want to put any added pressure on Dillon by telling him that.

"They're very attentive to their customers," Em said. "They probably don't want to rush us, but they want to be prepared."

"Then I'm guessing you've been here before."

"I'm here every few weeks. Nick and I have a standing dinner date on Wednesday nights. We rotate through our four favorite restaurants on the island."

"In that case, what would you recommend?"

"Normally, I'd go for the queso fundido, the Mexican street corn, grilled chicken tacos served with black beans and rice, and a frozen mango margarita. But a bellyful of cheese and beans, corn kernels stuck in my teeth, and tequila—my personal truth serum—don't seem like a very good combination for a first date." Em glanced up at Dillon who was staring at her with an open mouth and wide eyes.

Shit. Not a very ladylike thing to say, Emerie Roberts.

"Excellent point." Dillon rubbed his chin, amused by her candor. "What are the next best options?"

"The beef or chicken flautas are delicious. That's what I'm getting. And if you like pork, Nick usually gets the pork ribs or the braised pork shank. You can't go wrong with either."

"I'm more of a steak man, myself." Dillon buried his face in his menu again.

"Then I'd go with either the steak tacos or the steak fajitas."

He put his menu down and signaled to Sofia that they were ready. Once their orders were placed, Dillon said, "So you were going to tell me about yourself. Is Dexter your only sibling?"

"No. He's the eldest of three brothers. I'm the baby of the family and the only girl."

"So not surprising that you'd be a tomboy." Dillon sipped the Modelo Especial Sofia had brought to the table. "But then again, it was a fifty-fifty gamble that you would've ended up like my sister. She's the only girl, too. There's nearly a ten-year difference between us. My mom was so glad to finally have her baby girl that she pampered her and treated her like a little princess. Bought her all the frilly dresses and Barbie gear. All the things my mom wished she'd had growing up."

"My poor mom tried. All of my Barbies ended up with awful haircuts and missing limbs, buried somewhere in the backyard while I played ball with the boys."

"What kind of ball?"

"Basketball, racquetball, rugby, volleyball, billiards, and occasionally football."

"As in soccer?" Dillon asked.

"No. American football. The guys wouldn't always let me play. But in a pinch, I could be one hell of a wide receiver."

"Well, you are full of surprises, Emerie Roberts." Dillon's stormy gray eyes twinkled with amusement. "And I look forward to discovering every one of them."

Em's cheeks warmed, and the nervous tension she'd been feeling calmed.

Dillon was sweet, kind, dreamy, adorably nerdy, and far more fascinating than she'd have imagined. They had a lovely evening, so she gladly accepted his invitation to a second date. But in the back of her mind, she couldn't help comparing Dillon to Nick. And she couldn't help wondering where her friend was and who was with him tonight.

Chapter Twelve

———•••———

So...I get to meet the boyfriend." Nick dumped all his favorite seasonings into the ground beef as he prepared burgers for a night of watching basketball at her place.

"Dillon is *not* my boyfriend." Em elbowed her friend. "We've gone out twice, and he's a really sweet guy. So be nice, please."

"I will. As long as he passes the test."

"What test?"

"The 'is this dude good enough for my best friend?' test," Nick said, as if the answer should've been evident. "But don't sweat it, I'll be completely chill about it. Unless I need to bounce him."

Nick went heavy with the Worcestershire sauce before donning plastic gloves and kneading the heavily seasoned ground beef.

"Okay, first: maybe take it down a thousand. Second: you won't need to '*bounce*' Dillon. He's a genuinely good guy. If you give him half a chance, you might actually like him," Em said. She realized that her friend was protective, and she appreciated that. But this would be Dillon's first introduction to one of her friends, and she wanted it to go well.

Nick stopped kneading the meat and turned to her. "Do you like him?"

"I wouldn't have invited him tonight if I didn't."

"Can you see yourself with this guy? In the long-term, I mean?"

Em shifted her gaze from Nick's and folded her arms. She tried to maintain a neutral expression, but an involuntary frown furrowed her brows.

The truth was that she liked Dillon, and they got along well. There just wasn't a spark between them. But everything about him seemed so perfect. So maybe if they spent a little more time together, she would eventually feel the kind of attraction for him that she felt for Nick.

Em glanced back at her friend, wondering if he'd been able to read the thoughts floating in her head from the expression on her face.

If he had, Nick was gracious enough not to let on. He started forming the meat into perfectly shaped hamburger patties instead.

That was Nick. Everything in his life needed to be neat and perfect. No wonder he didn't consider her a good match. It was a miracle their friendship had survived their myriad of differences.

"Serious, adult relationships aren't just about sex and attraction, Nick. They're built on commonalities, admiration, friendship, respect..." Em ticked each item off on her fingers.

"Hey, who said anything about sex?" Nick looked like he was about to clutch a set of imaginary pearls.

"You just asked if I could see this going somewhere. How would I know that unless I kicked the tires?"

"She's using car metaphors about sex." Nick shook his head.

"Would you prefer it if I said yes, I could definitely see myself banging this guy?"

"No!" Nick held up a finger encased in latex and covered with ground meat. "I definitely would not."

"Fine. But could you please just be nice to the guy?" Em leaned her hip against the counter where Nick was working on the burgers. "And try to remember that this isn't about whether you like him or if my brothers or parents do. It's about whether *I* like him." Em jabbed her thumb to her chest. "And if I do, shouldn't that be enough for all of you?"

"Of course it is." Nick glanced up from forming his nearly identical hamburger patties. A deep furrow formed between his brows, despite his ready agreement. "But we care about you, Em. So forgive us if we're being a little overprotective."

"I'm not the same little girl you met twenty years ago. I'm a grown woman, and I can fend for myself. But thank you for caring." Em pressed a hand to his back.

There was a knock at the door, and Emerie drew in a deep breath and stood taller.

"That's them. So play nice, Nicky, or I swear to God, I'll put your ass in a time-out."

"As you wish."

Great. Nick was quoting Westley from *The Princess Bride*. That meant he was irritated. Which was rich, since he was the one who'd started this ridiculous conversation in the first place.

But she couldn't think about that now. She needed to focus on getting to know Dillon to see if there was any real possibility for the two of them.

Em opened the door. Dillon looked handsome in a gray sweater, dark jeans, and a black-wool winter coat. He held a bouquet of flowers, but there was something in his and Kassie's body language.

Dillon looked contrite, and Kassie looked pissed.

"Hey, Dillon. Hi, Kassie. What's wrong?" Em looked at Kassie, whose eyes didn't meet hers, then at Dillon.

"I was hoping we could talk for a second," Dillon said.

"Sure. Come on in and—"

"Actually, I was hoping we could talk out here," he said.

"Oh." Em's face heated. Coupled with the tension between Dillon and his cousin, his request wasn't a good sign. She lifted her chin and forced a smile. "Sure. Are those for me?" She indicated the bouquet in his hand.

"You really seemed to like the flowers at the restaurant the other night. I saw these at my aunt's floral shop, so I picked them up for you." Dillon flashed a sad smile.

"I can put them in some water, if you'd like," Kassie offered.

"Please." Em nodded to her friend who took the flowers from her cousin, then went inside, closing the door behind her.

"So..." Em pressed her back against the corridor wall. "I'm guessing you're not staying."

Dillon, who stood beside her, responded with the subtle shake of his head.

"Was it something I said? Or did? I'm not trying to make you change your mind," Em clarified. "I'd just really like to know what I did wrong."

"You didn't do anything wrong." Dillon turned toward her and shoved a hand into his pocket. "The thing is: I *really* like you, Emerie. But you're clearly in love with someone else."

Em's eyes widened, and she turned toward him, too. "What makes you think—"

"You probably don't even realize it, but you talk about your friend Nick like all the time. He's a big part of your life, so it stands to reason that a lot of your stories would involve him. But my last relationship ended...*badly*. The woman I was seeing for two years...she eventually broke it off because she realized she was in love with her 'work husband.' " Dillon used air quotes. "After I got over the initial shock and had a chance to think about it, I realized that the signs were always there. I'd just ignored them because I was so crazy about her. I can't do that again, Em. So as much as I like you and would love to see you again...I think it would be better for my own sanity if I didn't."

Emerie wanted to deny it. To insist that she wasn't in love with her best friend. But they both knew it was true.

"I'm sorry, Dillon. I didn't mean to—"

"I know." His cursory smile didn't activate the dimple in his right cheek. "Does he know?"

"Yes. But he doesn't feel the same." Em frowned. "So I'm trying really hard to move on."

"I'd bet everything I own that he'll eventually regret that choice," Dillon said. "For both of your sakes, I hope it isn't too late once he does."

"I doubt that. But it's nice of you to say." Em extended a hand and forced a smile. "It was a pleasure meeting you, Dillon. I enjoyed getting to know you."

"You, too, Emerie." Dillon shook her hand. "And if you ever find yourself *not* in love with your best friend, I'd honestly love to hear from you."

Dillon waved, then headed back toward the elevator.

Once he was gone, Em collapsed against the wall and groaned quietly. Dillon's words replayed in her head.

I'd bet everything I own that he'll eventually regret that choice. For both of your sakes, I hope it isn't too late once he does.

She'd spent the past few years believing the same thing.

So despite how well-meaning Dillon might be, he was wrong. She just needed to work harder at moving on with her life. Or at least do a better job of pretending that she was. Then eventually, it would be true.

———

Nick sipped his beer after saying good night to Kassie, who was leaving right after the game ended. He couldn't hear what she and Em were saying as they walked to the door. But from Kassie's apologetic expression and the bear hug she gave Em, he'd bet that the conversation had something to do with her cousin whom he'd dubbed *Villain* in his head. Because what else would you call a man who'd deliver breakup flowers in person when he was supposed to be meeting his romantic interest's best friend for the first time?

Nick scowled and rubbed his chin.

The moment he realized that Dillon wasn't coming in and that Em was upset, he'd wanted to follow the guy downstairs and give him a piece of his mind. But Em had made him promise to mind his own business, claiming that it was her fault—not Dillon's.

Nick found that hard to believe. Everyone loved Em. She was funny, compassionate, generous, and sometimes too damn honest for her own good. But there was something so adorably sweet and sincere about her that you couldn't stay mad at her for telling you the truth about yourself. Even if you wanted to.

Then there was Kassie. Her mood over the course of the evening wavered from sad and apologetic to Em to annoyed and angry with him. When Nick had asked Kassie if he'd done something to upset her, she'd just narrowed her gaze, folded her arms, and shaken her head before walking away.

Her cousin bails on Em two dates in, and Kassie was mad at him?

Nick could swear that the older he got, the less he understood the women in his life.

"Hey." Nick turned to Em when she sank onto the sofa, seated cross-legged, and hugged the large sofa pillow to her chest. "Tonight was really weird. I know you said everything was fine and you don't want to talk about it—"

"And I still don't," Em said quickly, then sighed. "I'm sorry. I didn't mean to snap at you. But I'm fine. Kassie's fine."

"Kassie was *not* 'fine.' I'm pretty sure she spent the evening plotting my murder. Why do you think I wouldn't let her make the drinks tonight?"

"Kassie would never hurt you, Nick. You are such a fucking drama king." Em shook her head but couldn't help laughing. Nick did, too.

He scooted closer to Em on the sofa and nudged her with his shoulder. "C'mon. If I did something inadvertently to upset Kass, I'd at least like to know what it is that I did."

"Like I said, it wasn't you. It was me."

"Then why is Kassie mad at me?"

"Because..." Em shifted her gaze from his, her voice wavering and her eyes watery. "Dillon is a really sweet guy. I like him, and he said that he really likes me."

"If he likes you so much, why did he bail tonight?" The muscles in Nick's back and neck grew tight seeing the pained expression on his friend's face.

"His previous relationship ended when his girlfriend finally realized that she was in love with her work friend. He said all the signs were there from the beginning, but he ignored them. My friendship with you...it gave him the same vibes." She shrugged.

"Oh." Nick leaned back against the sofa and dragged a

hand down his face. "So that's why Kass is mad at me. She thinks it's my fault things didn't work out between you and Villain."

"That isn't fair, Nick. Dillon isn't the villain in this debacle. If anyone is the villain, it's me. I'm the one who couldn't stop bringing you up."

She stood abruptly, gathering the trays filled with the remaining snacks.

"'What was your favorite vacation ever?' Nick and I took an amazing trip to Mexico five years ago. 'Have you ever been to Europe?' Nick and I have been talking about going there forever. Nick, Nick, Nick." Em mimicked herself in a mocking tone. "What an idiot. Of course the man thinks I'm in love with you."

Nick swallowed hard, his heart banging against his rib cage. He wanted to take Em in his arms, kiss her, and tell her how much he cared about her, too. But the little voice in the back of his head reminded him how that had ended for him twice before.

He squeezed his eyes shut and drew in a deep breath, trying to shake the desire to kiss Emerie and to tell her how he felt about her. The stakes were just too high.

Do not *sabotage another friendship. Three strikes and you're out.*

Losing Em and the group of friends they shared would mean losing everything that mattered to him aside from his parents. And his parents adored Emerie. She was the closest thing they had to a daughter. So they'd be pissed with him, too.

"Did you tell him that's not true?" Nick asked, his heart thumping loudly as he anticipated her response.

Em snapped her attention to his, her mouth twisted with a scowl as if she was angry that he'd had the nerve to ask.

"There was no point." Em deftly avoided answering his real question.

Are you still in love with me?

Em had moved so swiftly into this Soulmate Project. And since then, she'd remained focused on moving forward with finding someone else. He'd assumed that she'd shut down whatever feelings she might've had for him. But maybe he'd been wrong.

"The truth is that as much as I liked Dillon…I don't know. There was just *something* missing."

"Like what?" Nick really needed to know. "I mean…I think it would be helpful if we talked it out. Maybe it would help you recognize a doomed matchup from the start next time."

Em glared at him, completely unconvinced by his explanation. Still, she heaved a sigh and responded.

"Dillon is thoughtful and brilliant. He has this sort of dry sense of humor. Like you don't realize he was telling a joke until it hits you five minutes later because he's so cerebral." The corners of Em's mouth curved in a soft smile. "On paper, he's perfect. So why didn't I…" Em frowned, her words fading.

"So why didn't you want to rip Clark Kent's clothes off?" Nick teased, hoping to ease the tension Em was feeling. "Because you're looking for Superman, Em. A guy who doesn't exist."

Her frown deepened. Em dumped the leftover pretzels and chips in the garbage and put the rest of the cherry pie in the fridge.

"I'm not saying that the guy who looks good on paper *and* sets off all those fireworks isn't out there. Nor am I saying that you should settle for less than you deserve. Definitely don't do that." Nick squeezed her hand. "What I'm trying to say is you're putting so much pressure on yourself to find 'the one' that you're missing out on the whole point of dating."

"Which is?" Em tugged her hand free and folded her arms, one hip cocked.

"Dating should be fun. This isn't a biology experiment. Yes, the purpose is to learn about the 'subject' "—he used air quotes—"but dating also gives you the chance to learn a lot about yourself. What you like and don't like. What kind of person would drive you crazy in the long-term. What drives you crazy in bed." His gaze lingered on hers a moment longer than it should as he wondered—as he had so many times before—what would drive his friend wild.

A kiss on the neck? The gentle grazing of her nipples with his thumbs? A nibble on her earlobe? Riding his face with sheer abandon?

A shudder ran down Nick's spine and he squeezed his eyes shut, trying to push the thoughts aside.

"You should *enjoy* the process of dating, Em. Dating is not unlike life. It's not just about the destination. You should enjoy the journey. The rest will come to you."

Emerie eyed him suspiciously. "It seems unwise to take dating and relationship advice from a guy who is anti-relationships, don't you think?"

"I'm not anti-relationships," he countered. "Marriage and monogamy are beautiful things—when they work. But I'm honest with myself about my flaws. I just don't see a serious relationship working for me." Nick placed a hand to his chest. "Besides, you know the rule . . . those who can't do, teach." Nick winked.

Em picked up a dish towel and tossed it at his head.

Nick ducked, his fingers inadvertently ending up in what was left of the ranch dip. He smeared the dressing on Em's cheek.

She squealed with outrage, stuck her fingers in the last of the salsa, and smeared it across his lips. When she reached for the ranch dip, he grabbed her from behind and wrapped his arms around her, both of them laughing.

They had played and tussled like this lots of times before. But as he held Em in his arms now, her body pressed to his, Nick froze. His heart beat a mile a minute as he inhaled her soft floral and citrus scent and his body absorbed the warmth of hers.

He wanted to trail kisses down her neck and nibble on her ear. Find out if any of those things would drive Em wild. Make her want to rip off his clothes and invite him into her bed. His body reacted to the soft swell of her round bottom pressed against him. His dick grew painfully hard, and his breathing suddenly felt labored. Hers was, too.

Em seemed just as aware of the sudden shift in the mood. She glanced up at him, her eyes meeting his as her chest heaved with each uneven breath. He could feel the pounding of her heart, nearly in sync with his own.

Nick's gaze dropped to Emerie's mouth. Her full lips looked so tempting. Like they would be soft and sweet and taste like a slice of cherry pie. He wanted desperately to find out. But the one thing he wanted and needed even more was his friendship with Em. He couldn't afford to lose her the way he'd blown his other friendships.

"I should go," Nick said suddenly. "I need to prepare for a conference call with the San Antonio office. Did you decide if you'd like to go?"

"I have a big design project coming up, and I'm looking for a virtual assistant. Once I find someone, I have to train them." Em grabbed paper towels and wet them. She handed him one, and they both cleaned their hands and faces. "So I'll pass on San Antonio. But I'd love to go to

New York with you, if you still don't mind me tagging along."

"Hitting up one of my favorite cities with my best friend? C'mon. It's gonna be amazing." Nick collected Em's napkins and discarded all of them in the trash. "Also, there's the possibility that New York could be my new home."

"Wait...you're thinking of relocating to New York?" Em looked heartbroken. "I mean, I realize that when you moved back here, you said you wanted to move back to a major city at some point. But the timing seems sudden and—"

"This isn't me running away from what happened on New Year's Eve, Em. I promise. The opportunity to work on this special project was offered to me the following day. And the way it's been going, there's the possibility that I might be offered a position in our main office. Plus, when I was there last week, I reconnected with an old buddy I played with in LA. He runs his own recording studio. If I move to New York, I could pick up gigs as a session drummer."

"You loved doing session work when you were in LA." Em's smile was sad. "And you've always said that given the right opportunity, you'd love to move to New York. So this is exciting, right?"

"It is. But does the timing suck? Also, yes. Nothing is written in stone. It's just a possibility. Still, I wanted you to know, so it won't come as a surprise if it happens."

"This is what you want, so if you get the opportunity to chase your dreams, I'll be rooting for you. Like always." Em did her best to look happy for him, but all he could see was the heartbreak in her brown eyes.

Neither of them mentioned that he'd always hoped that she'd come with him if he moved to New York.

"Look, Em, maybe things didn't work out with Villain—"

"Dillon," she corrected with a warning tone.

"But maybe you'll find your love connection when we begin dance class."

Em looked doubtful. "At least it'll be fun, and we'll get to do it together. Given how quickly our lives seem to be changing, we should make the most of every moment we get to hang out together."

The reality of Em's words hit Nick squarely in the chest. He heaved a sigh and frowned. "I guess you're right."

The mood had turned somber as they discussed the logistics of dance class and Em packed a container of leftovers for him to take home.

Nick hugged Em tight and wished her good night. But on the drive home, he couldn't stop thinking about how he was going to extraordinary lengths to fight his growing feelings for Emerie because he valued their friendship above everything else. Yet, it was beginning to feel like he was losing her anyway.

He would do whatever it took to ensure that didn't happen.

Chapter Thirteen

• • •

Em hadn't signed up for dance classes to become the ballroom equivalent of Misty Copeland. But the owner of the dance studio, Idelle Willis, was a grand dame of modern ballroom dance and had been a contemporary of many incredible, groundbreaking Black dancers. So she took the lessons quite seriously.

"You think Ms. Idelle will notice if we sneak out the back?" Nick whispered in Em's ear while the older woman lectured another couple on holding proper position.

Em snorted, followed by a giggle she hadn't been able to hold in. She quickly straightened her expression and stood tall with her chin tipped when Ms. Idelle's attention snapped to her.

"Ms. Roberts..." Ms. Idelle walked toward them, her elaborate, bejeweled cane striking the floor of the dance studio with each step. "Perhaps you and Mr. Washington would like to demonstrate the proper hammerlock position."

"The hammer what?" Nick whispered in a slight panic.

"Of course," Em said without hesitation. She took her position while subtly nudging Nick into his, facing the opposite direction, their hands connected behind her back and across the front of his body.

The older woman walked around them, her long white hair pulled up into a severe bun, as she carefully examined their positioning.

"Move to an open hold," Ms. Idelle instructed, her expression unchanging.

Em could feel the tenseness and panic in her friend's grip.

Nick was a perfectly good dancer at the club or a back-yard barbecue. He could do the Wobble, the Cupid Shuffle, and the Cha Cha Slide with the best of them. But ballroom dancing required more structure. And while Nick had been a good sport for helping her tick another box off on the personal improvement part of her Soulmate Project, he'd been there to keep her company, not to learn to ballroom dance, and it showed. Em didn't care because she enjoyed the lessons and the time that she and Nick got to spend together two nights a week. So she'd do her best to guide him through without making it look like she was.

"Music, please." Ms. Idelle signaled to the instructors handling the music. She turned to them. "Let's run through those turns again beginning your basic bachata steps, if you please. One...and two..."

Ms. Idelle tapped her cane on the floor in time to the music as she called out each turn, observing them carefully. Once they were done, she raised a hand, and the music halted.

"Well done, you two." The older woman nodded approvingly. "Your progress is quite remarkable, Ms. Roberts. You're proving to be an excellent follow. You've already learned the subtle art of prompting your lead with almost no one being able to tell." The older woman winked, and the entire class laughed—including Nick.

Em was pretty sure it was the first time she'd seen the

older woman smile. Ms. Idelle was in her seventies and still gorgeous. But Em had Googled her. When she'd been a world-famous dancer fighting to make her mark in the world of ballroom dance with her late husband, the two of them had been an incredibly handsome pair. And despite the bigotry they'd faced, in the videos she'd seen of the two of them, Ms. Idelle had always looked regal and refined. But she'd also looked truly happy—despite all of the barriers they'd had to surmount.

"All right, class. Ms. Roberts and Mr. Washington have shown us how to execute the hammerlock and a two-handed turn into a cuddle position. Now let's see you do it. Open positions, please."

Ms. Idelle walked the group of twenty students through a variety of bachata moves several times, until she seemed confident enough that the group had mastered the moves. Then she called for the music—a pop song covered by a Latin artist with a bachata flavor.

"Okay, I take back every jab I ever made about your dancing. You are an excellent dancer," Nick noted as he led her through the basic combination of bachata sensual moves they'd learned that evening. He braced his hand lightly on her hip as she did a hip roll. "How did I not realize that before?"

"I don't know." Em shrugged as Nick lifted her arm over her head in preparation for a pretzel turn. "Maybe because you were too busy dancing with whomever you planned on sleeping with next."

She could feel the heightened tension in Nick's body with her shoulder leaning into his chest. He faltered slightly before leading her into a body roll.

"I'm not judging," Em said. "But you asked, and I answered."

"Fair." Nick seemed to recover as they unwound from their closed position and resumed the basic steps.

"Up next...shadow position with a hip pendulum followed by social position with chest and hip isolations and ending with that gorgeous slide," Ms. Idelle called out.

Em drew in a quiet breath, her heartbeat quickening as Nick went into his break forward motion, rotating her into shadow position so that her back was toward him. He wrapped his arm around her waist from behind, and they rocked their hips in a slow, sensual pendulum motion.

Em tried to focus on the gentle sway of their hips rather than how their close proximity made her heart race and her tummy flutter. She tried to ignore his breath warm on her neck and the way his subtle, delicious scent tickled her nose. To pretend that her skin didn't feel as if it might burst into flames in the wake of his gentle caress of her arm.

That she wasn't still madly in love with her best friend.

"It's not like we've never danced together," Nick noted.

Em snorted, and she could hear her mother's voice in her head, reminding her how unladylike the sound was. She cleared her throat as they hit the isolation movements. "Middle school doesn't count. Nor does whatever that was Sinclair had us doing at Dexter and Dakota's wedding reception."

"Actually, I was thinking about when we danced together our final night in Mexico." Nick sounded nostalgic. "It was just us and like one other couple in this dinky little dive restaurant. That was a great night."

"It was," Em agreed.

It was the night Nick had almost kissed her. The night she'd first realized that she had feelings for her best friend.

Nick's knee glided between her thighs, and she resisted the urge to clamp her thighs around his as they made the isolation movements together: chest, hip, hip, chest. Then he used the gentle pressure of his knee to lift the leg not holding her weight as they ended with a slide.

"Give yourselves a round of applause, ladies and gentlemen." Ms. Idelle nodded approvingly. "That was much better. You're all improving quite nicely."

Em had been relieved when Nick had volunteered to take the sampler dance class with a mix of salsa, bachata sensual, and other styles of dance. Taking a dance class had been something she'd always wanted to do... as a couple. But she just hadn't ever found herself in a relationship where it felt right. Or she'd asked and had been turned down by whomever she was dating. She'd never considered asking Nick. But she'd enjoyed the time they spent together the past few weeks.

Em was proud of the progress she'd made. She learned to relax, trust her instincts, and let go of her inhibitions. The lessons they learned in class were like metaphors she could easily apply to her own life.

She looked forward to dance class so much that she'd been spending less time focused on the dating part of the Soulmate Project. Dancing salsa and bachata sensual with Nick was fun and exciting. Scrolling through pages of strangers who could either be "the one," nice but not quite right, or a complete jerk was more anxiety-inducing.

"Before we end our lesson this evening, I'd like to try a little experiment." Ms. Idelle's eyes twinkled with mischief as she scanned their faces. "Mr. Clark, I'd like for you to try that routine again, this time with Eboni." She nodded toward her granddaughter, who was one of the dance instructors. "Ms. Roberts, I'd like you to try it with Carlos this time." She gestured for Em to leave Nick's side and join the other dance instructor in the center of the floor.

Em turned to Nick in a slight panic, but he placed a gentle hand on her back and whispered, "You've got this."

She nodded and released a slow breath, the tension easing.

Em joined Carlos on the floor, giving him a polite nod as they assumed a closed position.

"The Jacksons, the Tanakas, and the Kellys will round out our little group." Ms. Idelle walked over to the sound system, then nodded for her assistant to start the music again.

Em drew in a deep breath, her heart fluttering as she prepared to take on another challenge.

———

Nick gritted his teeth, his jaw tense, even as he forced a big smile for Emerie whenever she glanced his way.

Em was clearly nervous about being a part of Ms. Idelle's impromptu exhibition. So he needed to reassure her that she was more than capable of nailing this routine with the Jeffrey Dean Morgan–looking dude holding her in his arms. Half the women in the room were swooning over the man—including the women there with their partners.

"Lucky girl," one of the other dance students whispered loudly to her friend.

"You realize I'm right here, right?" her husband grumbled. "And so is her boyfriend."

"He's not her boyfriend. They're just childhood friends." The woman—who clearly had no idea how whispering worked—waved a dismissive hand.

What the woman had said was true. So why did it bother him so much?

The woman's husband glanced over at him, but Nick

kept his attention on Em moving in time with the music as Carlos held her in his arms.

The fact that Carlos was a much better dancer than Nick came as no surprise. After all, dancing was the man's livelihood. But what did surprise Nick was how incredibly graceful Em looked floating on the dance floor in Carlos's arms.

Had she been holding back before because she was afraid of making him look bad?

Nick was mesmerized by Em's sensual, fluid movements. He couldn't pull his gaze away from the slow rock of Em's hips in those navy leggings. A laser-cut design down the sides showed flashes of her brown skin from her hips to her ankles. The long-sleeve top knotted at her back showed hints of her back and belly as she moved.

Carlos's fingertips grazed Em's exposed skin, and Nick clenched his hands into involuntary fists, his short fingernails digging into his palms. He gritted his teeth, his nostrils flaring. Heat enveloped his neck and his cheeks.

"You sure they're just friends?" the man whispered.

Nick sucked in a slow breath and exhaled quietly. He forced himself to relax, so that when Carlos turned Em into pretzel position and she was facing him again, he could give her a big smile.

Em seemed to relax, and her stiff expression softened into a more natural one as Carlos walked her toward him before he turned her again and they retreated in the other direction.

"She's quite good, isn't she, Mr. Washington?"

For a woman with a cane that struck the floor loudly, Ms. Idelle could move with the stealthiness and grace of a cat whenever she chose to. The older woman was standing right beside Nick, and he hadn't seen or heard her coming.

"She's fantastic. I had no idea she was such a good dancer." Nick returned his attention to Emerie and Carlos on the dance floor.

"And you're sure that the two of you are just friends?" Ms. Idelle said the words as if she seriously doubted their veracity.

"Yes, ma'am." Nick didn't take his eyes off of Em. She was relaxed now, having fun, and the competitor in her was really going for it as she turned it up a notch, hitting every move a bit harder. More sass, more sexiness, while still maintaining her precision.

He was proud of her, even if he wanted to chin check that Carlos guy because he seemed to be enjoying it a little too much.

"We've known each other since we were kids."

"And the two of you aren't romantically involved?" Ms. Idelle turned to him expectantly.

Telling the woman it was none of her business didn't seem like an option. She'd probably swat him on the behind with that blinged-out cane of hers.

"No, ma'am." Because the erotic fantasies he'd had about Em didn't count.

"Then you won't mind if I ask her to partner with Carlos in the dance exhibition I'm planning?"

Ms. Idelle cocked one of her thinly drawn eyebrows, as if daring him to object.

Another project that would put distance between them? *Great.* But what was he going to do? Beat his chest like some caveman and declare that she was his?

"Of course not. Not if that's what Em wants," Nick added, hoping she didn't.

"Oh, she will. I'm certain of it. Look at the fire in her eyes when she dances." The woman tipped her chin toward

Emerie, swirling on the dance floor to the music. "She enjoys the battle. It'll serve her well in every facet of her life."

The entire room oohed, aahed, and whooped in response to Carlos and Em's hip pendulum which looked a thousand percent sexier than the one he and Em had done earlier.

Nick sighed quietly, his face pinching with an involuntary frown as he looked on at his best friend. There was no way in hell that Em would turn down the chance to be a star on the dance floor. And since she was so excited about dancing, he wanted that for her, too.

After all, what kind of friend would he be if he didn't want to see Em happy?

There was more cheering in response to Em and Carlos's chest and hip isolations, followed by loud applause for the entire group of dancers.

But as Nick watched Carlos and Em embrace in celebration of their flawless performance, his gut knotted.

Either you want to be the only man in Em's life or you're willing to set your ego aside and be the friend she needs as she searches for the man who wants to be.

Dexter's advice echoed in Nick's head, and his shoulders tensed. He'd made his choice. Now he needed to get his shit together and follow through with supporting his best friend in her decision to find a life partner. Just as he'd supported her through every other area of her life for the past two decades.

"Oh my God, can you believe that? I felt like a professional out there." Em was standing in front of him, bouncing on her heels.

"You were an absolute star, kid. Way to go." Nick hugged Em tight, lifting her off her feet momentarily, which made her laugh.

"It was no surprise to me. You have incredible potential, Ms. Roberts. In fact, I'm banking on it." Ms. Idelle nodded approvingly. "We're putting on an exhibition at The Foxhole. I'd like for you and Carlos to do a routine together. What do you say? Ready to show Holly Grove Island what a talented dancer you are?"

"Just me?" Em pressed a hand to her chest. She turned to Nick, her brows furrowed. "I don't know if—"

"You should do it, Em. Don't worry about me. This will require lots of additional practice. With work and the band, I wouldn't be able to squeeze in extra practice anyway," Nick said. "Besides, you took this class to challenge yourself by doing something outside of your comfort zone. This is the perfect way to do that."

Em's frown softened. "You won't feel slighted?"

He definitely did. Before this class, he'd actually believed he was the better dancer. But Nick was thrilled to see how Em was blossoming as she executed the steps of her Soulmate Project.

"What I'm going to be is your biggest cheerleader. Now c'mon. You know you want to do this. Say yes, already."

"Okay, I'll do it." Em bounced up and down excitedly. "Thank you for believing in me, Ms. Idelle."

"You just need to believe in yourself as much as your friend and I do." Ms. Idelle perched both hands on her glittery cane. "Now go ahead and work out a practice schedule with Carlos."

Em hugged Nick again before running off to talk to the dance instructor who would be her partner for the exhibition.

"I don't know how much I believe that your sole interest in Ms. Roberts is friendship." Ms Idelle eyed him cautiously. "But you are a good friend indeed, Mr. Washington." The older woman's voice softened. "Now...before next class, work on making those steps a bit smaller and not flapping your arms. We aren't stepping over potholes or trying to land a plane, are we?" Her eyes danced with quiet amusement. "I'll see you next week."

He couldn't help chuckling as the grand dame hobbled toward another couple.

Nick caught a glimpse of Carlos's wide grin as he stared at Emerie, and he gritted his teeth.

What in the hell is going on with me lately?

He and Em had been friends through her high school and college boyfriends. Through the handful of relationships she'd had in her twenties, including the few she'd had since he'd realized that he was attracted to Em. They were friends. He needed to let go of whatever romantic feelings he might have for her. So why had it suddenly become so hard to ignore them? And why was he suddenly resentful of every guy who looked Em's way?

Emerie's admission on the beach that night had tugged at the thread that had kept his feelings for her safely tucked away. Buried down deep where they wouldn't make a mess of the friendship he valued so deeply. In the past, whenever those feelings would resurface, he'd simply reminded himself of what a mess he'd made of past friendships when he'd tried to turn them into something more. And of how whatever fire or passion might've existed between his parents— who'd been best friends before marrying in college—had evaporated long ago. That wasn't an eventuality he wanted for himself and Em, either.

"Nick, right?" One of the other students—a curvy brunette with a huge smile—approached.

"Right." Nick forced himself to tear his gaze away from Emerie. "And you're..."

"Bethany," she volunteered quickly, tucking her hair behind her ear. "Is it true that you and your partner are just friends? Because I always assumed you two were a couple. You're definitely giving established couple energy."

"We've known each other a really long time." Nick tried not to seem rude or impatient. He cast another glance at Carlos, who'd casually draped his long arm over Em's shoulder.

He clenched his fists, forced a smile, and returned his attention to Bethany.

"So then you're both single, right?" Bethany's brown eyes danced, and her grin widened.

"Right," Nick said, preparing himself to let the woman down easily. She was pretty and seemed nice enough, but between work and everything that'd been going on with Em, Nick had been too busy and distracted to bother with dating.

"Awesome." Bethany tossed her dark hair over one shoulder. "I was considering asking her out. Do you think she'd be interested?"

"Oh." Wow. He'd definitely read the room wrong. Bethany was interested in Em—not him. "She's currently on a quest to find Mr. Right, so . . ."

"Got it." Bethany stared across the room longingly at Em.

Join the club, sis.

"Can't blame a girl for trying, right?"

"Not at all." Nick flashed her a sympathetic smile. "In fact, I'm sure Em would be flattered that you were interested in her. Good night, Bethany."

"Good night, Nick," Bethany called over her shoulder.

"She's very pretty." Em approached him with a teasing lilt to her voice.

"She thinks you are, too. In fact, she asked if I thought you'd be interested in going out with her. But don't worry. I let Bethany down easy. I told her you're currently on the quest for 'the one.'"

"Aww. That's sweet." Em flipped her hair. "I'll have to tell Sin that her makeover game is even stronger than we thought."

"I think it's that effervescent personality, that contagious smile, and those heart-stopping bachata hips that had just about everyone in this room *hyp*notized." He emphasized the first part of the word. "Get it? *Hyp*notized? See what I did there?"

"I get it, all right." Em did a hip pendulum followed by a couple of hip isolations and a head roll. Nick was sure his heart went into overdrive. He clutched at his chest like Fred Sanford threatening to join Elizabeth in heaven, which made Em laugh.

She finished off her impromptu performance with a spin.

"Very nice." Nick clapped, surveying his friend. "I have to admit that those little dance outfits of yours don't hurt, either."

"This?" Em glanced down, as if she needed to remind herself of what she was wearing. "It's just a pair of leggings and a T-shirt. The same thing I've been wearing for about a decade now."

Now it was Nick's turn to scoff. "I'm pretty sure you know just how fucking hot you look in that outfit. Yes, it might *technically* be just a pair of leggings and a T-shirt. But laser cutouts and an off-the-shoulder, belly-baring top are a definite upgrade from what you used to wear." Nick rubbed his chin as he studied her body. "You look...*incredible*, and you've got the moves. Is it really any wonder why

Ms. Idelle selected you? Or why Bethany and a handful of other people—including Carlos—can't keep their eyes off you?"

Nick was chief among the folks mesmerized by Emerie, despite trying hard not to be.

A soft smile lit his friend's eyes as her gaze met his, neither of them speaking for a few moments.

"Thanks, Nicky," Em said finally.

Nick grabbed Em's coat from the rack, holding it up as she slid it on. Then he put on his own coat, and they headed to the parking lot.

"Wanna grab something to eat, maybe play a couple games of pool?" Nick asked.

"Sorry. I'm meeting Carlos at The Foxhole. He thought it would be good if we had a chance to see the space. Plus, we can grab a meal and get to know each other a little bit so we can begin putting together our plan for the exhibition."

Why did it feel like he was beginning to develop a tick in his jaw every time Em mentioned Carlos's name? "Be careful with that guy, Em."

"What do you mean?" Em lowered her voice to a whisper.

"He's been doing this a long time, and he's definitely into you. Just feels like this get-to-know-you date is part of his MO."

"First: it's not a date. Second: is this the part where you pull out your six-shooter at high noon and declare that this town isn't big enough for two fuckboys? Especially when one is a silver fox with Zaddy vibes?" Em's raised eyebrow vibrated with well-deserved condemnation.

"This isn't about me," Nick assured her. Though it sounded like a load of bullshit, even to his ears. "But we always look out for each other. And that's what I'm trying to do here."

"Well, it sounds a tad bit *hyp*ocritical." Em emphasized the first part of the word. "*Hypocritical*? Get it? See what I did there?" She imitated his voice, then burst into laughter.

"Not funny, and I do *not* sound like that." Still, he couldn't help chuckling.

"Whatever, dude. I'm just saying take it down a little and relax. I'll be fine."

"You're right." Nick held up his hands. "I'm gonna chill out and let you handle your business."

"Good." Em's broad smile was contagious.

His scowl softened, and his heart seemed to expand in his chest. He was proud of Em. She was focused and determined. She was investing in herself and expanding her business. Things she'd been hesitant to do before. His friend had never lacked confidence in sports—where she often excelled. She'd been less assertive in other areas of her life—like her relationships, career, and business. Nick loved seeing Em's growth, her assertiveness, and confidence. It made his friend—who'd always been beautiful and sexy—infinitely more so.

He loved that for her. And he loved *her*.

The playful look in Em's dark eyes as they sparkled... it did things to him. And all the head games he'd employed to ignore his attraction to his best friend just didn't work anymore.

Nick stared down at Emerie, his heart beating faster and his pulse racing. Em was so damn beautiful standing beneath the moonlight on a chilly February night. His eyes were drawn to her full lips. And he couldn't help wanting to step closer, slide his hands beneath her coat, rest them on those mesmerizing hips, and capture those sensual lips in a greedy kiss.

She gazed up at him, nibbling on her lower lip. Everything around them had gone quiet. The moments felt like minutes.

Nick sucked in a breath and stepped closer to Em. But he was startled by a man's voice.

"See you at the restaurant?" Carlos called to Em as he eyed Nick.

Nick glared at him.

Right back at you, playa.

"I'll be there in ten minutes," Em said.

Carlos climbed into his banana-yellow Corvette with a smug look on his face.

Is that my future?

A middle-aged man with nothing to show for his life but a list of conquests and a neon-colored sports car that screamed midlife crisis?

"Nick, are you all right? You've been kind of weird tonight."

"I'm good. Just text me when you get home. I won't be able to sleep until I know you're okay."

"I will. I promise." Emerie's expression softened. "And I really do appreciate you looking out for me."

"Same, kid," Nick said, meaning it.

Meeting Emerie had changed his life, Nick was sure of it. The resentment and anger he'd harbored as a lonely kid had been a recipe for disaster. He'd been on a bad path—despite having parents who loved him and neighbors who cared. But the concern and genuine friendship Em had shown him had pulled him out of a dark place.

His parents loved him. He never once doubted that. But neither of them was particularly demonstrative of their affection for him or each other. It was his friendship with Emerie and his relationship with Dakota and her family that taught him to be a more open, loving human being. His parents taught him how to be focused, organized, and disciplined. How to excel at one's chosen craft. They'd taught him the importance of knowing one's history and of giving back to one's community. And he would always be grateful to them for that. But it was Emerie, Dakota, and their families who showed him the beauty of unconditional love.

They'd helped make him the man he was today as much as his parents had.

"Stop worrying so much. Go home and get some sleep. You have a big meeting in the morning." Em lifted onto her toes and kissed his cheek.

"Right." Nick massaged the tension in the back of his neck. The dance class had gotten him out of his head for a couple of hours and made him forget his concerns about the work meeting. But now this date with Carlos that Em didn't even realize was a date had given him something else to be uneasy about.

"Hey, there are a couple of good basketball games on Friday night. Want to meet at Blaze's?" Nick opened Em's door for her.

"Friday is Valentine's Day, so Kassie and I are just gonna hang out." Em slid into the front seat and started her car. "But if you don't have plans, you're welcome to join us."

He'd forgotten about Valentine's Day. Normally, he went out of his way to avoid scheduling a date on holidays and at weddings because those always felt significant, and he didn't want to send mixed signals to someone he was trying to keep it casual with. But between work and being wrapped up in his best friend's life more than he should, he hadn't been out with anyone since before New Year's Eve.

"Sounds great. What time should I come through?"

"Seven. Bring pizza *and* beer." Em's quirky smile

reminded Nick of the one she'd flash when they were kids. That smile could get him to laugh, no matter how grumpy his mood.

Nick groaned quietly as Em drove away. Emerie Roberts was his person.

She knew him inside and out, understood him and loved him unconditionally, despite his faults. Em's very existence made his world better and each day brighter whether they were in the same room or on opposite sides of the country.

Nick cherished that. And he had done his damnedest to be the same for her—no matter what that entailed. He should be grateful for Carlos's interruption. Because he'd been seconds from leaning in and kissing Em and unraveling the beautifully complicated friendship they'd spent two decades weaving.

He needed to pull it together. Because more and more, he was flirting with the idea of crossing the line with his best friend.

Chapter Fourteen

—•—•—

Emerie returned to her living room and set out a fresh batch of nachos. She set the warm dish on her coffee table, along with the pizza and a variety of snacks. Elaborate Valentine's Day dates were nice—and every girl should experience at least one. But Em much preferred hanging out with Nick and Kassie for a casual evening.

"So tell me more about Harrison Dunbar, III." Em folded a leg beneath her on the sofa. Kassie's creamy skin—the color of the sand on Holly Grove Island Beach—flushed at the mere mention of the man's name. "He isn't one of *the* Dunbars, is he?"

"He's their eldest son." Kassie smiled sheepishly.

Nick and Em exchanged a subtle glance. The Dunbars were a powerful family, but not well-liked there on the island. Still, they were a frequent topic of conversation around town.

Dunbar Real Estate Development had built an upscale community called Fox Grove on the far side of the island. They were looking to expand the gated community, which had much of the island up in arms.

"How'd you two meet?" Em asked.

"At a fundraiser for the botanical gardens a few months ago. We had a little polite conversation, but nothing big. But then...this Soulmate Project of yours inspired me to join a couple of dating apps, too. Harrison saw my profile on the app and swiped right. We've been talking online and by telephone the past couple of weeks. We're going on our first date next Saturday."

"What's Harrison like?" Nick mumbled through a mouthful of pizza.

Translation: Is he a pompous asshole, like his parents? It was something Em had wondered, too.

"He's handsome, tall, incredibly charming, and he has the most commanding presence," Kassie said dreamily, a big smile spreading across her face. She scooped up a nacho oozing with four different types of cheese and piled high with ground beef, black beans, black olives, and a healthy dollop of sour cream. "I don't think I've ever met anyone quite like him."

Kassie talked excitedly about her and Harrison's plans for their date the following weekend, and Em was excited for her friend who'd always been a shy wallflower.

"Harrison sounds amazing, Kassie. I'm glad the Soulmate Project is working for at least one of us."

This time, Nick and Kassie exchanged looks. Kassie's registered as guilt with a hint of pity. And Nick's furrowed brows indicated concern. She immediately regretted her comment, but it was too late to take it back.

Nick shifted his attention to Em. "You haven't talked much about this dating experiment of yours lately. How's it going?"

Em had been expecting the question. Still, her neck stiffened, and her cheeks warmed beneath her friends' stares. Nick's simple question shouldn't feel like judgment, but it did. She shrugged, pushing her nachos around her plate.

"I've been preoccupied the past few weeks. There's dance class, I'm revamping my business brand and my website. Then there's the influx of new clients that are the direct result of implementing Dakota's new marketing strategy." Em licked melted cheese from her fingers, and Nick's nostrils flared.

"Not ladylike. I know," Em said in response to Nick's wide-eyed stare.

Her mother and Sin often reminded her of that. She didn't try to behave like an ogre. But clearly, being raised with three older brothers, she'd adopted a lot of their boorish habits.

Nick's eyes widened. "I didn't…I wasn't—"

"You've taken on a lot," Kassie cut in, and Nick seemed relieved. She set her mostly empty nacho plate on the coffee table and turned toward Em. "But wasn't the point of all those things to put yourself in the ideal mental, physical, and emotional space to meet the right guy?"

Emerie frowned, shifting her gaze from Kassie to Nick and then back again.

She could usually count on Kass to let her off the hook whenever a topic was uncomfortable. But not this time.

Nick and Kassie stared at her expectantly.

"The self-improvement and business development are a huge part of the larger plan to find Mr. Right. But there are only so many hours in the day." Em felt guilty for not being straight with her two closest friends. She collected a few empty paper plates and carried them to the kitchen, dumping them in the trash.

"But isn't that kind of like a tennis player lifting weights to increase the power of their backhand, but then becoming a weightlifter instead?" Nick asked.

Em swallowed hard, her neck and face hot and her gut tightening as she hovered on the edge of the living room.

She could've just quietly chosen to go on this quest for a lifelong companion. But she'd chosen to announce her intentions to her friends and family, not only because she needed their help, but because she knew they'd keep her accountable. Nick and Kassie were doing that right now. So why did she feel persecuted rather than relieved?

Maybe because it'd felt safer to spend more time with her friends and to work on her business than to put herself out there like she had with Dillon. Maybe it was because she was afraid Dillon was right. That she wasn't ready to find the right guy because she hadn't let go of her feelings for Nick.

"We're not trying to badger you," Kassie said calmly. "But you said this is what you want, so we'd like to support your efforts. If your goals have changed—"

"They haven't." That much, she was sure of. Em stood taller, sifting her fingers through her hair. "And I didn't do all of this just to give up when things start to feel hard. But I made such a big deal about it. I suddenly have this panicky fear of failing spectacularly."

"You're not 'failing,' Em," Kassie said gently. "You're allowing fear of failure to prevent you from even trying. And I know you well enough to know that you'll regret giving up far more than running into a few relationship snafus."

Kassie did know her well. What haunted her most were the opportunities in her life that she'd talked herself out of. Like the design jobs she'd been hesitant to pursue because she didn't think she was talented enough. She'd been wrong. She was a gifted graphic designer. And with the help of her virtual assistant, she was becoming better at handling the business side of entrepreneurship, too.

"I guess I have been a little gun-shy since Dillon," Em admitted.

"I love my cousin. But he isn't the only fish in the sea." Kassie walked over to Em and took both her hands. "I real-ize that you might have to kiss a lot of frogs before you find your prince. But you can't win the game if you're hanging out on the sidelines."

"More sports analogies. *Great*." Em groaned.

"We're speaking in a language we know you under-stand." Kassie poked Em's arm and grinned. "Now are you ready to climb back on the horse and try again? You've been rejecting every guy who pops up on those dating apps. But they can't all be terrible."

Before Em could respond, Kassie's phone rang.

"It's Harrison." Kassie grinned in response to the cus-tom ringtone.

"Speaking of Prince Charming," Em teased as her friend hustled to grab her phone from the coffee table before it stopped ringing.

Em glanced over at Nick. He was frowning, but she wasn't sure why.

Was Nick interested in Kassie?

"You okay?" She tapped Nick's foot with her own.

He was lost in thought and oblivious to their conversation—something that happened more often lately. Her guess was that the stress of this work project, the travel, and the pros-pect of relocating to New York was beginning to wear on Nick. Maybe he was feeling like he was in over his head but was reluctant to admit it for fear of letting Dexter down. But whenever she asked, he'd just claim everything was fine.

"I'm good," he assured her.

"You don't look good. You look—"

"I'm so sorry to bail on you guys, but Harrison sent me a surprise. He wants to video chat." Kassie bounced on her heels excitedly.

"That's sweet, Kass." Em pressed a hand to her chest, happy for her friend. "Don't you dare apologize. Go on. Don't keep the man waiting. We'll be fine."

Kassie hugged Em, then she whispered something to Nick before hurrying out the door.

Em locked the door behind Kassie and flopped onto the sofa beside Nick. She turned up the TV volume, carefully eyeing her friend. He still seemed lost in thought, but the best approach was never to badger Nick. She'd learned to work her magic and coax the truth out of him.

"More nachos or beer?" Em set the remote on the coffee table and focused on the game. Their team was getting their asses handed to them. But the second half of the game was just beginning. Em was nothing if not optimistic when it came to her favorite sports teams.

"No." Nick reached for the remote and muted the TV. "I want the truth. What's the real issue with this dating thing? And don't tell me you're afraid of failure. You're one of the most badass women I've ever known. You went skydiving for your thirtieth birthday, Em. Shit that even I consider too dangerous." Nick jabbed a thumb to his chest. "You've suffered more sprains and breaks than any guy I know, and it's never stopped you from getting back out on the court. You are fucking fearless, Emerie Roberts. You always have been. So level with me. What's *really* going on with you?"

Why did her friends have to be so damn perceptive? Usually, she found it endearing. Tonight, she wished they'd play along and take her at her word.

"I'm gonna get a bottle of water." Em stood abruptly, her throat feeling parched again. "You want one?"

"No, Em. I don't want water or a beer or more nachos." Nick caught up with her in the kitchen, grasping her hand before she could open the refrigerator. "I want you to talk to me. You were so enthusiastic about this plan. But now you'd rather go to dance class, update your business plan, or do *anything* except go on an actual date. So what's going on? If you've changed your mind about this, no one is going to be disappointed in you."

"Are you kidding?" Em tugged her hand from his and collapsed against the kitchen island. "Everyone in this town is invested in this Soulmate Project. And I can't be upset about it because I'm the one who chose to announce my plans to all of Holly Grove Island. Which, in hindsight, was a foolish decision."

Em shook her head and sighed, her heart racing.

"Don't get me wrong...I'm grateful that they all care so much. I just don't want to let them down. And I don't want to let myself down, either. You know I never give up or chicken out once I decide to do something. I was terrified before I tandem jumped out of that plane. But I went through with it because you were all there expecting me to do it. But this time, I..." Em swallowed hard, the words stuck in her throat.

"But this time...*what*?" Nick's tone was gentle, his eyes searching. Em wanted more than anything for Nick to put his arms around her and tell her she didn't need to resume her search because he'd finally realized that she had been the perfect woman for him all along.

But he didn't. Because that was the way things ended in her fantasies about Nick, not in her reality.

"I feel like I'm in over my head," she admitted.

"Why?"

"Because I haven't done this in a really long time. And the relationships I have been in...I wasn't the pursuer."

"I'm pretty sure you walked up to Billy Johnson, kissed

his cheek, and *told* him he was your boyfriend." Nick chuckled.

"I was eleven," Em reminded him. "Life was simpler then. Things are different now. I'm looking for the man that I'll want to start a life with. Raise a family with. The stakes are so much higher and—"

"Hey, just breathe. Everything is going to be fine." Nick squeezed her bicep, and the pressure eased the tension that made her feel as if she was going to hyperventilate.

She sucked in a deep breath, as he'd advised. The spinning in her brain and the sense of panic that had been swirling in her chest subsided.

"Better?"

She nodded.

"Good." Nick released her arm, and she immediately missed his reassuring touch.

"I know it's like riding a bike, and it all comes back to you. But I haven't been with anyone for a while. Since before you returned to town." Em shifted her gaze from his. "I feel like a novice at this again."

Nick nodded thoughtfully and rubbed his chin. He leaned against the island. "And what would make you feel more comfortable?"

"Practice," Em joked. "That's what I'd normally do to shake the rust off in tennis or volleyball. But this is a completely different situation."

After a few moments of awkward silence, Nick asked, "What if it wasn't?"

"What do you mean?" Em studied her friend's face. Surely, he wasn't suggesting that...

"You're intimidated by dating and intimacy because you're out of practice. So what if we practice?"

"Okay, I'm going to need you to spell this out for me."

Em's heartbeat thumped so loudly that the sound reverberated in her ears and her voice quavered. "You're proposing that we practice doing *what*, specifically?"

Nick's gaze dropped to her mouth. "Come here."

Em placed her trembling hand in Nick's, and a zing of electricity danced along her palm. He tugged her forward so she was standing directly in front of him. He slid his arms around her waist, as he'd done many times during their bachata sensual dancing. But this time, he eliminated the space between them that Ms. Idelle always reminded them was appropriate for social dancing.

Nick's fresh, woodsy scent teased Em's nostrils as her chest rose and fell with quick, shallow breaths. Her skin felt warm wherever their body touched: her breasts, pressed to his hard chest; their thighs; his hands on her waist. Em's knees felt unsteady, and she couldn't speak. If she did, the faltering of her voice would reveal just how nervous and utterly turned on she was by her best friend holding her like this.

In dance class, their bodies weren't in full contact. And there were so many other things to think about. Ms. Idelle. The other students. The need to keep time with the music and follow the directions that had been called out. Here, there was only her and Nick and the sound of her own breathing.

Nick cupped her cheek and leaned in, his dark eyes locked with hers.

"Is it okay if I..."

"Yes." Em nodded a little too eagerly. One side of Nick's mouth curved into that devilish smirk she'd often wished he'd flash at her.

He leaned in slowly. So slowly, it felt as if time had stopped.

"Relax, Em." Nick pulled back and met her gaze again. "There's so much tension in your body. You're about to kiss someone. You're not getting robbed at an ATM."

Emerie snorted, and the tension that had made her feel like a tightly wound spring eased.

"That's more like it." Nick's gravelly voice lowered to a seductive whisper that vibrated through her body, culminating low in her belly. "Now about these arms...they're just hanging at your sides. That reads 'unengaged passive observer.' At this stage, he needs to know you're feeling him. That you want him as much as he wants you."

"Okay." Em swallowed hard.

Her gaze was glued to his as she lifted her arms. She rested her hands on Nick's shoulders, prepared for the next instruction as if they were in dance class.

"Better. But I need to know that you *want* me to kiss you, Em," Nick whispered, his dark eyes glinting. "Fuck that. I need to know that you're *desperate* for my kiss. That in this moment, it's all you can think about."

Yes, yes, and yes.

Em's hands were shaking as she lifted them higher, cradling Nick's whiskered face. Her gaze descended to the lush lips she'd fantasized about tasting for the past several years. Then she lifted onto her toes and closed the remaining space between them, her lips crashing into his.

———

Nick wasn't prepared for the dizzying feeling that hit him the moment Em's soft, full lips met his. Or the way her strong, toned body would melt into his as his mouth glided over hers.

He loved the feel of her buttery, smooth skin beneath his

fingertips as he pressed them to the bare skin of her back beneath her shirt.

The gentle glide of his lips over hers escalated—along with his heart rate. He devoured the lips he'd spent so much time fantasizing about.

Nick tipped her chin, and her lips parted. He swept his tongue inside her warm mouth, swallowing Em's soft gasp.

She wrapped her arms around his waist, pulling their lower bodies closer. As if she needed more contact between them.

He needed it…craved it, too.

Nick walked a few steps forward until Em's back was against the wall. He lifted her arms, as they had done in dance class. His pulse raced, and his heart beat in his chest like a drum as he devoured her mouth. He grasped both of her wrists with one hand, pinning them to the wall over her head. His other hand glided down her side, lingering on her hip.

He palmed the firm, round bottom that had teased and tortured him as he'd stood there, mesmerized by the sensual swaying of her hips during her electrifying dance with Carlos. He gripped her flesh, evoking another gasp from Em's soft, sweet lips.

Nick deepened the intensity of the kiss they both seemed so desperate for.

His skin was feverish, and the sound of rushing blood filled Nick's ears. His heart raced like he'd taken off in a sprint at full speed.

So many times, he'd wondered what it would be like to kiss Emerie. Would there be any sexual chemistry between them? Or would it feel awkward?

He now had a definitive answer.

Their raw desire for each other was evident from the

rapidly escalating kiss that was supposed to be a simple demonstration. A practice kiss that would ease Em's nerves and make her more comfortable with the idea of kissing someone else.

Only deep down, Nick knew that was complete bullshit. He'd kissed his best friend because he was attracted to her. Because he couldn't stop imagining what it would be like to kiss her. Because even though he knew all the reasons he shouldn't, he desperately wanted to take her to bed and worship every inch of her deep brown skin with his hands, his lips, and his tongue.

Nick pressed a knee between Em's thighs. She settled onto it and responded with a breathy moan. The sensual sound induced an instant response from his body, and Nick shuddered at the sensation that crawled up his spine.

Had he ever felt such a deep, desperate ache for anyone? Because right now, he wanted to run headfirst through the wall of reasons they shouldn't be doing this. Nick intensified their kiss, pinning her body between his and the wall. He glided his hand up her taut belly and teased one pebbled tip with his thumb as he palmed her breast.

Em's breathy exhalations made him desperate to touch more of her skin. To tease the stiff peaks with his tongue until she was riding his thigh and chasing her release.

Nick settled his hands on Em's hips, using gentle pressure to guide her hips back and forth, as he had when they'd danced together in class. Only this time, he prompted her body to move against his, increasing the friction of their contact as she glided along his thigh. Em's breath came in short bursts, her arms draped around his neck as she kissed him eagerly.

A knock at the door stunned them both, halting their kiss. Nick stepped back, his chest heaving as he dragged a hand down his face.

They stood there staring at each other, neither of them speaking. Em's face registered confusion. His, no doubt, revealed guilt.

What am I doing?

This was supposed to be a way to help Em get comfortable with intimacy again. To alleviate her anxiety about getting back into the dating game. Not a way for him to satisfy his own nagging curiosity about kissing her.

There was a reason curiosity had killed the fucking cat.

He'd sworn that he wouldn't act on his attraction to Em because he was afraid of what it would do to their friendship. He'd learned the hard way, not once but *twice*, that friendships and sex didn't mix. So this time, he'd use the head above his shoulders rather than being led astray by the still-hard one below his belt.

"I got carried away." Nick cleared his throat. "I'm sorry. You good now?"

The confusion in Em's brown eyes shifted to disappointment. She lowered her gaze and nodded but didn't speak.

Nick's gut knotted, and his chest clenched at the pained look on Em's face.

He was a complete ass.

The way he'd kissed and groped Em just now...Of course she expected it would lead to something more. That was what he wanted, too. But it wasn't in the best interests of their friendship. One of them needed to keep that in mind.

There was another knock at the door, heavier this time.

"Em, it's me, Kassie. I left my wallet here."

Em's eyes widened. Sadness, panic, and a hint of guilt flashed across her face.

"You should get that." Nick placed a hand on Em's shoulder, startling her from her temporary daze.

Em tugged her shirt down and ran her fingers through her hair, reminding him of how his had sifted through the soft strands during their heated kiss.

"Coming!" Em called.

She gave him one last look filled with hurt and disappointment. Then she crossed the living room to open the door for her friend.

Nick leaned back against the counter and cursed beneath his breath.

His growing feelings for Em had made him anxious and a little edgy the past few weeks. But what he felt now was worse. He'd moved beyond wonderment or fantasy. Now he knew just how amazing things between them could be.

Now that he'd had a taste of Em, how could he not obsess over just how much he wanted her?

Chapter Fifteen

· — ● — ·

Emerie's legs felt unsteady, her pulse racing as she made her way toward the door.

She drew in a deep breath, trying to ignore the fluttering in her belly and the pulse between her thighs. The moment felt surreal. Like she'd just stepped out of one of her vivid fantasies about her best friend. But this wasn't her imagination.

Moments ago, Nick's tongue had been halfway down her throat, and she'd been shamelessly riding his knee like a cowgirl on the rodeo circuit.

Em's cheeks and forehead flamed with embarrassment. She tried her best to pull it together, hoping her friend wouldn't notice.

Emerie drew in a deep breath, plastered on a broad smile, and opened the door.

"Hey, Kass." Em stepped aside so Kassie could enter. "Sorry it took so long. I...*we* were in the kitchen."

Em stopped short of claiming not to have heard her friend knocking. The volume on the television was still muted.

Kassandra stared at Em for a moment with one eyebrow

cocked. She shifted her gaze to Nick who was lingering in the kitchen. "Sorry if I'm interrupting."

"You're not interrupting," Em said.

She should be grateful. If Kassie hadn't returned when she did, she and Nick might've ended up in her bed. And if their kitchen make-out session had made things awkward, she could only imagine how unbearable it would be if things had gone further.

Despite what Nick called it, their kiss hadn't felt like practice. Every moment, every touch, had felt incredibly real.

Her hands were still shaking, her belly was still fluttering, and her head was still spinning.

"Here's your wallet." Em retrieved it from the coffee table and handed it to Kassie. "How was your chat with Prince Charming?"

The suspicious look on Kassie's face was quickly replaced by a bashful grin and flushed cheeks.

"It was great, actually. That's another reason I came back. I wanted to tell you what he sent me."

"I can't wait to hear it. Another mojito?"

"Please." Kassie beamed.

Em was happy for her friend. Kassandra was hardworking and focused, sweet and considerate. She cared deeply about the Holly Grove Island Arboretum and Aquarium, where she was the director of programming, and about the preservation of the flora and fauna on the island. Kassie was dedicated to the staff, interns, visitors, and the community. And she often found time to help her mom, who owned a florist shop on the island. If anyone deserved love and happiness, it was Kass.

She'd inspired her friend to be open to finding love, and Em was glad of that. Yet, despite the big makeover, the rebranding of her business, and venturing into online dating, she had yet to find a serious prospect for herself. Em drew in a deep breath and fought back the hint of envy that had crept in.

She walked into the kitchen where Nick hovered on the other side of the island, like a spider on a wall trying not to be noticed.

"Can I make you a mojito, too, Nick?" Em cast a glance in Nick's direction without meeting his gaze.

"No, thanks. In fact, I should head out. There are a few things I need to do." Nick tapped the counter lightly. "I'll see you both later."

"But there are still five minutes left in the fourth quarter," Kassie noted suspiciously. "You *never* leave a close game with minutes left."

Em's shoulders tensed, and she bobbled the glass she was grabbing from the overhead cabinet, nearly dropping it on the counter.

"Are you okay, Em?" Nick asked.

"I'm fine. Thank you." Em's tone was sharper than she'd intended. Without glancing back at Nick, she set the glass on the counter and opened the fridge.

"It's a home game. I'm confident they'll close this one out," Nick said. Something they both knew wasn't true. Their team had blown more fourth quarter leads than most of the teams in the league. And both teams were desperately trying to climb in the standings for the NBA Eastern Conference. But given the situation, it was better not to mention that.

"Have a safe drive home," Em called, her head practically buried in the fridge. She was thankful that the chilled air cooled her burning cheeks.

Em set the limes and sprigs of mint on the counter. Then she grabbed the bottle of rum and gathered everything else she'd need.

"Text me to let me know you got home." Em forced

herself to glance in Nick's direction once she heard him open the door.

"I will. But you should lock up behind me."

Nick wanted to say something to her. Maybe to apologize again. But Emerie wasn't in the mood for another apology. When she didn't respond, Kassie sprang into action, saving them all from the uncomfortable silence.

Em was relieved that Kassie had spared her another awkward conversation with Nick tonight. Yet she was curious about what he'd wanted to say.

"Don't party too hard, you two," Nick said.

"We won't," Kassie said before bidding Nick a good night and returning to the kitchen. She climbed onto a stool at the breakfast bar and propped her chin on her fist. "So exactly how long have you two been making out like a couple of horny teenagers?" Her lips were pursed, and her dark eyes twinkled with amusement.

"I…what makes you think…I mean…" Em faltered, searching her brain for a way to sidestep the question without lying to her friend. Her head was still spinning, and she was still trying to process exactly what had happened between her and Nick.

"The first clue was you flashing me with those headlights when you answered the door." Kassie indicated Em's chest.

Emerie glanced down at her nipples still visible through the thin fabric of her shirt. She should've taken Sin's advice and invested in a T-shirt bra. Em folded her arms over her chest.

"But the dead giveaway was the smears of your tinted gloss Nick still had around his mouth." Kassie grinned proudly. "So…how long? After Dillon, I assume."

"Of course." Em tried not to sound so defensive about her friend's question. "Today was the first time Nick and

I have ever kissed. I swear." She sighed heavily, replaying the night's events in her head. "I honestly still can't believe it happened."

"Does that mean you two are official now?" Kassie clapped her hands together excitedly.

Em drew in a shaky breath and blinked back unexpected tears. She responded with a subtle shake of her head.

"I don't understand." Kassie's countenance fell. "You two kissed, and clearly you were both feeling it. Nick was definitely shook just now."

"I know." Em rubbed her forehead, her voice faint and her chest aching with the reality that she'd kissed her best friend and yet, nothing between them had changed. At least, not for him.

"Oh, hon." Kassie scrambled off her stool and wrapped Emerie up in a bear hug. When Em tried to pull out of the hug, Kassie held on tight. And it was exactly what she needed.

Emerie squeezed her eyes shut, trying to keep the tears from falling. But the more she fought to hold them in, the faster fat tears rolled down her cheek, wetting her friend's sweatshirt.

"Sit down, sweetie." Kassie guided Em to a stool. "I'll make the drinks. You just relax. We can talk about it if you want to; if not, I'll understand that, too. All right?"

Em nodded, sniffling. She tore off a paper towel and dabbed her face as her friend washed her hands at the sink and started to make their drinks.

"How was your call with Harrison?" Em asked. Kass had come downstairs excited to share her news. She hated that the attention had been shifted from Kassie to her and Nick's drama.

"It was good. Great, actually." A dreamy look softened

Kassandra's expression, and Em smiled, too, happy for her friend.

At least one of them was moving in the right direction.

"Harrison had the most beautiful bouquet of flowers delivered to my apartment." Kassie pulled out her phone and showed Em the gorgeous bouquet of twenty white roses and five white lilies. "He also sent a certificate for the spa at the resort. And he included enough so that it'll cover my spa treatments and yours. He said he knew I'd enjoy it much more with a friend."

"The man certainly has good taste." Emerie returned the phone to her blushing friend. "And he's thoughtful and generous."

She had yet to meet Harrison. But maybe the gossip about him and his family being snotty, self-centered assholes who thought they were better than the rest of them was wrong. Or perhaps Harrison wasn't like the rest of them. For Kass's sake, she hoped so. Because she was really into the guy.

"He said since he couldn't be here with me on Valentine's Day, he was thankful I had a friend to keep me company." She used the stainless-steel cocktail spoon to crush and stir the mint leaves and sugar in the bottom of two collins glasses.

"Well, please thank him for me." Em smiled. "Are you nervous about your first official date when he gets back?"

"A little," Kassie admitted. She quartered two limes, dropping all but two of the pieces into their glasses. She used a muddler to express the lime juice. "But I'm also really excited. I love my job, and the work I do is important, but my career shouldn't be the totality of my existence. Your willingness to face your fears and be open about wanting love...I found it inspiring. And it forced me to be honest with myself about what I want."

"You're looking to settle down and become Mrs. Harrison Dunbar, III?" Em asked cautiously. The question wasn't meant to demean or tease. She just hadn't ever heard Kassie express any desire for marriage and kids.

"I don't know." Kassie hunched a shoulder as she added rum and ice to the stainless-steel cocktail shaker. "I'm not going into this with that kind of expectation. Besides, I'm sure his parents would rather see him with some blue-blooded heiress so they can consolidate their families' wealth."

"Well, your mom does own her own florist shop." Em grinned. "And bonus points to Harrison for ordering the flowers from her. Smart man."

"He is. And a sweet one, too." Kassie added two craft ice spheres to each glass, then divided the icy rum from the cocktail shaker between them. She topped off the mojitos with club soda, a slice of lime, and sprigs of mint.

Emerie took a sip of the refreshingly minty drink. It wasn't summer, but she didn't care. It was never the wrong season for a mojito.

"This is really good, Kass. Well done." Em fist-bumped her friend, then took another sip of her drink.

"Thank you," Kassie said proudly. She took another sip of her own drink, then turned her stool toward Emerie's. "Now… about what happened tonight between you and Nick…"

Em should've known they'd revisit the conversation. At least she had liquor now.

She heaved a sigh and recounted what had happened after Kassie left.

"You asked your best friend, who you're trying to get over being in love with, to kiss you so you'd be more comfortable kissing someone else?" Kassie's tone conveyed bewilderment and a hint of reverence. "Wow. That's a lot to take in. I'm trying to decide if you're diabolically brilliant or have completely lost your mind. But I'm leaning toward the latter. Em, what were you thinking?"

"I was joking," Em said. "I didn't think Nick would actually kiss me. But once he pulled me into his arms… I knew it was a terrible idea, but…" She pressed a hand to her forehead and groaned.

How could she have made such a mess of things?

"You couldn't resist the chance to finally kiss him." Kassie placed a hand over Em's. "And maybe a part of you hoped it would make Nick see how right you two are for each other?"

Em nodded, frowning. How could she have been so foolish?

"So how was the kiss?"

"Amazing." Was she sporting the same dreamy look Kassie had when she'd talked about Harrison? "In college, I dated a guy who I considered to be a great kisser. But I've honestly never had a kiss that felt like *that*. It was this total-body experience. My skin is all feverish and tingly, and I can't stop reliving every moment of it."

"Sounds like a lot more than *practice*," Kassie said.

"It was for me." Em rearranged the sprigs of mint in her drink. "But Nick clearly doesn't feel that way."

"Not true." Kassie's cheeks flushed. "Because the other thing I noticed as Nick made his escape was the hard-on he definitely didn't have before I left."

"Oh my God." Em cupped a hand to her mouth, and they both dissolved into giggles. "We really were acting like a couple of hormonal teenagers, weren't we?"

"I think you were behaving like two people who have a serious thing for each other, even if one of you is too bone-headed to realize it." Kassie sipped her drink. "Why else would he volunteer to help you practice kissing?"

"I don't know, Kass. But that kiss was a complete mind-fuck. I have no idea what's happening with us anymore," Em said. "I tell Nick how I feel, and he says he doesn't feel the same. *Fine*. But then I go on this soulmate quest, and suddenly, he's been hovering over me like an overprotective lover. And then he kisses me like…*that*. But then he says, 'You good now?' Like we were practicing three-pointers out on the basketball court. As if he didn't just kiss me with so much passion and intensity that it felt like my entire soul was sucked out of my body." Em huffed, getting angry and confused all over again.

She drained the remainder of her mojito, setting her empty glass on the counter harder than she'd intended.

"Nick is bullshitting you and maybe himself, too. You know that, right?" Kassie said.

"Maybe." Em shrugged. "I don't know anymore. I'm not sure he does, either."

"So…what are you going to do?"

"What am I supposed to do, Kass?" Em turned to her friend, then sighed. "I'm sorry. I'm just frustrated and confused. I've been trying so hard to move my feelings for Nick back into the friend zone. But he's doing everything he can to keep me pining over him like a lovesick puppy."

"Another mojito?" Kassie climbed off her stool.

"Please."

Kassie worked in silence, preparing the mint leaves and sugar, then cutting the limes and muddling them.

Emerie's phone signaled an incoming text message, and she checked it.

Nick.

Made it home. Sorry I lost my head and got carried away tonight, but the kiss was perfect. If this is really

what you want, you don't need to worry. You'll be fine.
But if you don't, no one will blame you for changing
your mind. Good night.

Emerie felt a hint of nausea. How could the kiss have
meant everything to her yet so little to him?

"See what I mean?" Em set her phone in front of Kassie
after she sat down with their drinks. "Despite his physical
reaction to the kiss, it didn't mean anything to him."

"I don't believe that, and neither do you," Kassie said.

"It doesn't matter what I believe. It only matters what he
does." Em sipped her mojito. This one was stronger than
the last.

"Maybe it isn't my place to say this, but I love watching the two of you interact because you have such a special
connection. The kind that only happens once or twice in
a lifetime. So maybe it's worth broaching the subject with
Nick again, now that he's had time to think about it."

"Do you have any idea how humiliating it was for me
to be completely vulnerable with Nick and lay my heart on
the line only to get rejected?" Em felt a deep ache in the pit
of her stomach, remembering that night on the beach. She
shook her head. "I can't put myself through that again. If
Nick says I'm not the one for him, then I need to respect
that and move on."

"Right. Of course." The space between Kassie's brows
furrowed. "Sorry if I overstepped. It's just…I realize that
Nick is your best friend. But you're mine. I want you to be
happy, Em. And you deserve to be."

"Thanks, Kass. I appreciate that." Em was grateful to
have such good friends. "I want you to be honest with me.
Even when I'm not ready to hear it. That's what best friends
are for, right?" She squeezed her friend's arm.

"Good. Because here's something else you need to hear." Kassie took a deep breath and sat taller. "You began this journey because you said you were ready to find Mr. Right and settle down. But it seems you've gotten cold feet. Have you changed your mind?"

"Definitely not."

"Then stop hanging out by the side of the pool and jump in with both feet, the way you jumped out of that plane on your thirtieth birthday."

"Sometimes the dating pool seems really shallow, and I'm pretty sure there's pee in it." Em shuddered. "Seriously, some of these guys make Marcus look like the cream of the crop."

"That is so gross, yet, sadly accurate." Kassie sighed in commiseration. "Will you meet a lot of Mr. Wrongs? *Probably*. But eventually, you will find Mr. Right. But only if you put yourself out there and try."

Kassie picked up Emerie's phone and handed it to her.

"Open up your dating app."

"Right now?"

"Yes, *now*. Just think of me as a mama bird. It's my job to give you a gentle shove out of the nest. And if that don't work, I'm fully prepared to go with the foot-in-the-ass method." Kassie grinned and Em dissolved into laughter.

"Okay, fine." Em unlocked her phone and opened the app. "Now I suppose you want me to swipe right."

"Yes, I do. Because it's the first step in your stated goal of finding a mature, emotionally available man who is *actually* interested in a serious relationship."

Touché.

"But first...we need to edit your profile." Kassandra maneuvered through the app, then started typing something. "There!" she declared proudly, showing Emerie the screen. "Now it's perfect."

Em scanned the profile to determine what had been changed. Finally, she spotted it under the "What I'm Looking For in a Partner" section.

" 'He needs to be an exceptional kisser'?" Em read the words aloud. "I cannot believe you just added that." She hit the edit button to remove it.

"Before you do that…" Kassie held up a hand. "Wasn't the point of your practice kiss with Nick to make you more comfortable with intimacy and discover what you like?"

"Yes, but—"

"Well, you just discovered that you want someone whose kiss will turn you inside out and make you feel like you're floating. Right?"

Nick's kiss had made her feel all those things and more.

"Right."

"Then don't be afraid to ask for what you deserve. That's what you told me about my job, and you were right. If I hadn't asked for that promotion, I would never have received the title or the additional pay. So now I'm returning the favor. Isn't the Soulmate Project about you stating *exactly* what you want and then going after it fearlessly?"

"Yes."

Em realized that she'd given in to the gratification of spending so much time with Nick. Their dance classes had begun to feel like dates. But they weren't. Nick still wasn't hers, and he never would be. She needed to stop fooling herself into believing otherwise.

"Then ask for what you want. Bad kissers need not apply." Kassie grinned. "Now, are you ready to *really* begin this search for Mr. Right?"

Kassie had been half right about why Em hadn't swiped right on the dating app. Yes, she'd gotten a case of cold feet. But that was because a part of her had been holding out hope that Nick would change his mind. Especially after he'd agreed to take bachata lessons with her. But if the kiss they'd shared tonight hadn't changed his mind, nothing ever would. She needed to let go of her childish dream and move on.

"Okay. Let's do this."

Kassie squealed and gave her a big hug.

They'd been scrolling through potential dates for nearly an hour. Finally, Em settled on a profile that intrigued her.

She nibbled on her lower lip, her hand hovering over the screen. "Here goes," she muttered as she swiped right.

Kassie cheered and hugged her again. "I'm so proud of you!"

Em was proud of herself, too. She also felt a sense of panic and dread. And not only about whether the guy would respond.

"What if Nick sees that line we added? That'd be really weird and awkward."

"The man just gave you a tonsil massage. I'm pretty sure things are going to be weird and awkward for a bit either way," Kassie noted. "Besides, Nick doesn't strike me as the dating app type."

"He isn't. Mostly because gorgeous women seem to just fall into his lap whenever we're out," Em grumbled.

"Perfect. Then he's never going to see it or know that it was his kiss that inspired it," Kassie reassured her.

Em sighed quietly with relief, hoping that was true.

Chapter Sixteen

Nick sat at his parents' kitchen table, trying his best to keep up the illusion of following their conversation. His mother and father—both professors working at the same university—were top experts in molecular biology and astronomy, respectively. They shared an apartment near the university during the semester, coming home to Holly Grove Island mostly on the weekends or during breaks.

As usual, most of the conversation went over his head. It was just as well tonight. It had been a little more than two weeks since he'd kissed Emerie, and his brain was still scrambled. He couldn't stop thinking about the kiss or what might've happened between them had Kassie not returned when she did.

"What's going on with you tonight, son? That's the third time one of us has been speaking to you and you've zoned out." Timothy Washington sat across the kitchen table from Nick with his arms folded as he carefully assessed him.

"Sorry, Dad. I've got a lot on my mind. The project at work and..." Nick's voice trailed off. He rubbed his chin and frowned.

"And this Soulmate Project of Em's, I'd imagine." Evelyn Washington set her fork down and folded her arms, too.

Her expression was "who you think you're fooling?" but her tone was compassionate.

"That, too." Nick stabbed the last of his steak and took a bite.

He was trying his damnedest not to pout about the fact that Em would be going on her second date with some dude she'd connected with on the app. But based on the softening of his mother's expression, he was failing.

"I was so sure that you and Em would eventually end up together," his mother said. "They don't say it around you, but your aunts have been referring to her as my daughter-in-law for the past couple of years."

His shocked expression was met with her quiet chuckle.

"Emerie Roberts is an absolute sweetheart. More importantly, she's the *perfect* woman for you, Nicholas. She adores you. Quite frankly, you're the only person who seems oblivious about it."

His mother's bright smile shifted to a deep frown.

"We were so surprised to hear that Em was suddenly on a quest to find her soulmate. But you said you applauded her bravery and supported her efforts. So I've kept my opinions to myself. But in the weeks since Em began her search, you seem sadder every time we talk. And tonight, you're agitated and distraught. So what's *really* going on?"

Nick couldn't help thinking of when he'd asked Em the same question. The question that had led to the most incredible kiss of his life.

"It's nothing." He stood quickly, grabbing his dishes and stacking them with theirs before taking them all to the sink and rinsing them. He started loading the dishwasher.

"Don't worry about the dishes, sweetheart." His mother closed the dishwasher door and guided him back to his seat. "Right now, I'd much rather hear what's troubling you."

"I screwed things up with Em." Nick heaved a sigh.

He'd barely been honest with himself about his feelings. Now he was confessing them to his parents? But it was nice to have someone to discuss this with. He was tired of endlessly debating the situation with himself. He'd been hoping to either convince himself that things with Em would be different or make peace with his decision.

"You blew it *how*, son?" his father asked.

"On New Year's Eve, Em told me that she wanted to be more than just friends. I said that I didn't see her that way, and that I love her as a friend."

"You didn't!" His mother slapped a hand to her forehead and groaned. "Why on *earth* would you say that instead of telling her the truth?"

"My friendship with Em means everything to me. She's the one person in my life who is always there when I need her—no matter what."

His parents exchanged a hurt look. But in their usual calm, logical, and scientific approach to parenting, neither objected.

Instead, his father said, "Seems like that's all the more reason for you two to be together."

"I was sure that if Em and I got involved, it would spell the end of our friendship. I've dated women I was friends with before. Both relationships ended badly," he admitted.

"Well, your father and I were best friends who fell in love, and it worked out just fine for us." His mom gestured toward his dad with a proud grin. "We've been married for nearly forty years and counting."

"You *were* best friends," Nick emphasized the past tense. "But that's *not* the relationship you have now. You barely had time for me growing up, let alone each other."

"Nicholas Fabian Washington!" His father's voice boomed

like a clap of thunder. "How dare you imply that your mother and I were neglectful. Do you have any idea how many sacrifices—"

"Tim, please." His mother put a hand on his father's arm, halting his rant. "I'd like to hear what Nick has to say. Wouldn't you?"

His dad rubbed his whiskered chin and huffed. "Fine. Let's hear it."

"And let's *actively* listen to what our son has to say." She squeezed her husband's arm, her eyes warm and pleading. "What's important here is understanding why our son feels this way, not preparing a rebuttal."

His father heaved a sigh and clamped a reassuring hand over his mother's. "We're listening, son."

Nick shifted his glance from his mother to his father. His brows furrowed, and his gut tightened in a knot. This was a conversation he'd danced around his entire life. But if understanding his parents' relationship could give him any insight into how he and Emerie could truly have both love and friendship without one relationship sabotaging the other, it was a conversation worth having. No matter how painful it might be.

"Can I be brutally honest?"

His parents exchanged a worried look, but both quickly agreed. "Of course."

Nick pressed his palms to the table and met his parents' expectant gaze. "Yes, you've been married nearly forty years, and I admire that. But you each exist in your own little bubble. That's not what I want for me and Em. I don't want to lose the bona fide friendship we've always shared."

"What exactly is that supposed to mean?" his father demanded indignantly. He took a deep breath and lowered his voice after Nick's mother clamped a hand on his wrist.

"I mean…perhaps you could further explain that statement. After all, we provided for you and made sure that you had all the things we didn't have growing up."

Nick's parents were good people, and they'd done their best to raise him while also making their mark on the world. He realized that. But his resentment over feeling like science, history, and the greater good always came ahead of him had built an invisible wall between him and his parents. As an adult, his relationship with them felt formal and superficial. That was the reason they didn't normally have honest conversations like this. He didn't want to hurt his parents. But this discussion had lingered in the back of his head, like an open wound that never quite healed. Maybe finally getting the words off his chest was the best thing he could do for his relationship with his parents.

"You're both accomplished career professionals, and I respect that. I'm proud of the barriers you've broken in your respective fields. And I'm in awe of the tenacity and determination you've both shown in the face of bigotry and misogyny." He looked at his father, then his mother. "But those accomplishments came at a price. Your relationships with me and with each other are the sacrifices you made to achieve those goals."

His father looked outraged. His mother gasped, genuine hurt marring her beautiful face.

"I realize we couldn't be there for your basketball games and band performances as much as we would've liked. But your father and I were doing important work. And just as importantly, we were making a path for other Black scientists. We're both committed to reaching down to help young, Black STEM professionals climb that ladder because other folks are working hard to destroy it rung by rung."

"I know, Mom." Nick nodded. "And I understand how important and how necessary that work is. I feel that same pressure as a corporate VP. That's why I was willing to take on this additional assignment. But as a ten-year-old kid, I just wanted my parents to care as much about me as they cared about molecules and undiscovered galaxies. I wanted to matter to you as much as getting your work published or securing funding for your programs. I wanted...*needed* to feel like *I* was a priority in your life." Nick's jaw clenched as the tension and bitterness built in his chest. He tried to tamp those feelings back into the little box where he'd been storing them his entire life.

"Your father and I love you very much, Nicky." His mother squeezed his hand. The corners of her eyes were damp. "You mean the world to us, sweetheart. And you have *always* been our priority. I'm sorry if you didn't always feel that way."

Nick forced a pained smile. "I know, Mom. And I'm not saying any of this to make you feel bad. I just need you to understand why I'm worried that getting romantically involved with Em would destroy our friendship."

Oh yeah, genius? Then why did you kiss her?

Nick tried to shut out the voice in his head condemning him for being both stupid and selfish. He never should've kissed Emerie. But he couldn't bring himself to regret it.

"I realize how difficult it must've been for you to level with us about your feelings, son." His father finally broke the awkward silence that had settled over them. "Believe me, there were countless moments when I felt like the shittiest father alive because it was Oliver who taught you how to throw a ball and ride a bike instead of me." There was pain in his father's voice and expression. "The Jones family was a godsend. Evelyn and I were only able to do the things we did because we knew that you were with them. And that they cared for you as if you were their own. Maybe we became a bit *too* reliant on them. We both regret that. But I promise you that nothing we've accomplished means more to us than you, Nick." His father's voice trembled with a hint of emotion.

"That means a lot, Dad," Nick said honestly, surprised at how much lighter he felt getting those words off his chest and hearing his parents express their regret.

"So...about Em. She embarked on this Soulmate Project following your rejection." His mother dabbed the corner of her eyes with a napkin and tried to sound more upbeat. "Do you think it's her way of trying to make you realize that you two belong together?"

"At first I did." Nick was ashamed that his ego had allowed him to believe that Em would go through with such an elaborate plan simply for the sake of spurring his interest. "But I was wrong. Em wants to settle down and start a family. To have children of her own."

It made Nick's chest ache to think of Emerie falling in love with and marrying someone else. Having a kid with him. He already hated this guy she was going out with tonight. But he hated himself even more.

He should've admitted the truth to Em. That he wanted to be with her, too. But not at the expense of their friendship. Then they could've worked through their concerns whether they chose to move forward with a relationship or not.

"And what do you want, son?" His dad frowned, rubbing his beard. "Because you've never given any indication that you're ready to settle down and give us grandkids."

"Or..." His mother narrowed her gaze at his father before returning her attention to him. "Perhaps you haven't considered marriage and a family because you couldn't imagine yourself taking those steps with anyone other than Emerie."

Nick felt like a light bulb had flipped on in his head. He squeezed his eyes shut and rubbed his forehead.

His mother was right.

His relationship with Emerie had been the primary one in his life. Whenever a woman he'd been dating had threatened to interfere with that relationship, he'd ended things. Because his friendship with Em was the relationship he would protect at all costs.

Nick had always thought the reason he hadn't considered marriage or starting a family was because he wasn't cut out for it. But these past few months had made him see things differently. Because Emerie Roberts was the one person he could unequivocally say he wanted to spend the rest of his life with. He couldn't imagine spending forever with anyone else.

And while Em had been going on dates with Marcus, Dillon, and now this Alan dude from the dating app who sounded like a pretentious asshole, Nick couldn't remember the last time he'd been out on a date or had even wanted to go out on one. He'd come up with one excuse after another as to why he couldn't go out with other people. But the truth was that he'd become focused on Em and her quest for love.

Faced with the possibility of losing her, it had become increasingly clear that Em meant *everything* to him. That she was already more than just a friend. And she had been for some time.

Nick laughed bitterly. "All this time, I'd convinced myself that I loved Em as a friend. But that's not true. I just plain love her. So much. I've been a complete idiot. Why didn't I recognize this before?"

"You've been friends for so long, sweetheart." His mother placed a gentle hand on his cheek and smiled. "In situations like this, love can come on so gradually...you don't really notice it until you're forced to make a choice. Em's decision to move on with her life finally put you in that position."

"We Washington men can be a bit oblivious when it comes to love." Tim chuckled. "Good thing we fell in love with brave, smart women who light a fire under our asses."

His parents exchanged a smile as his father squeezed his mother's hand, then kissed the back of it. There was so much love in their eyes.

Had he been wrong about his parents' relationship? Maybe they weren't as demonstrative with their affections as some of his friends' parents were. But now that he was truly paying attention, the love, respect, and camaraderie between them was evident.

"I really fucked this up, didn't I?" Nick pressed a hand to his mouth and groaned.

"You stepped in it up to your—"

"Tim!" His mother shot his father a look, then flashed Nick an encouraging smile.

"The situation isn't ideal," she noted. "But there's still time to fix it. You need to tell Em how you really feel about her. If you don't tell her now, you'll lose her."

"She's going on a second date with this guy later tonight."

"Then you'd better get over there. *Right now*," Evelyn added when he sat there staring at her. She clapped her hands to punctuate each syllable. "You don't have a single moment to lose."

"You expect me to just show up there while she's getting ready for her date and tell her I don't want her to go on it?" Nick asked.

"*Yes!*" His parents' response was immediate.

Nick jumped up from his seat, his heart thumping against his rib cage.

Am I actually doing this?

"About what you said earlier...Your feelings are absolutely valid, sweetheart. And I'm glad you finally got them off your chest." His mom squeezed his hand.

"And you were right about your mother and me being so focused on our academic careers that we neglected our relationship. We ran into a really rough patch after you went off to college. We even tried living apart for a bit and discussed the possibility of ending our marriage," his father admitted.

"Why didn't I know this?" The news hit Nick in the chest like a sledgehammer. He'd been so preoccupied with himself and making the most of his college experience that he'd had no clue his parents' marriage had disintegrated so badly.

"Because we worked very hard to ensure you didn't know," his mother said. "We thought it would negatively impact your academic career. But you were more aware of our relationship woes than we were at the time." She sighed. "The time your father and I spent apart was the most devastating period of my life. It didn't take long before I realized—"

"Before *we* realized..." his father interjected.

She smiled and squeezed his father's hand. "It didn't take long before we realized what a big mistake we'd be making if we walked away from the life we'd built together. We were both raised to believe that parents shouldn't openly show affection in front of their children. That likely has some bearing on your misconceptions about the current status of our relationship. But rest assured that the love and passion we have for each other burns brighter than ever."

She eyed his father flirtatiously, and his old man responded with a grin and a chuckle.

"Okay, okay... you're still really into each other. I get it. Let's not go from zero to sixty here." Nick held up a hand.

"You're the one who was worried about our sex life," his dad said.

"Ew... gross. No, I was worried about your seeming lack of connection and companionship. As far as I'm concerned, I was delivered by the stork. End of story."

His parents laughed.

"Whatever floats your boat, son," his father said, still holding his mother's hand tight.

Nick was happy that his parents had revived their marriage. That they'd found a way to still be happy and in love after nearly four decades.

"But we have fallen into some of those same bad habits that nearly derailed our relationship back then," his father acknowledged. "I don't ever want to go there again. So I'm glad you brought it to our attention, son. I plan on working hard to rectify that."

"Me, too." His mother smiled back, her eyes filled with happy tears. She turned toward Nick. "As for your concerns about your relationship with Em diminishing if you get involved romantically... I don't believe that to be true. You have two decades of love and friendship. You've seen each other through highs and lows since you were kids. I doubt that was the case with those other friends you dated. It certainly wasn't for your dad and me."

"That's right, son. You two will be building your relationship on a rock-solid foundation. Doesn't mean you won't run into the occasional problem. Just means that you have enough love and respect for each other to work your way through them," his father added.

"Thanks, Mom." Nick kissed his mother's cheek. "Thanks, Dad." He hugged his father. "Thanks for dinner and the talk. But there's somewhere I need to be right now."

"Good luck, sweetheart. Send Em our love."

Nick grabbed his coat and hurried to his car. His brain was spinning, and his heart raced as he thought of what he'd say when he showed up at Emerie's door.

Chapter Seventeen

Em got out of the shower, toweled off, and applied her luxurious new scented body lotion. Maybe she hadn't found her soulmate yet, but her new self-care routine had her skin soft and glowing. So at least there was that.

Emerie walked into her bedroom closet and sifted through a few of the sexy, daring, or ultrafeminine looks that she wouldn't have imagined she could pull off, just a few months ago. Through this experience, she'd gained a growing sense of confidence. And though she still hated the fuss and muss, she loved her new look. She pulled a skirt from the rack and examined it. But it didn't quite feel right for a Friday night date. It was more of a Sunday brunch look.

She halted at the sound of knocking. There was silence, followed by another round of knocking—harder and longer this time.

Kassie lived in Emerie's building. She was likely popping in to keep Em company and dish about her latest date with Harrison while Em got dressed for her second date with Alan—the first dating app candidate who'd been worth a second look.

Em yanked off her towel and slipped on a short robe before going to the front door and checking the peephole.

"Nick?" She opened the door. "What are you doing here? I'm getting ready for my date."

"I know my timing is shitty, but I *really* need to talk to you, Em. Could you spare like ten minutes?"

Emerie was prepared to tell him they needed to do this some other time. But Nick's tone was urgent, and he seemed nervous and unsettled. The opposite of his usual laid-back demeanor.

Em clutched her robe—holding it together where it was falling open and revealing peeks of cleavage. She opened the door and gestured toward the living room.

"Ten minutes is all I can spare, so start talking." Em folded her arms as she studied her friend, who seemed more rattled than she'd ever seen him before. "What's going on, Nick? The past few weeks you've been acting...I don't know...weird."

Honestly, things had been strange for her, too, in the weeks since their kiss. But Nick hadn't brought it up again, and neither had she. Besides, between Nick's work and the band and her increased client load, dance practice, and now dating...they hadn't seen each other much since that night. Still, Nick's tense vibe was surprising.

"So what's this about, Nick?"

"The past few weeks have been rough for me. Between my work and all of your practice for the dance exhibition, we don't get to spend much time together anymore."

Em wasn't sure what to make of Nick's admission or where he was going with this. But she'd spent the past several years captive to Nicholas Washington's charm. She wouldn't let that deep, sexy voice and that penetrating gaze sway her again.

"You're saying you're upset because the dance exhibition is taking away from the time I spend with *you*?"

"No. I mean...yes. But I—" Nick swallowed hard, and his forehead glistened with beads of perspiration, despite it still being winter in the Carolinas.

Had he run up the stairs rather than taking the elevator?

"Look, Em, I realize that sounds—"

"Selfish? Immature?" she offered.

"I was thinking *petty*, but okay. I can see your point," Nick conceded. He sighed heavily and dragged a hand through his hair. "Look, Em, you're the shining star of that class. I am *thrilled* that you're getting your chance to shine. I'm just..."

Nick's words faded and her friend looked more flustered than she'd ever seen him.

"You're just...*what*, Nick?"

"Jealous of Carlos because he gets to spend so much time with you during practice. And of this guy Alan, who you're going on a second date with. And who the hell ever else you've been spending time with on that damn dating app. Because...God, this does sound incredibly selfish and immature, but I swear it comes from a place of absolute sincerity."

"*What* comes from a place of sincerity?" Em's head was spinning. "You didn't even finish your sentence. Why would you be jealous of Carlos or Alan or anyone else I'm spending time with?" The volume of Em's voice was climbing, as was her frustration with Nick.

A few months ago, she would've been over the moon to hear Nick proclaim how much he missed spending time with her. But she'd told Nick how she felt about him, and he'd rejected her. And she was growing tired of his self-centered little games. So she didn't feel that warm, fuzzy feeling she would've a few months or even weeks ago. What she felt was incandescent rage.

"What the fuck is this, Nick?" Em seethed, her heartbeat going a mile a minute.

Nick took a half step backward, clearly aware that she was angry. "I'm just trying to say that I miss you, Em. I miss *us*."

"Now that you're no longer my complete focus, suddenly you miss *us*." Em stressed the final word, her chest heaving with each breath. "You don't want me, but you don't want anyone else to have me, either. Does that just about sum things up?"

"Shit." Nick huffed. "That makes me sound like a complete dick. And maybe I am. But it's true. You and I are more than just friends, Em. We're...we're..."

"We're *what*, exactly, Nick?" Emerie demanded, stepping closer, her hands balled into fists at her side as she stared up at her best friend.

The question was one she'd considered a lot lately. That "practice" kiss a few weeks ago had confirmed that there was something more than just friendship between them. But they clearly weren't lovers, either. So where did that leave them? In some weird, gray space in between the two?

Em stared at Nick, waiting for a response. He seemed to search her face for an answer of his own, neither of them speaking. Then suddenly, Nick stepped forward, cupped her jaw in his large hand, and pressed his lips to hers.

Em gasped, surprised by her friend's action. But as his lips moved over hers with a heat and intensity that made her body instantly react, the stiffness in her spine and the anger that fueled it began to dissipate.

She hated to admit it, but she still had feelings for Nick, and she wanted him.

She pressed her hands to Nick's chest and leaned into him, her heartbeat filling her ears, and her pulse racing.

Nick tilted her head slightly, and her lips parted the

tiniest bit. His tongue swept between her lips and glided against hers as he deepened the kiss.

Em sank into him, loving the feel of her body melting into his as he captured her mouth in a hungry kiss that made her wonder if he'd been as starved for this as she had.

Nick's hand drifted down her neck, then down her side, and settled on her hip. He pulled her closer, their lower bodies flush, removing any doubt about whether Nick was attracted to her. The feeling of him hard against her belly was more pronounced given that she was wearing absolutely nothing beneath the thin, satin robe.

Em settled into the kiss, into the feel of Nick's arms around her, the taste of his warm mouth, and the way he held her as if she belonged to him and no one else. Because that was what she wanted, too.

A knock at the door startled them. Nick suspended the kiss but didn't let go of her. They stared at each other, neither of them speaking. There was more knocking.

"Emerie, it's Alan. I know I'm kind of early but…"

Em slapped a hand over her mouth, her heart racing as the dreaminess of the kiss faded and she came back to reality. "It's Alan."

"I heard." Nick heaved a quiet sigh.

"What the hell am I doing?" Em paced the floor, one hand pressed to her forehead as she whispered beneath her breath. Suddenly, she stopped and turned to Nick. She poked his chest. "No, what the hell are *you* doing? Did you just wake up today and decide to choose violence?"

"No, of course not. You know me better than that, Em." Nick seemed genuinely hurt by her accusation. "I'm here because—"

Alan knocked again. "Emerie? Would it be better if I—"

"Just a minute, Alan. I'll be there in a sec!" Em called.

She sucked in a deep breath. She needed a moment to think; a moment to breathe.

Twenty minutes ago, she was floating on a cloud, trying to decide what to wear for her second date with Alan, and now her head was spinning, her temples were throbbing, and she felt like she was in the midst of a panic attack. Em was going to strangle her best friend.

"I can get rid of him," Nick said. "I'll just explain that—"

"The only person I'm getting rid of tonight is you, Nicholas Washington." Emerie grabbed her friend's elbow and dragged him toward her bedroom.

"Wait...you're still going out with that guy after we kissed?" Nick protested as she ushered him into her bedroom.

"Yes, I'm still going out with Alan." Em closed the door behind them. She shoved a finger in Nick's direction. "You don't get to waltz in here and try to stake your claim on me because someone else is finally interested."

Nick winced and lowered his gaze.

Good. At least he had the decency to be ashamed of himself.

"Look, I know my timing is sus. But Alan isn't the guy for you. You deserve better."

"And you know this *how*, exactly?" Em tightened her loosening belt, then folded her arms as she glared at Nick.

He shifted his gaze from hers. "I just do."

Em heaved a sigh and shook her head. She wasn't sure what had gotten into Nick. He was behaving like a puppy peeing on fire hydrants to mark his territory. But this time, she wouldn't give in to his selfish antics.

She'd initiated the Soulmate Project because she was tired of the roles that she and Nick had fallen into. Tired of playing the faithful, lovelorn sidekick to Nick's charming playboy. Emerie was ready to find the person she was *meant* to be with, and no matter how much she wanted him to be, that clearly wasn't Nick.

Alan was the first of her dates she'd liked enough to consider a second date with. She wasn't about to let Nick ruin things with the best prospect she'd had since Dillon.

"Well, *bestie*, your concerns have been noted. Now unless you want to climb out of my sixth-floor window, I suggest you park your ass in that chair, stay in this room, and stay quiet. I'm going to let Alan in, get dressed, then we'll be on our way. Then you can leave and lock up behind you."

"But, Em—"

"*No*, Nick," Em said firmly. "I am *not* letting you mess this up for me. You promised you would help me with this. That you would be my wingman the way I've been for you all this time. This is the exact opposite of helping." Em's anger receded, and there was just hurt left behind. She placed a hand on her friend's arm, and her eyes pleaded with his. "Please do this for me. We can talk about everything else later."

Nick dragged a hand down his face and sighed. He nodded solemnly. "If that's what you want."

"Thank you." Emerie slipped the shower bonnet from her head and tossed it onto the bed. "I'll be back in a few minutes. Remember…stay in here and do *not* make a sound."

Em closed the door behind her, hurried toward the front door, stopping in front of the mirror long enough to fluff up her hair, flattened by the shower cap.

Em put on her biggest smile, then opened the door a crack. She peered at the handsome man standing on the other side. He smelled like soap and cologne. The two cloying scents clashing.

"Sorry it took me so long, Alan. But I'm still getting dressed. Did we get our signals mixed up? I thought you weren't coming for another half hour."

"No, you're right. That was the plan, but I found myself in the area earlier, and I was eager to see you again. So I thought I'd take a chance on seeing if you were ready." He flashed a grin that was probably intended to be sexy but missed its mark by a mile. "Mind if I come in and wait?"

Em stared at him a moment, her brain churning. If she'd been there alone, she probably would've asked him to wait in the car. But while he didn't give her stalker vibes, she felt more confident knowing Nick was in the other room.

"Sure. Have a seat." Em gestured toward the living room. "I shouldn't be long. Can I get you a drink? Water, juice, soda, coffee, maybe?"

Alan rubbed his beard as he took in her bare legs beneath the short robe. He cleared his throat. "Juice would be great. What are the options?"

"Cranberry or white grape." Em pulled her robe tighter, suddenly self-conscious.

"Cranberry would be great. If you have a splash of vodka to go with it...even better." Alan chuckled, his dark eyes twinkling.

Em grabbed a glass and pulled a bottle of cranberry juice from the fridge, ignoring his suggestion about the vodka. They weren't supposed to be having cocktails at her place before they went to a movie theater off-island. She handed him the glass.

Alan took a sip and practically coughed. "Just juice, huh?" He studied the glass as if the liquid inside had offended him.

"We can go for cocktails *after* the movie." Em flashed a smile. "And if we're going to make it to the theater in time, I should get dressed. I'll be as quick as I—"

"Actually…" Alan set his drink down and caught her hand.

The zing of electricity she'd felt when Nick had taken her hand earlier was notably absent. There was only the sensation of chilliness and the roughness of Alan's palm.

Em's gaze dropped to their joined hands, then up at Alan again.

"I was thinking…it's opening weekend. The theater will probably be really crowded. Not ideal. What if we see the movie next weekend or the weekend after that? By then, the crowd will have died down a bit." Alan grinned.

"Sure. Okay, I guess." Em shrugged. It was the ninth or tenth installment in a dying action movie franchise. She honestly couldn't care less about the movie. She'd checked out three or four movies ago. She only kept seeing the movies because Nick loved the franchise.

"So what should we do tonight? Dinner? Billiards? The Foxhole maybe? There's live music there tonight." Em didn't yank her hand from his, but she took a half step backward.

"Actually…" Alan drew the word out, and Em's shoulders tensed instinctively "…I was thinking we could do dinner and a movie here. There must be something on one of the streaming services neither of us has seen, and we can order in. I discovered a fantastic Asian fusion restaurant that delivers to the island."

So that's why Alan had shown up to her apartment a half hour early.

He was hoping to make it a Netflix and Chill night. But that wasn't going to happen. They'd had one date and a series of messages on the dating app. She barely knew the man. And in the history of her dating life, she'd never slept with someone she didn't know well and feel totally at ease with. She and Alan certainly hadn't reached that stage.

"Actually, I was really looking forward to going out tonight." Em tugged her hand free as subtly as she could manage. "Bought a new outfit just for the occasion."

"And I'll bet you look amazing in it." Alan stroked his full beard and scanned her legs again. "But I promise to appreciate it just as much if you wear it here."

Em took a full step backward this time. "Seems pointless to get all dressed up if we're just hanging out at my place."

Alan stepped forward, his legs much longer than hers. "Good point. I happen to think you look pretty damn amazing just the way you are. No need to get dressed on my account."

Em wasn't afraid. But Alan clearly either wasn't taking the hint or simply didn't care what she wanted. Neither was acceptable.

"*Actually*..." Em repeated what had become the word of the evening. "On second thought, it's been a long, exhausting day for me. I'm not feeling great. Perhaps we should take a rain check on the entire evening." She folded her arms.

"After I came all this way, you want me to leave?" Alan folded his arms, too. He glared at her. "I'm sorry if I offended you by suggesting we stay in tonight. But isn't the point of this to get to know each other and see if there's something here? It would be much easier to accomplish that in the comfort and quiet of your apartment than in a crowded movie theater or restaurant."

"Maybe I haven't been clear enough." Em kept her voice steady, despite her growing uneasiness and his increasing agitation. "I'd like you to leave my apartment. *Now*. Please."

Em moved toward the door, but Alan grabbed her arm. His grip was tight, but not painful.

"Emerie, I think there's been a misunderstanding. You're taking this all wrong. I—"

"I think she asked you to leave more than once, *bruh*."

They both turned toward Nick's voice as he stalked toward them like a train barreling down a railroad track. His expression and body language were far more menacing than Alan's.

"Who the hell is this?" Alan's tone was accusatory.

"The guy who won't ask you twice to take your fucking hand off of her." Nick was standing toe-to-toe with the man, staring him down.

Alan released her arm and stepped back.

"This is Nicky," Em said. Her face was hot, and her gut churned. She wasn't sure who she was more pissed at right now. Alan for being a pushy jerk or Nick for riding in on his white horse without giving her a chance to resolve the problem herself. "He's the childhood best friend I told you about."

"I thought Nicky was a woman." Alan frowned.

"Clearly not." Nick grinned like a cartoon villain.

"Nick came by to tell me something. Then you arrived earlier than we'd agreed and—"

"What kind of game are you two playing?" Alan shifted his gaze between the two of them. "What was the plan, Emerie? You already have a man? Were you two planning to rob me or is one man just not enough for you?"

Okay, she was *definitely* more pissed at Alan. But she was more angry with herself. How could she have liked this guy enough to give him a second date?

"I was supposed to meet you downstairs. *You* invited yourself in," she reminded him, her voice rising.

"And she asked you to leave. So take the hint and get the hell out before I help you find the door." Nick's hands were balled into fists at his sides, and a vein bulged in his temple.

"Please," Em added.

Alan snatched his jacket off the couch and put it on.

"Gladly. Because it seems things just aren't working out for us." He strode toward the door Nick held open.

"And what was your first clue about that, Casanova?" Em yelled after Alan as he strode down the hall. She slammed the front door and locked it. "Asshole!"

Emerie heaved a sigh, her back pressed to the closed door. Between another failed candidate and whatever was happening with Nick, the Soulmate Project was officially in trouble.

Chapter Eighteen

—•—•—•—

I told you that guy wasn't right for you." Nick shoved his hands in his pockets.

Em, who seemed to have momentarily forgotten he was there, turned her full ire on him.

"I thought I told you to stay in the bedroom." She slapped his arm.

"And I was." Nick forced himself not to rub at his stinging flesh, no matter how badly he wanted to. "But clearly that guy wasn't taking the hint."

"I could've handled it. Now I look like a deranged maniac trying to pull some sort of scam on the dating app. I wouldn't be surprised if they kick me off after this." Em stomped toward the kitchen, smoke practically pouring from her ears.

He followed her. "Maybe you could've handled him on your own. But I sure as hell wasn't going to cower in the bedroom while I waited to see if he tried to assault you. This is serious, Em. Guys like that are bad news. They feel entitled because they treated you to dinner once or paid for a couple of drinks. I've seen his kind before."

The anger in Emerie's expression faded, and she seemed

to realize how wrong things could've gone with Mr. Second Date.

"You're right. Things could easily have gone sideways. I'm glad you were here. Thank you for standing up for me, like you always have, Nick." Em kissed his cheek and sighed. "I could use a cranberry juice and vodka now. How about you?"

"Please." His skin tingled in the wake of Em's kiss. Since Em's admission on New Year's Eve, every touch, every graze of his skin, felt more meaningful. More so since he'd come to terms with the depth of his feelings for her.

"Two cranberry juice and vodkas coming up." She pulled out two glasses, added craft ice to each, then poured their drinks. Em handed him a glass, then sank onto the stool beside him and took a long, deep gulp.

She was more shaken by the experience than she was letting on.

Nick turned to her on the barstool, his heart still thumping from the confrontation.

"You were doing a great job of handling the situation, Em. But when I heard that guy pushing you like that, I couldn't help imagining..." Nick swallowed a large gulp of his drink and heaved a sigh. "I lost it. Even now, I'm sitting here thinking about following him out to his car and beating his ass just for putting a hand on you."

Emerie set her drink down and squeezed Nick's hand. "Alan isn't worth it. Besides, it's your job to look after me, and it's mine to ensure that you don't mess up these talented hands. It'd be tough to perform at the next wedding with busted knuckles. Not to mention that we don't want to ruin that pretty face of yours."

They both laughed, and it eased the pressure that had been building in his chest. Nick tightened his grip on her hand.

He'd always known how much Em meant to him as a friend. She was the reason he'd returned to Holly Grove Island rather than staying in LA or moving to New York where he could've continued his music career. But Em meant more to him than he'd realized. And she was so much more than a friend.

Em slipped her hand from his and drained the remainder of her drink. Another clear sign that she was shaken by what had happened with Alan. She climbed down from the stool. "I should go and get dressed. Not that I have plans for tonight anymore."

"I could take you to the movie." Nick stood, too. "I mean, we've seen every single one of those together anyway. No point in bucking the trend now, right?"

"I guess." She shrugged. "But if it's all the same to you, I'd rather not go out tonight. I think I'll just stay in and binge-watch a murder mystery series. I'm feeling pretty stabby right now. Another night, maybe?"

"Of course." Nick rubbed his chin. "But about tonight, if you'd like some company..."

Em halted, quickly turning back to him. She stared at him in silence for a moment, and he figured she was about ten seconds away from telling him off. But then she folded her arms and sighed.

"Actually, I'd love some company. But if you already have plans, you don't need to babysit me. I'm fine."

"Em, there is nothing more important to me than making sure you're okay. Go ahead and change. I'll order our usual from Lila's Cafe."

"No! Ms. Lila knew about my date tonight. If you have our usual delivered here, she'll know something's up. I really don't feel like explaining anything to her or to my brother and Dakota, because it'll take about ten seconds for the news to get to them."

"Okay." The pained look on Em's face made Nick want to hunt Alan down even more. "There's that new barbecue joint. We can try that instead. I'll go pick up our order."

"Thank you, Nick." Emerie hugged him like she didn't want to let go.

He didn't want to let go, either. He wanted to keep her in his arms and close to his heart—where she'd be safe.

Nick rested his chin atop Em's head. Inhaled her subtle citrus and vanilla scent—a combination of her body and hair products.

He loved her smell. Loved the warmth of her body. The feel of her skin. When she finally pulled out of his hold, he felt her absence more acutely than he ever had before.

"You good?" he asked. It was a question he'd been asking her for as long as he could remember.

"I'm good." She studied his face. "I'm just...confused."

"About why Alan thought he could bully you into letting him stay? That wasn't about you, Em. Guys like that... they're assholes. Period. End of story."

"It's not Alan I'm confused about. I'm confused about why you came here tonight. About why you kissed me." She searched his face. "When I told you I had feelings for you, you said you didn't feel the same. And then you volunteer to kiss me, but only as practice, so that I'd be more comfortable kissing someone else. But it felt more real than any kiss I've ever had." Em paced the floor as she spoke. Something she did while trying to process information.

Nick swallowed hard, his throat dry, and his chest burning. God, he'd been an idiot. He needed to level with Em about how he felt. Starting with that kiss.

"That kiss felt real to me, too," he admitted.

She frowned, seemingly confused by his confession. "But you didn't say anything. Instead, you let me go on making one failed dating attempt after another. Then you come over here while I'm preparing for my date and kiss me. And I still don't understand why—"

Nick stepped forward, cupped Em's face, and captured her lips in a kiss. It was easier to show her how he felt than it was to admit he'd been so afraid of losing her friendship that he'd been terrified to take this chance.

He was prepared for her to shove him away and declare that he'd missed his opportunity, and she was no longer interested. Instead, she wrapped her arms around him, erasing every inch of space between them.

Nick kissed Em greedily. His tongue teased open the seam of her full lips and glided along hers. He ached with his growing desire for her. Feelings he'd tried hard to conceal from Em and from himself. Because letting the genie out of the bottle would change everything for them.

Em tugged his T-shirt from his jeans, her hands roaming his back. His skin seemed to catch fire in the wake of her touch, which was tentative at first, then increasingly sure.

Emerie lifted the edge of his shirt, and he helped her pull it off before dropping it onto the floor. She dropped soft, butterfly kisses on his bare chest, sending electricity down his spine.

"I want you, Em." Nick lifted her chin, forcing her gaze to meet his. "I was just so afraid of risking the friendship we've built."

"I know," she whispered, her gaze meeting his as her hands glided down to his waist. She unfastened his belt. "But we don't have to choose, Nick. We can have both. We're *lifelong* friends. Nothing is going to change that."

Nick's heart flooded with all the emotions he'd bottled

up for so long. He kissed her again, his heart beating like a drum. He hoped she was right.

———

Be brave. Be bold. Go for what you want. Lifelong regret is far worse than temporary embarrassment.

In her head, Em repeated the words she'd read in one book or another about becoming the badass woman she was always meant to be. All of those clichés like "no risk, no reward" were, perhaps, tired and trite, but they had a lot of truth to them. She'd dreamed of this moment so many times. And it wouldn't be happening if she hadn't put herself out there and told her best friend exactly how she felt about him.

She was in love with Nick. And she had been for the past few years. But she'd been afraid of being rejected. More importantly, she'd been afraid that their friendship wouldn't be able to survive the aftermath of said rejection.

But she'd been wrong. Not only had their friendship continued, but they were here, in her bedroom, both of them half dressed. A situation she fully intended to resolve.

As the intensely passionate kiss escalated, she helped him out of the rest of his clothing. When Nick loosened the belt to her robe and pushed the garment off her shoulders, he regarded her reverently.

"Wait…you've been naked under this thing the entire time?"

"I'd just hopped out of the shower. Maybe if either of you had called before you dropped by, I would've had time to get dressed." Emerie laughed, and Nick did, too.

"Point taken." Nick scanned her naked body, his eyes wide.

She'd seen his bare chest at the beach and on the

basketball court lots of times. He'd never seen hers. Nick swallowed hard, his Adam's apple working as he took her in. His chest rose and fell rapidly.

"Em, you look…incredible."

Her cheeks warmed as she surveyed his body. "You, too."

Nick leaned in and kissed her neck, then her shoulder. He lifted her onto the bed, and they both scrambled beneath the covers.

Em lost herself in their kisses. Part of her feared that this was all just an incredibly vivid dream. That she'd wake up to realize that Nick wasn't there at all.

But if this night was real, Em wanted to remember everything about it. The taste of Nick's kiss. The way his tongue felt gliding against hers. The softness of his lips and the prickliness of his bearded chin as he trailed kisses all over her skin. Down her neck. Across her shoulders. Over her chest. The sizzling heat of his skin as his body lay atop hers.

Em gasped softly when Nick covered one of the beaded tips of her breasts, aching for his touch, with his warm mouth and sucked. Her eyes drifted closed and her heels dug into the mattress as soft murmurs escaped her lips.

Emerie squirmed beneath him as he licked and sucked, the sensation going straight to her sex and deepening the ache she felt for him. And when he did the same to the other nipple, she nearly came undone.

Nick kissed his way down her stomach, then spread her thighs. He glanced up at her and smiled. She'd never be able to think of that sexy, mischievous smirk of his again without remembering this moment.

Her breathing was shallow as her chest rose and fell.

"Just breathe." Nick dropped one kiss, then another on

her inner thigh. His gruff, sexy voice was muffled as his lips grazed her skin. "It's only me. All right?"

Em sucked in a long, slow breath and nodded, not trusting that her voice wouldn't waver. She didn't bother telling her best friend that it was precisely because it was him that this moment felt so amazing and yet, so strange.

But before she had the chance to consider why that was, she was startled by the sensation of Nick's tongue on her slick, sensitive flesh. Each stroke evoked involuntary sighs of pleasure emanating from deep in her throat. The sensation building until her legs trembled and it felt like the room was spinning. She clutched the sheet beneath her.

"Oh my God, Nick." Em tipped her head back, her eyes screwed shut as his tongue teased her sensitive clit, taking her higher and higher until she shattered into what felt like a million glittering pieces.

She lay there, trying to catch her breath as Nick trailed lazy kisses up her inner thigh.

"Watching you fall apart like that? That was the fucking hottest thing I've ever seen," Nick muttered between kisses as he continued to move up her body.

"Well, it was the most amazing thing I've ever experienced." Em wrapped her arms around his waist as she stared into his hooded gaze. She kissed the lips that tasted of her. "In fact, it just might be my favorite thing *ever*."

"I don't know." Nick grinned, kissing her again. "It's early still. There's a lot of night left." He winked. "Speaking of which...I need to grab a condom from my wallet."

She indicated the nightstand beside her bed. "I believe it was you who told me to never trust that a dude will A: have condoms on hand and B: that they'll be in usable condition."

"Good girl." Nick's voice was low and sexy, and there

was something in his heated gaze that made her belly flutter.

When he reached for the handle, Em found enough clarity to think of what else she kept in that drawer.

"Let me get it." She leaned up on her elbows, but it was too late.

Nick had already opened the drawer, and from the way his eyes lit up, he'd obviously seen what she was hoping he wouldn't.

That sexy half grin slid across his sensual lips as he shifted his gaze back to hers.

"Don't you dare say a word." Em covered Nick's mouth with her hand, her cheeks and forehead suddenly hot. "It's embarrassing enough just knowing that you've seen my—"

"Vibrator?" Nick murmured from beneath her hand, then chuckled. He kissed the palm of her hand, and she dropped it from his mouth. "No reason to be embarrassed. It's completely normal. What isn't is how weird people get about self-pleasure."

"That's nice of you to say. But somehow, I doubt you have a drawer with Fleshlights."

"True." He chuckled when she poked his shoulder. "But that's only because my hand works just fine. Between you and me...those Fleshlights creep me out."

"Me, too." Em smiled. There was something comforting about Nick's determination to ease her anxiety during the awkward moments bound to happen with this transition in their relationship. And she loved that he could make her laugh, no matter the situation.

"Now you know all of my secrets." Em stroked his cheek.

"Funny." He nuzzled her neck. "I thought we told each other pretty much everything. But I guess we've both been holding things back." Nick met her gaze again. "So many times, I've wanted to tell you how I feel, but I was worried that we'd lose this incredible friendship it's taken us a life-time to build. I don't have that with anyone else, Em. And a part of me, even now, is terrified of losing it. Of losing you."

Em's vision blurred as her eyes filled with tears and her heart expanded. Her mouth stretched into a wide smile as she cupped Nick's face.

"You can't get rid of me that easily, Nick Washington." Em laughed. "And no matter what happens tonight, you'll always be my best friend."

Nick breathed out a quiet sigh of relief. "Promise?"

Em nodded. "I do."

He captured her mouth in a tender kiss that quickly escalated to one filled with heat.

Her nipples tightened, and the slick space between her thighs throbbed. His dick—thick and heavy—was pinned between them as their bodies writhed and their hands roamed each other's bare skin.

Nick tore open the box of condoms, retrieved one, and sheathed himself. He pressed himself to her entrance, and she shuddered with the delicious sensation of Nick slowly pushing inside her.

Her thighs fell open to accommodate Nick as he lay between them, his body stretching hers. He shifted his hips in a torturously slow glide. With each movement, the pleasure built, coiling inside her like a spring desperate for release but not quite there.

Nick cocked an eyebrow and grinned, halting his move-ment long enough to reach into the drawer.

"Nick, what are you—"

The sound of the garishly pink vibrator whirring to life made it clear what Nick had in mind. Before she could object, he held the toy to her already sensitive clit. Em nearly screamed at the intense pleasure that shot through her.

The sensation was dizzying.

"Good. Now you hold it," Nick said, repeating his demand when she hesitated. His lips grazed her ear as he whispered, "Show me *exactly* what you like."

Em took a breath, squeezed her eyes shut, and repositioned the buzzing toy to just where she needed it as Nick moved his hips again.

The combined sensations took her higher than she'd ever been. She cursed and moaned, feeling like she might crawl out of her own skin. Until finally, the overpowering sensations exploded inside her like fireworks on the Fourth of July.

Nick continued to move inside her, faster now, until his back arched, and he cursed and groaned, her name on his lips.

When he met her gaze, there was something in Nick's eyes that made her heart squeeze and her tummy flutter. Her vision blurred with unshed tears as he captured her lips in a kiss that warmed her from the inside out. He tumbled on the mattress and gathered her to his chest, his chin resting atop her head.

"That was incredible, Em." He kissed her lips again.

"Yes, it was." Em dragged a hand through her hair, her heart still racing, and her skin tingling.

"Let me take care of this, then I'll be right back." Nick kissed her again and climbed out of bed, just as his phone buzzed in the pocket of his jeans, discarded on the floor.

"I'm expecting a message from work." Nick retrieved his phone and checked the message.

"Is it the message you were waiting for?" she asked.

"No." There was something odd in Nick's expression.

He set the phone face down on the edge of the nightstand. "Be back in a sec."

He kissed her again before treating her to a prime view of his bare ass as he made his way to her en suite bathroom.

Em waited until she heard the click of the door before doing a little dance, beating her fists on the mattress and kicking it with her heels as she made a silent scream of joy.

She and Nick had slept together. Not in her very vivid imagination, where it usually happened. In real life. In her bed. And it was absolutely amazing.

They'd ventured into uncharted territory. It had been a little awkward at first, and she'd been slightly overcome with emotion. But it had been worth the risk. Regardless of what happened next, they'd both committed to putting their friendship first. Because it was just as important to her as it was to Nick. And she wasn't prepared to lose her most meaningful connection—even if it meant that what had happened between them tonight could never happen again.

But she'd much rather have it all. The friendship. A romantic relationship. And the kind of sex that had felt like a revelation on human sexuality and a master class in female pleasure. One she'd strongly advise that her past partners take.

Honestly, Em felt like she'd unlocked a new level on one of those video games she and Nick often played. And she couldn't wait to find out what additional levels of sex and pleasure were in store for them.

Em smiled contentedly and stretched like a cat, accidentally toppling Nick's phone onto the floor.

Nick was hard on his phones, so he had a tough-as-nails hard-shell case. Hopefully, it had done its job.

Em retrieved the phone, and it buzzed in her hand, startling her. She glanced at the lock screen. There was a text message from a gorgeous Black woman with blond locs named Tiffany.

Where are you? I expected you half an hour ago?

She drew in a deep breath, her muscles tense, and her hand shaking. Her temples throbbed, and her throat felt gritty and parched.

Em squeezed her eyes shut and reminded herself to breathe. She and Nick weren't in a relationship. In fact, nothing about what had happened that evening had gone according to plan. If it had, she'd be on a date with that awful Alan. Besides, she knew exactly who her best friend was. So was she really surprised that Nick had other plans this evening?

She slowly, deliberately, unclenched her muscles and tried to be reasonable about the situation.

Nick could've been with Goldilocs tonight. But instead, he'd come rushing to her place to "rescue" her. She should feel good about that, shouldn't she?

The phone buzzed again. This time, a photo appeared in the text message. Em juggled the phone, nearly dropping it to the floor again.

Dayum. Goldilocs was stacked. No wonder she wasn't shy about sending a pic of herself in a super tight white tank top sans bra and a barely-there miniskirt with the message:

You really gonna keep all this waiting, Nick?

Em pressed a palm to her throbbing eye and shook her head. She reminded herself of the logic she'd just estab-lished and all the reasons she shouldn't get bent out of shape about Goldilocs's text messages. And maybe she was a glutton for punishment, but when the phone buzzed again, she couldn't help looking at the message.

Only this one wasn't from Goldilocs. The message was from Ellen—a buxom brunette with big, soulful eyes—who declared that she was in town and feeling lonely.

Em glanced down at her body. Average breasts. More muscular than curvy. Built more like a brick than a brick house.

No wonder Nick preferred those other women.

She wasn't a curvy girl, and she'd always been just fine with her body. But seeing the two women currently vying for Nick's attention...Em couldn't help thinking that she clearly wasn't Nick Washington's type.

Was he settling for her because he was afraid of losing her to someone else? If so, how long would it be before he was ready to move on to someone who was more his type? And speaking of moving on...would Nick really be able to settle down in a monogamous relationship? Because she had zero interest in becoming fuck buddies. Yes, the sex was amazing. But she needed more than that.

The phone buzzed again. Em's stomach knotted, and her chest ached. She couldn't look at it. Couldn't bear seeing more of the messages from Goldilocs, Ellen, and whoever else might be vying for Nick's time and talents tonight.

Em pulled her knees to her chest and wrapped her arms around them. Her eyes burned with tears.

How could her night with Nick have been so damn amazing and yet, a monumental mistake?

Chapter Nineteen

◆ ● ◆

Nick finished up in the bathroom, washed and dried his hands, then stood in front of the mirror. He dragged a hand across his forehead, still in disbelief.

Tonight, with Em, had been perfect. Better than he'd imagined . . . and he'd imagined them together plenty.

In retrospect, it seemed silly that they'd been afraid to admit their feelings for each other. From now on, they could be straight with each other about everything.

Nick's heart beat faster. He still hadn't told his best friend everything. He'd admitted his attraction to her, and there was no doubt about their incredible chemistry. What he hadn't told Em—what he'd barely come to terms with himself—was that he was in love with her.

Now that he'd finally admitted as much to himself, Nick realized that the signs had always been there. He'd been fighting his feelings for Em for years out of a desperate need to preserve their friendship.

But the more he acknowledged his feelings for her, the more confident he was that they could make this work. They could have a romantic relationship and a close friendship without compromising either.

"I love you, Em. I think I always have," Nick whispered the words beneath his breath, surprised at how good it felt to say them aloud. But now he needed to confess his feelings to her.

Nick stepped out of the bedroom and glanced at the spot where he'd left Em glowing, sated, and a little emotional.

She wasn't there.

Maybe she'd gone to the kitchen to make them a snack. An idea he was totally on board with. But first, he needed to tell Em how he felt.

Nick slipped on his boxer briefs and ventured into the living room. Em was seated on the sofa wearing an old T-shirt and a pair of shorts. She sniffled and dragged a finger beneath her eyes, wet with tears still. But this didn't look like an emotional reaction to the two of them being together. There was deep hurt in her dark brown eyes.

"Em, what's wrong?" Nick sank onto the sofa beside her.

Before he could drape an arm around her shoulder, she sprang to her feet, as if the last thing in the world she wanted was his touch. She retreated to the other side of the coffee table.

A lump settled in Nick's throat, and another knotted his gut.

He'd been gone maybe five minutes. What the hell had happened?

Nick quietly assessed his best friend. She was pacing the floor, and her arms were wrapped around her torso. Something she did whenever she was upset.

Right now, she was clearly upset with him. But he had no clue as to why.

Nick retraced his every word and every action. But he couldn't think of anything that would've caused Em to react this way.

"What happened between us tonight…It was a mistake. We shouldn't have kissed, and we definitely shouldn't have…" Em gestured toward the bedroom. And even beneath her brown skin, Nick recognized the flush of her cheeks.

"Okay." Nick stood, but he didn't move toward her. He kept his voice even and his expression calm, despite all of the emotions swirling in his chest. "But just a few minutes ago, you were literally saying how amazing it was."

"And it was." Her soft, wistful expression was quickly replaced by a pained one. More tears welled in her eyes, and she brushed them away before they could fall. "But I think it'd be best if we didn't do this again."

Nick's heart was heavy. He felt every ounce of the pain reflected in the brown eyes that had always greeted him with a smile and made him feel like everything would be okay, regardless of what was going on in his life.

"Sweetheart, I get that you're upset," Nick said calmly. "But at least tell me what it is that I've done."

"That's just it. It isn't what you've done. It's who you are, Nick." Em wiped away more tears and sniffled. Her gaze didn't quite meet his. "You're Holly Grove Island's very own fuckboy. But I didn't call this the Find a Fuckboy Project for a reason. That's not what I'm looking for. I'm looking for someone I can build a life with. Can you honestly say you've ever even considered settling down with someone?"

"I'm clear on what you want, Em. And yet, I'm here," he said. "Would I be here if I hadn't at least considered it?"

Em frowned, her shoulders sagging. She wasn't pleased with his response. But before he could think of a better one, she spoke again.

"You've been my best friend for two decades, Nick. As long as you were the center of my world, you were fine with things the way they were. I finally decide it's time to start living my life and get serious about finding love rather than waiting for you to decide you want me, and suddenly you realize that you're into me?" she asked incredulously.

"It's not like that, Em. You make it sound like—"

"You're only interested in me now because someone else has the audacity to want to play with your favorite toy." Tears rolled down her cheeks, and she wiped them away angrily.

The pain and devastation in Em's voice ripped a hole in his chest. He hadn't developed feelings for her because someone else was interested in her. But he had been prompted to finally act on his feelings because...

Shit. Em was right. He was a selfish asshole who probably didn't deserve her.

"You're an amazing friend, Nick, and tonight was incredible. But I'm not interested in joining your list of friends with benefits. I need more than that. It was unfair of me to expect you to become someone you're not." Em's eyes finally met his.

"Did you ever consider that maybe I'm ready for a change in my life, too?" Nick asked.

Em tilted her head as she regarded him carefully. She shook her head. "No. You've always said not everyone is meant to be in a monogamous relationship," she reminded him.

Shit. Shit. Shit.

He'd definitely said that. *Repeatedly.* At the time, he'd meant it because he couldn't imagine wanting any woman other than Em in his life long-term. And he'd been sure that if he got involved with Em, it'd destroy their friendship. So he'd been content to keep things the way they were.

He'd been unfair to Em, not realizing that their friendship alone wasn't enough.

As he stared into his friend's eyes now, it was clear that nothing he could say would convince her otherwise. He needed to figure out how to show Emerie that she was the only woman he wanted in his life.

"Okay." Nick sucked in a quiet breath. "But can I at least ask what led to such a sudden change of heart?"

"Reality." Em's expression hardened. "By the way, I think those *work messages*—" she used air quotes "—you were waiting for came through."

Now he had a pretty good idea what had flipped the switch on their evening.

He'd seen that message from Tiffany come through before he'd gone to the bathroom. And he'd left his phone on the nightstand because he hadn't wanted Em to think he was trying to hide something from her. But she'd evidently seen the message, and now she was both pissed and doubtful that he was capable of being a one-woman man.

He didn't blame her for jumping to conclusions. But she was wrong. He hadn't made plans with Tiffany or anyone else tonight. In fact, he hadn't gone out with anyone in months because his thoughts had been consumed by Em and this Soulmate Project of hers.

Nick opened his mouth to tell Em that he understood her apprehension. Until she'd started this Soulmate Project, he also doubted his desire and capacity to settle down.

He snapped his mouth shut.

Even in his head, that argument sounded weak. He'd only be reinforcing Em's doubts.

"I get why you feel the way you do right now, Em. And I'm sorry. We were having an amazing night, and I was looking forward to talking about what this could mean for us. But maybe we should talk about it another time. I'll get dressed, and we can watch a movie like we'd planned."

"Actually, I could use some time alone."

"Sure." Nick's heart sank. "I'll get my things and go."

Em tucked her hair behind her ear and nodded. "Thanks for understanding."

Nick took a few steps toward the bedroom, then stopped. He turned back to his friend, the silence between them louder than the scream happening inside his head.

"We promised each other we wouldn't let sex destroy our friendship. I meant what I said, Em. I hope you did, too."

"Of course I did, Nicky." Emerie took a few steps toward him. "But tonight has been a lot. I just need some time to process everything."

"Fair enough." Nick resisted the urge to insist they talk through whatever Em was feeling. If he ignored her request that he leave, how was he any better than Alan?

Nick got dressed, grabbed his phone, and shoved it into his back pocket before making his way to the front door where Em was waiting for him.

"Em, I need to know we're still okay. That tonight hasn't ruined our friendship."

"You can't get rid of me that easily." She repeated the running joke between them and flashed him a sad smile. "You should be so lucky."

"I am lucky," he said. "Because I couldn't ask for a better best friend."

"Same." Em's eyes were suddenly filled with sadness. "When do you leave for New York again?"

Nick sighed. He didn't like leaving town with things this way. But he couldn't force Em to talk to him. "Tomorrow afternoon. It was supposed to be three days, but I might end up flying from New York to the new property in Virginia."

"Then safe travels. Text me to let me know you arrived safely."

"I will." He didn't miss the fact that she'd asked him to text rather than call.

She gave him an awkward hug, the vibe between them so different from before. "Good night, Nick."

Nick frowned deeply as he cradled her to his chest. "Good night, Em."

He left her apartment and returned to his car. His phone buzzed again, and he pulled it from his pocket. Nick scrolled through the messages from Tiffany and Ellen.

He had no idea which messages Em had seen or how she'd come to see them. But it was no wonder she'd been upset.

Nick dropped the phone in the cupholder and slammed a fist on his steering wheel.

He'd finally stopped fighting his feelings for Em, they'd had an amazing night, and then his past had come stomping in to sabotage things as quickly as they'd begun.

He was in love with Em. Nick knew that now. He wouldn't give up so easily. Maybe this trip to New York was well-timed. It'd give her a few days to cool off and give him a few days to think of what he needed to do next. Because he would need to be armed with more than just words if he was prepared to prove to Em that she was the only woman he wanted.

Chapter Twenty

— • ● • —

Em sank into a booth across from Kassie at Blaze of Glory and took a sip of the drink her friend had ordered her.

She was exhausted. Her legs and abdomen were sore, and so were her arms. She'd had a long day handling client graphic design projects followed by two hours of dance practice with Carlos and Ms. Idelle. She'd bypassed a shower and opted for a long soak in a hot tub where she'd fallen asleep. Which was why she'd kept poor Kassie waiting for her on their girls' night out.

"Sorry I'm late, Kass. But practice was brutal today." Em set her glass down, removed the pick, popped the maraschino cherry in her mouth, and chewed.

Kassie giggled. "You're savoring that cherry like it's a premium cut of steak."

"I'm starving." Em rubbed a hand over her belly. "I haven't eaten since . . . I don't remember when I last ate. And now that you mention it, a steak sounds great."

"I'll let Blaze know that we're ready to order." Kassie caught the owner's eye and raised a hand.

He nodded and held up a finger as he poured someone

else a drink. Once he was done, he made his way over to them with his electronic pad and pen in hand.

Blaze was in his forties with a scruffy red beard, the same spiky crew cut he'd been wearing since he'd first returned to town after enlisting with the Marines, and wary blue eyes that seemed to change with his mood, like the ocean, visible outside of the bar and grill.

"What can I get for you ladies tonight?" Blaze asked. He keyed in both of their orders, then cocked a head and rubbed his bearded chin as he studied Em. "You just missed your partner in crime. Nick was in here ordering the same thing about an hour ago. Haven't seen you two together in a while."

It'd been two weeks since she and Nick slept together. Emerie had thrown herself into her graphic design work, marketing her business, helping her mother convert her childhood bedroom into a craft room, and very intense practice for the dance exhibition coming up in less than two weeks. And Nick had been on business trips to New York and Virginia. That was why she'd barely talked to her best friend. Not because of the awkwardness of the two of them having slept together. That was the story she'd been telling herself... and Nick.

Em opened her mouth to say as much to Blaze and Kass, but he was a human lie detector, and she was practically an empath. There was no point of trying to bullshit either of them. But being honest with them meant facing her own feelings about what had happened between her and Nick. Something she wasn't ready for.

"We've both been really busy, and Nick's been traveling a lot," Em said. Her cheeks burned as both Blaze and Kassie stared at her, then exchanged a look.

"Well, he's here now, and the dude looks like he lost his

best friend. Never seen Nick like that before. Maybe you want to check on him." Blaze tapped his fingers on the edge of the table. "Your appetizers will be out in a bit."

Em drew in a quiet breath and frowned. Part of her felt guilty about avoiding Nick. But she couldn't help being angry at him, too.

"I was going to try and be all subtle and clever about bringing up the fact that you've been avoiding Nick. But since Blaze already put it out there...you wanna talk about it?"

Em sipped her drink. "I'm not avoiding..."

Kassie hiked an eyebrow and folded her arms on the table.

Em sighed. Lying to herself was one thing. But she felt badly about lying to her closest friends.

"Okay, so maybe I am avoiding him."

"Why?" Kassie leaned forward. "You aren't mad at Nick for tossing Alan out on his ass, are you? That dude was trash."

"No, it's not that." Em drew in a deep breath and worried her lower lip with her teeth. "About that night...I didn't tell you the entire story."

"Okay. So what else happened?" Kassie lowered her voice and leaned in closer. "Did you and Nick get into a fight?"

"Yes." Em glanced around to see if anyone else in the bar was listening. "But he also kissed me again."

Both of Kassie's eyebrows shot up, and she clapped a hand over her mouth, seemingly holding back a squeal.

"Oh my God! Nick is into you," Kassie whispered loudly. "I knew it! Wait..." Kassie narrowed her gaze at Em for a moment. Suddenly, her big brown eyes widened. She pressed a hand to her chest. "You two didn't just kiss. You slept with Nick, didn't you?"

Em shushed her friend as she glanced around again. "Yes. All right? But I'd prefer it if the entire bar didn't know."

"I'm sorry, Em." Kassie squeezed her wrist. "I'm just surprised and happy. But wait...if you two finally hooked up, what's with the disappearing act?" She lowered her voice. "Was the sex terrible? It's Nick, so I just assumed he'd be...well, you know...good at it."

"It was amazing," Em confessed.

"Okay. So you want him, he wants you, the sex is crazy good. I'm not seeing a problem here." Kassie frowned, thoroughly confused by Em's dilemma. "Was it something he said or did after this amazing sex that ruined things?"

Em's stomach twisted in knots, and her chest ached as she thought about Tiffany and Ellen and all of the other women Nick had slept with. Gorgeous, voluptuous women who could easily be lingerie models. Women she could never compare to.

Over appetizers and another round of drinks, Em told Kassie about the text messages and about her ensuing argument with Nick.

Kassie popped a smashed potato into her mouth and chewed thoughtfully.

"I can understand why seeing those text messages would've been so unnerving. Especially at such a pivotal moment." Kassie chose her words carefully. Em knew her friend well enough to realize that there was a "but" coming. "But if Goldilocs was expecting Nick, yet he came to your apartment to rescue you instead—"

"I could've handled Alan," Em interjected. She was no damsel in distress.

"I'm sure you could have." Kassie nodded. "We never want to imagine that we could become the victim of sexual assault. Yet, so many of us have." Lines formed on her friend's forehead. She swallowed hard. "So please don't downplay how serious a situation like that could become. All right?"

"I won't. I promise." Em took both of Kassie's hands in hers and nodded. It was the second time in the five years that they'd been close friends that the other woman had alluded to being a victim of assault. When Em had pressed Kassie about it, her friend had quickly changed the subject. "And if there's anything you'd like to talk about… *anything*—" Em stressed "—I'm here."

"I know." Kass grabbed a jalapeño popper. "But the only thing I want to talk about right now is why—after you finally got exactly what you wanted—you're avoiding Nick."

Em nibbled on a smashed potato. "What I want with Nick isn't just sex. It's a relationship. It's—"

"A soulmate." Kassie picked up another potato, too.

Em nodded solemnly.

"We all know what you're looking for, Em. And Nick really cares for you. I can't believe he would get involved with you unless he's prepared to deliver on that happily ever after." Kass sipped her drink. "Have you considered that maybe he's realized that's what he wants, too?"

"I wanted to believe that." Em traced a finger through the condensation on her glass. "But those text messages reminded me of what I've always known." Em frowned. "Nick is an eternal bachelor who doesn't do relationships. I was wrong for expecting him to suddenly change."

"But Nick didn't actually tell you that he doesn't want a relationship. Right? You're basing your decision on those text messages, which he didn't solicit—"

"And his past history," Em noted.

"True," Kassie conceded. "But you've come to your own conclusion rather than allowing Nick to make a decision for himself. That doesn't seem fair, Em."

"Was it fair of Nick to deny that he had feelings for me and then start acting like some jealous boyfriend the moment someone else showed interest?"

"No. Nick should've been honest with you. But maybe he was still coming to terms with his feelings about you. Just like you've been struggling for years to come to terms with your feelings for him."

"Maybe there's a *reason* we're both struggling with this," Em said. "And maybe that reason is that we're better off staying friends."

"You don't really mean that, Em." Kassie's accusation was softened by her tone and empathetic expression. "You're just scared."

Em groaned quietly and swirled her drink. Kassandra was right. Nick had been worried about how a romantic relationship would impact their friendship. And now she was worried that she could never be enough for him.

"Maybe I am afraid. But given the situation, don't I have good reason to be?"

"Okay."

Em knew Kassie well enough to know that the word didn't signal agreement. She was simply tabling that line of discussion for now and moving on to another one.

"But if this is all for the best, it still begs the question: why are you avoiding Nick?"

"He seems to think it's some sort of punishment," Em said.

"Is it?"

Em drained the rest of her drink, then shrugged.

"I don't know. At first it was just . . . awkward, you know?

But the more I thought about everything...the more upset I got."

"Are you angry with yourself for sleeping with Nick? Or are you angry because someone texted him at a really inopportune time?" Kassie nibbled on another potato.

Em didn't miss her friend's implication that she was being unfair to Nick. That he wasn't the one who'd initiated the contact with those women. They'd reached out to him.

It was a fair point. But those messages had fed her insecurities. Someone was always calling or texting him. Flirting with him as if she was invisible. And yes, they'd only been friends then. But every single incident had tugged on a little string, like the unraveling of a sweater, eroding her confidence and feeding her doubts about whether Nick would ever want her.

"Both," Em said. "I've spent all this time pining over Nick and wishing that he'd look at me the way he looks at every other woman on the planet. The moment I give up the dream and move on, suddenly he's interested, and we tumble into bed. But now what?"

"Maybe if you give Nick a chance to explain himself, he'll surprise you," Kassie said.

"Or maybe I've been naive, and Nick was right all along. This could be the beginning of the end of our friendship."

"I know you'd both be putting a lot on the line. But the only way to find out is to try. Yes, there's a chance that Nick will disappoint you. But there's an even greater chance that the two of you might find everything you've ever wanted from a relationship. After all, he's been spending most of his time hanging out with you. I can't recall the last time I saw him on a date. Can you?"

Em opened her mouth to respond, but the last time she'd seen Nick with someone else was when that tourist had kissed him on New Year's Eve. That had been months ago. Then again, maybe he'd been more discreet about his dating life, worried that he'd hurt her feelings.

Kassie's cell phone rang, and a look of alarm replaced her friend's smile.

"What is it, Kass?"

"This is the maintenance manager at the aquarium. If he's calling me at this hour, it can't be good. Excuse me while I take this." Kassie hurried toward the exit to take her call.

A pretty server approached the table with Em's steak and Kassie's crab cakes.

Em thanked the woman, who seemed reluctant to leave.

"You're Nick Washington's friend, right?" the gorgeous, young Black woman asked.

Em's stomach knotted. Still, she forced a broad smile.

"Taneeka, right? Yes. I am Nick's friend. Why? Did he leave something behind when he was here earlier?"

"You could say that." The girl flipped her beach waves over one shoulder, her long, mink eyelashes fluttering. She reached into her apron pocket and handed Em a piece of paper with a floral print folded in half and sprayed with the same perfume the girl was wearing. "He left before I got the chance to slip him this. It's my phone number," she added.

"Yes, I figured as much," Em deadpanned. She rocked onto one hip and slipped the note into the back pocket of her jeans. "I'll be sure he gets it the next time I see him."

"Promise?"

"Promise." Em offered the woman a weak smile.

The woman turned to walk away, then turned back toward Em. "You two are just *friends*, right?" Taneeka emphasized the word.

How the hell was she supposed to answer that?

"Yes," Em said after a beat of silence.

Regardless of the fantasies she'd entertained about them becoming a real couple, that clearly wasn't in the cards for them. So it would be best if they just remained friends and forgot about that one incredible night they'd shared.

She needed to come to terms with that, and so did her best friend.

Taneeka walked away, though she didn't seem convinced by Em's delayed response. Then someone played Em's favorite Dua Lipa song on the jukebox, and it felt like a lightning bolt struck her.

The dance exhibition was two weeks away, but she had an inspired idea that would require her and Carlos's final number to be completely revamped. Ms. Idelle had been worried that while Em's bachata steps were technically accurate, they lacked fire and passion.

If Ms. Idelle wanted fire and passion, she'd give it to her. But it would translate much better with a salsa routine. Em just hoped that Carlos and Ms. Idelle would be on board with choreographing a new routine. One that would be much better suited to Em's personality and style.

When Kassie returned to the table, Em borrowed a pen from her friend and jotted down a few notes about the new routine. It would be dramatic and have lots of flair. And by the end of the night, she'd be ready to resume her Soulmate Project and let go of the unrealistic fantasy that she and Nick would ever really be anything more than friends.

Chapter Twenty-One

—•◦•—

Nick entered The Foxhole—a space all too familiar to him. His band played live music at the venue every other month. And he, Em, and their friends were no strangers to the venue's excellent happy hours. So why did it feel so strange as he'd stepped through those doors tonight?

Maybe it was less about the place and more about the fact that he and Em had only exchanged a few brief text messages since she'd declared that she needed a little space to figure this all out.

It was a fair request. Besides, he needed time and space to figure his own shit out, too. He was clear on his attraction to Em and how much her friendship meant to him. But what had become evident in the past several weeks was the depth of his feelings for his best friend.

Nick had been working through that realization and its repercussions. Trying to let go of his fear that he'd inevitably fuck up his relationship with Em was a difficult task when it'd only taken him one night to do just that.

"Hey, Nick. Haven't seen you here in a while." Diane, one of the bartenders on duty, grinned, her thick lashes fluttering. Her voice—a low growl—could barely be heard over the music playing in the background and the din of disparate conversations.

"This marketing project I'm working on for one of our new resort properties has been keeping me busy," he said. "I've been traveling a lot."

"Must be nice." Diane grinned, impressed. "Call me if you could use a little company." She winked.

Nick groaned. It was the kind of harmless flirtation that came as naturally to him as breathing. But since he'd come to terms with his feelings for Em, those interactions no longer seemed harmless. They were a reminder of why Emerie had buried herself in her work, extracurricular activities, and family obligations for the past month. Anything to avoid talking to him.

"I'll have a Godfather." Nick's demeanor was polite, but not encouraging.

"Wait...you don't want your usual?" Diane looked up from the bottle of imported beer she was pouring, evidently for him.

"Thought I'd go with something different tonight." Nick ignored the woman's shocked expression.

"Perfect. I'll take that beer. And can I get a frozen peach margarita, too?" Rett leaned against the bar. He thanked Diane when she gladly handed him the beer she'd poured.

"I'll get your frozen margarita for Sin," Diane told Rett. Then she turned to Nick. "And your Godfather. Back in a sec."

"So it's not just my cousin you're pissing off lately." Rett sipped his beer. "Apparently, you're frustrating every woman you come in contact with." He turned toward Nick with one elbow perched on the bar. "Looks like Holly Grove Island's golden boy has lost the Midas touch with the fair women of our town."

"You got jokes tonight, I see." Nick glanced over at Rett. "I'mma give you a pass because I know you old married—"

"*Almost* married." Rett held up his beer mug.

"I know you old *married* fellas—" Nick emphasized the word again "—don't get out much."

"Oh, so now you got jokes. Touché." Rett chuckled. "But seriously, man, what's up with you and Em? Because clearly you did something to piss her off."

"Em and I are fine." Nick felt a rock form in his gut. He hated lying to his friend, but he wasn't about to confess to having sex with the man's cousin. Particularly not when she'd declared that it would be better if they pretended it had never happened. "We've both been really busy. She's been practicing like crazy for this dance exhibition, and I've been working on the opening of our newest resort in Virginia."

Nick thanked Diane when she brought his Godfather. He stuffed a five in the tip jar. That seemed to alleviate her previous annoyance with him for not flirting with her *and* daring to order something other than his usual.

"I'm aware." Rett nodded sagely. "But there is definitely something else going on with you two. And just so you know, it's been the topic of discussion on the family group chat. So you might want to try a little harder to come up with a viable excuse." Rett drank more of his beer.

"That obvious, huh?" Nick took a healthy gulp of his drink.

Nick had spent the past four days in New York, most of it in marathon meetings with the marketing team there. But he was concerned about the growing distance between him and Emerie. He'd returned to Holly Grove Island yesterday for one reason only—to attend Em's performance tonight. Afterward, he hoped they could talk before he had to return to New York for another important meeting.

Despite the strain between them, he was confident that

he and Em would work things out. After all, they'd been friends for two decades. This wasn't the first time they'd gotten into a little tiff—as his mother called their past minor disagreements. Granted, things had never gone on quite this long. Especially not since he'd returned to Holly Grove Island a few years ago. But he was sure they'd work it out, just the same.

"Neither of you is good at hiding your feelings," Rett noted. "You're walking around here like the Grim Reaper and she's been either super quiet or hella moody. Doesn't take a rocket scientist to figure out that something went down between you two and that Em's Soulmate Project is probably at the root of it," Rett said.

Was it awful that he was both gutted that he was the root cause of his best friend's distress while also feeling a glimmer of hopefulness at the fact that Em was miserable without him, too?

"Me, her brothers, her father...none of us are thrilled about this whole thing, either. But from what I've heard, she made her feelings clear, and you took a pass. And no one is blaming you for that," Rett continued before Nick could object. "But you made your choice. Now she's trying to move on, but you seem determined to sabotage the whole thing."

Nick refrained from noting that the men Em had selected thus far weren't shit to write home about. That would make him sound bitter. Besides, he realized in retrospect that though he hadn't done so consciously, on some level, he *had* been trying to sabotage Em's Soulmate Project. And he owed Em a sincere apology for that.

Nick polished off the remainder of his drink and requested another.

"That kind of a night, huh?" Diane retrieved the glass. "Don't worry. I've got you."

"I won't argue with anything you've said." Nick rubbed his chin. "And I know things have been weird between us the past few weeks. But we'll work it out. We always do."

"I don't know, boss. This feels...*different*." Rett set his partially consumed beer on the bar. "Look, I know you're both grown-ass, intelligent adults fully capable of figuring out your own shit. So normally, I'd keep my two cents to myself," Rett continued. "But as a friend, and as Em's cousin, I'm rooting for you two to win. Honestly." Rett placed a hand over his heart, his tone and expression sincere. "Because you two misfit toys clearly belong together."

Nick and Rett both laughed.

"We definitely do." A pained smile made Nick's chest ache as he thought about the past few weeks of awkwardness and silence between him and Emerie. Nick stared into his glass. "I really miss her."

When Nick looked up, he met his friend's compassionate gaze.

"Then you should tell her how you feel." Rett gently shoved Nick's shoulder.

"What if telling her how I feel changes everything between us?"

Rett's deep belly laugh surprised him.

"You're worse off than I thought." Rett shook his head, then drained the rest of his beer. He placed a large hand on Nick's shoulder. "That ship has sailed, been hijacked by pirates, and set afire in the middle of the ocean," Rett said. "Things will never, *ever* be the same between the two of you again. And that's okay. All relationships grow and change over time, Nick. But as the unofficial president of the Misfit Toys Club, I can tell you that whatever you're feeling for Em isn't going to just go away, no matter how hard or how long you try to bury your feelings."

"But it was different with you and Sin. You two were frenemies—not best friends," Nick pointed out.

"True. But we both love Dex and Dakota. We're part of the same friend and family group. Both love this town. So trust me, there was a lot on the line for us, too."

Nick hadn't thought about that. Friend groups were ecosystems that needed to be carefully balanced. One Bitter Betty or Gloomy Gus could send the entire thing spiraling. Something he'd discovered more than once during his college years.

"I've been telling myself that I'm just giving Em the time and space she needs. But the truth is, maybe I've been avoiding the conversation because the idea of having it scares the shit out of me. And based on how things have gone so far, I don't know that instinct is wrong."

"Putting your heart on the line, it's scary as fuck, and it isn't always pretty. But if you love Em—and it seems you do—getting your happy ending with the woman you love is worth it," Rett assured him.

"Thanks, Rett. I appreciate the talk. It helps a lot," Nick said gratefully. His friendships with Dexter and Rett and their families were important to him and part of the equation he was trying to balance. "Looks like the show is about to begin, but the next round is on me." Nick signaled to Diane that he wanted to order another round for Rett.

"Thanks." Rett nodded. "But I didn't come over here just to chat. I was sent to collect you so you won't spend the entire exhibition hiding out over here thinking we're all mad at you." Rett gestured toward the large table where Sinclair and Dakota were looking over at him like two concerned older sisters. "You're not just Em's friend, Nick. You're our friend." Rett placed a hand on his chest. "Don't let those sweet smiles fool you. If I come back without you, those two gorgeous women will have my hide."

A wave of emotion swept over Nick: familial love, friendship, gratitude, and a sense of relief. The people at that table meant the world to him. They had for most of his life. He was just as worried about disappointing them as he was about hurting Em. So it meant everything that they wanted him there with them, despite the difficulties he and Em were going through.

Nick released a quiet sigh of relief and nodded at Dakota and Sin. "In that case, the next round for the entire table is on me."

Rett clapped a hand on Nick's shoulder, then the two of them made their way over to the table after Diane brought their drinks.

The knot in his stomach slowly unfurled as the two women's faces lit up and Dexter, whose arm was draped around his wife's shoulders, gave him a subtle nod.

But before he could take the seat that Sin indicated was his, Em and Dex's mother, Ms. Marilyn, popped up from her seat and wrapped him in a big hug.

"Good to see you, sweetheart." Ms. Marilyn smiled. "I'm glad you made it, and I know Em will be, too."

"I hope so." Nick gave her a pained smile. They all ordered their next round of drinks and settled in for the show.

He couldn't stay long, but he hoped that he and Em could finally talk before he had to go.

———

Em paced back and forth in the private party room at The Foxhole serving as the green room for the dance exhibition performers.

"A few more paces around the place, and you're going to

wear a hole in that floor." Ms. Idelle's gravelly voice broke Em out of her swirling cloud of dark thoughts.

What if she forgot her steps? What if she tripped and fell? (She was definitely going to play dead and let them carry her off on a stretcher.) What if she sucked? But the most pervasive concern was whether she'd gone too far with the song selection for her and Carlos's final performance.

"I'm a little nervous." Em clasped, then unclasped her hands.

"You're a natural, Ms. Roberts. More importantly, your performances are filled with a freedom and joy that I find inspiring. The crowd will, too."

Effusive praise coming from Ms. Idelle was a rarity. A gift Em was appreciative of. Particularly coming just moments before she stepped out on that floor.

"Thank you, Ms. Idelle. This opportunity and your confidence in me both mean a lot."

The older woman, whose silvery, shoulder-length strands were pulled into a regal topknot, assessed her carefully.

"It isn't the dance you're concerned about, is it?" Ms. Idelle came a few steps closer and lowered her voice. "This is about your friend, Mr. Washington, and your sudden change in the song selection. No doubt a message to him?"

Em's cheeks heated as she glanced around the room to see if Carlos or the few remaining folks there to help with makeup and costumes could hear their conversation.

"Yes." Em nodded. "It seemed like a great idea at the time. But now..." Em shook her head and dabbed at the corner of her eyes. "I'm not so sure."

"I see." Ms. Idelle nodded thoughtfully. The older woman slipped her hand into Em's and offered a warm smile. "The passion with which you've performed since you made the change tells me this is what's on your heart.

Something you need to express. And evidently, this performance is the best vehicle for that message. I realize that this is a moment of vulnerability for you, Ms. Roberts. But it is in such moments that we truly find our voice and often a sense of bravery we never realized we possessed."

Em looked up at the older woman whom she so deeply admired. During an illustrious career that had taken her all over the world, Ms. Idelle had broken racial boundaries and triumphed again and again in the face of overt bigotry, blatant colorism, harmful stereotypes, and exhausting microaggressions. But Em couldn't help thinking that what Ms. Idelle was hinting at was more of a personal nature. She wondered what the older woman's story was.

"What if it was a mistake?" Em asked quietly. "What if it changes things in a way we can't rebound from?"

"I've been watching you two." Ms. Idelle smiled. "You share a love and friendship I envy. But true love and genuine friendship cannot exist if we are not living in our truth."

The woman's words struck a chord that seemed to vibrate through Em's chest. Ms. Idelle was right about everything. She'd chosen to perform this song because both she and Nick needed the message. The song was empowering, and Em felt every word, every note.

"Thank you, Ms. Idelle." Em squeezed the woman's hand and smiled. She sucked in a quiet breath and tipped her chin. "I know how important this exhibition is to you and to the school. I won't let you down."

"Never doubted it." Ms. Idelle's usually stern expression gave way to a ghost of a smile before becoming serious again. She made a shooing gesture. "Now go on. Carlos is waiting for you. Your finale is up next, and I need to get back out there to make your introduction."

"Yes, ma'am." Em turned to walk away, but turned back and hugged the older woman, taking her by surprise.

Em hurried to join Carlos, who flashed her a confident smile.

"Don't worry. You're a natural." Carlos tucked Em's hand in his elbow, then straightened his collar. "Just feel the music and the passion that prompted you to choose this song. Show everyone out there the skill and confidence you've demonstrated to us every night at practice. All right?"

Em nodded. Then, when Ms. Idelle announced their names, she and Carlos crossed the room and stood under the spotlight.

Butterflies flitted in Em's stomach, and she tried to maintain her composure as her adorably rowdy friends and family hooted and cheered her on.

The opening notes of "Don't Start Now" by Dua Lipa began, and she let go of her inhibitions and fears, got lost in the music, and focused solely on her partner—an experienced dancer who'd won countless dance competitions.

The audience clapped in time with the beat and sang along with the catchy lyrics of the song about a woman telling her ex that he'd had his chance, and he'd blown it. He didn't care before, so he shouldn't start now that someone else was interested.

With every movement executed successfully, Em relaxed and got more into the playfulness and joy of the empowering song. Her hips swayed, her shoulders shimmied, and she nailed each and every step whether they were synchronized or part of the push and pull of the scene.

When they nailed the tricky footwork, followed by a challenging lift, Em knew they were home free. Her confidence soared, and she put a little more sass and drama

in each and every step until the final part when she shoved
Carlos's shoulder, gestured for him to take a hike, and did
her final spin and pose.

The entire club erupted with applause, most of them
jumping to their feet.

The lights were blinding, but she could hear her mother's
and Sinclair's voices clearly as they yelled their encouragement. She blew a kiss in the direction of where her family
and friends were seated.

"You were incredible." Carlos hugged her, lifting her off
her feet, before putting her down and lifting their joined
hands before they both took a bow.

They'd nailed the performance, and there was something
about it that felt freeing. Maybe Ms. Idelle was right. It was
something she'd needed to do. Em glanced over toward the
table where her family and friends were. She was sure that
she'd seen Nick there when she and Carlos had first walked
onto the dance floor. But he wasn't there now.

She'd gotten the message across to her best friend, and it
seemed that he'd quickly come back with a response.

Chapter Twenty-Two

◆—◆—◆

After the dance, Ms. Idelle had introduced Em to a few of her colleagues and some potential students. Then there was a sample dance class, where she, Carlos, and the other students and instructors danced with members of the audience. The dance floor was nearly full. Em looked around the space, but there was no sign of Nick.

At the end of the classes, the regular DJ took over, and people started to dance, many of them trying out some of the new steps they'd learned.

"You two were marvelous, darling. I'm so very proud of you." Ms. Idelle hugged Emerie. "You were the star of the evening. The crowd adored you."

"To be fair, a third of the place was probably family, friends, and neighbors," Em said.

"Never downplay a compliment, Ms. Roberts," Ms. Idelle said sternly. "They were impressed because your performance was outstanding. Now I think your friends are eager to see you." The elegant grand dame of dance swept her hand in the direction of the table brimming with Em's friends and family who looked on eagerly.

"Yes, ma'am." Em gave them a subtle wave. Her heart

was bursting with the love and support radiating from the people at that table and a sense of pride in what she'd accomplished. "I hope the night was successful."

"It was indeed." The older woman's eyes twinkled. "We've nearly sold out the introductory class sampler passes. In fact, we might need to consider adding a class or two." She winked. "Now go on. Celebrate the night with the people you love. And never take that privilege for granted."

Something about Ms. Idelle's reminder made Em's chest tighten. She immediately glanced at the table and then at the bar. Nick wasn't at either place.

Em swallowed back her disappointment, broadened her smile, and joined her family at the table.

"Oh my God, sweetheart! You were amazing!" Em's mother pulled her into a bear hug, rocking her back and forth before gripping her shoulders and holding her at arm's length. Marilyn Roberts's eyes were filled with pride as she regarded her. "I had no idea my baby was a modern-day Josephine Baker and Ginger Rogers all rolled into one."

Em opened her mouth to say she wouldn't go that far, but she remembered Ms. Idelle's admonition about not downplaying a compliment.

"Thanks, Mom. I'm glad you liked it." Em smoothed back her hair, held in place by hairspray and countless pins, a few of which were currently digging into her scalp. "I didn't know how you'd feel about some of the racier parts of the routine. Or my outfit..."

Em placed a hand to her bare belly, suddenly conscious of the short, flared skirt under which she wore a pair of spandex biker shorts so she wouldn't flash the crowd during the lifts and spins.

"Those were my favorite parts." Her mother grinned, laughing at Em's shocked response. "What? They were really good, and you two had so much chemistry. If I didn't know better—"

"Mom!" Em said. "No. Just...*no.*"

"Okay, fine." Her mother shrugged. "That means my baby is not only a talented dancer, but you gave us *a bit of theater* as well." Her mom said the words like a thespian quoting Shakespeare. Then she added a little shoulder shimmy, similar to the one Em had incorporated in her routine.

"Not bad, Mom. Maybe you should consider taking dance classes." Em grinned.

"Girl, I already bought my introductory sampler pass. But don't worry, I'll make sure we don't end up in the same class. I can't have you interrupting my flow while I'm on the dating scene." Her mom fluffed her hair.

Sinclair, Garrett, and Dakota laughed. Dex and Em both said, "Mom!"

"These two are no fun." Her mother huffed. "I'm headed to the bar to get another drink."

Em accepted hugs and congratulations from Dakota, Sinclair, Dex, and Garrett before finally dropping into one of the empty chairs. She fielded her family's questions about the performance as she subtly glanced around the space in search of Nick.

He'd promised to be there, and she was sure she'd seen him there at the table earlier.

"Nick's gone." Dex leaned in closer and spoke quietly. "He left not long after your performance."

"Oh." She swallowed hard and folded her hands on the table. "Did he say why he left so early?"

Em tried to sound as nonchalant as possible. As if it didn't matter to her that her best friend had bolted before talking to her. Especially given how little they'd communicated in the past few weeks. She realized that was on her, but still.

"He tried to wait for you, but he had to get to the airport," Dex said.

"Nick's leaving town?" Em wasn't able to hide how startled she was by that news.

Everyone at the table turned toward her, but then Dakota asked Sin and Rett about their latest renovation project to distract the group and give her and Dex a little privacy.

Emerie could've kissed her sweet, thoughtful sister-in-law. She flashed her a grateful smile instead.

"Nick's been out of town for the past week, Em. He flew in late last night so he'd be here for your performance. But he's flying out on a red-eye so he can be at a critical meeting first thing tomorrow morning. He didn't tell you any of this?" Dex lowered his voice.

Em shook her head, her cheeks and forehead burning. The lack of communication had been on her. Nick had tried calling and texting a few times. She'd responded with brief text messages or terse conversation and hurried off the phone because she'd either been working on a client project or headed to or from practice. But the past week, the calls and messages had become sparser. A knot formed in her stomach.

"What the hell happened with you two, Em?" Dex rubbed his chin. His dark eyes, filled with worry, studied hers.

Em shifted her gaze from Dex's. She didn't address her brother's question. "Where has he been this past week?"

"Same place he's headed now...New York." Dex's raised eyebrow indicated that he was keenly aware of her attempt to dodge his question. "The same place you're supposed to be meeting him this weekend."

Em sighed softly. The night she and Nick slept together,

their planned trip to New York had seemed so far away. She was sure that this would all have blown over by then. But instead, she'd gotten a little deeper into her feelings every day. She was hurt, angry with herself for caring, and missing her best friend. She honestly hadn't imagined that nearly four weeks later, she'd still be avoiding him.

She'd missed him by maybe thirty minutes, and she felt the loss so acutely that it caused her physical pain.

"I should call Nick." Em stood suddenly. "To thank him for coming all this way—"

"Just for you to give him the finger but in interpretive dance?" Dex shook his head and chuckled.

"I didn't...I mean...I wasn't—"

"Baby Girl, that message was about as subtle as taking a sledgehammer to someone's pinkie," Sinclair said, then sipped more of her frozen margarita. Her Southern drawl was always a bit heavier after a couple of drinks. When everyone at the table looked at her, she shrugged. "What? We all know it's true. Em gave 'im a lil' somethin' to think about. Maybe that's just what our friend needed."

"Amen." Em's mother returned to the table, raising her dirty martini in agreement with Sin.

"Okay, maybe no more to drink for either of you." Dakota pointed a finger and gave a warning glare to her best friend and then to her mother-in-law. "And perhaps Em would rather *not* talk about this. At least not right now."

Sinclair and Marilyn made sullen faces but reluctantly agreed.

Em leaned down to hug Dakota. She whispered in her ear, "That's why you're my favorite sister-in-law."

"Same." Dakota squeezed her hand. She tipped her chin in the direction of another table. "Kassie and her family have been waiting to talk to you."

Emerie excused herself, then went over to the table where her friend Kassie and her parents were seated. All three of them stood to hug and congratulate her. Then Kassie's parents got out onto the floor when the DJ played "Sparkle" by Cameo.

"I can't believe how amazing you were out there tonight." Kassie bounced on her heels and hugged Em again. "I'm so proud of you, girl."

"Thanks, babe. Harrison isn't here with you?" Em asked.

"Unfortunately, he had business in Atlanta this week. But he's taking me to some new, pricey seafood restaurant this weekend." Kassie smiled sheepishly. "Now come on. I need to show you something."

Kassie grabbed Em's hand and led her toward the green room. Em's purse and her phone were still there, and she needed to call Nick.

When they stepped into the room, being guarded by one of Ms. Idelle's grandsons, Kassandra gestured to three arrangements of flowers.

"Oh my goodness." Em lifted a dozen red roses bound in white wrapping paper. She inhaled them, then pulled out the card. They were from her mother, Dex, Dakota, and little Olivia. She set them down, then pulled the card from a small arrangement of flowers. It was from Kassandra and her parents.

"Aww...thanks, babe." Em hugged her friend. "They're gorgeous."

"Thank you. But that..." Kassie gestured to a larger arrangement of tulips, roses, peonies, and snowball viburnums in soft pink, white, and coral set in a stunning crystal vase. "That is my *pièce de résistance*."

"Wow, Kassie. This arrangement is incredible." Em

inhaled the fragrant roses and vibrant tulips. "But you shouldn't have."

"And I didn't," Kassie grinned. "I mean . . . yes, I put the arrangement together. But they're not from me."

"Who are they from?" Em quickly shifted her attention to the card buried in the arrangement when her friend simply shrugged, her eyes dancing with that sweet, adorably goofy smile of hers.

Em lifted the card and read it. "To a truly incredible woman and the best friend a man could ever have. I am so damn proud of you for going after your dreams and standing up for yourself." Em turned the card over. "I'm truly sorry I hurt you, Em. I hope you'll still join me in New York."

"This is Nick's handwriting." Em held up the card.

"I know," Kassie said. "He insisted on coming into the shop and writing out the card himself. And he apparently had a lot to say."

"You read it?" Em asked.

"No. But I did see him write it. It took a couple of tries to get the entire thing on one card and as neatly as he wanted it." She grinned. "But whatever he wrote . . . I hope his words and the flowers helped. Because both of you have been pretty miserable these past few weeks."

"I didn't get to see him before he left." Em frowned as she sat on the edge of the table.

"I know, and Nick was bummed about that, too." Kassie parked her butt on the table beside Em and draped an arm around her waist as they leaned their heads together. "But he said he hopes you still plan to join him in New York this weekend."

That morning, Em noted on her calendar that she only had twenty-four hours left to cancel her reservation for New York. She honestly hadn't been sure whether she should still go. But now…she wanted nothing more than to see Nick.

She missed him, and she missed their friendship. And despite being hurt and angry, she hadn't been able to stop thinking about what an amazing night they'd shared.

"New York," Em said. "I'm leaving in two days, and I still haven't packed. And I need to wrap up a couple of design projects before I go and let my clients know I'll be on vacation." Em rattled off one item after another, her brain filled with all of the things she'd been procrastinating on because she'd still been sulking and hadn't been ready to commit to the trip with Nick.

"Relax, babe. Everything will be fine," Kassie assured her. "Your assistant will help you with the business items, and I'll help you get organized and packed."

Em thanked her friend, a sense of relief settling over her. She traced the delicate, pink petals of a peony and smiled softly. Em wasn't sure what would happen with her and Nick. But she did know that she loved him and that she wanted him as a friend, a confidant, a lover, and her everything. But if she couldn't have it all, she would ensure that they didn't lose their friendship. No matter what.

"I should call Nick and thank him for the flowers." Em dug her purse out of its hiding spot and rummaged through it for her phone. "Try to catch him before he gets to the airport."

"Then I'll give you some privacy," Kassie said. "Just call me when you're ready, and I'll help you pack up your things and transport the flowers to your car."

By the time Em pulled out her phone, Kassie was already making her way out the door.

Emerie pulled up her list of favorites and stared at Nick's handsome, smiling face. Her heart started racing again.

Nick had penned that incredibly sweet note and laid out

a small mint for the most elaborate floral arrangement she'd ever received.

Was he still proud of her after seeing her performance that Dex had described as "the finger but in interpretive dance"? Or was he as hurt and angry as she'd been when she'd seen those text messages? Did he still want her to join him in New York?

Em sighed, her hands trembling slightly.

Of course Nick still wanted her to join him in New York. Hadn't he asked Kassie to remind her of that *after* he'd seen her performance?

"Stop being a frickin' baby, Emerie Roberts, and make the damn call," Em whispered to herself.

She dialed Nick and put the phone to her ear, her eyes squeezed shut.

With each ring, Em's heart thudded harder. Her body swayed the tiniest bit in response.

"Hey, beautiful." Nick's deep, gravelly voice sent electricity down her spine.

Em couldn't help smiling. "You've never answered the phone for me like that before."

There was a beat of silence followed by a quiet groan. "I know. But trust me, I was thinking it."

Em nibbled on her lower lip, unsure how to respond to his admission. She swallowed hard, her throat suddenly dry.

"Thank you for coming back here to support me. And for the lovely flowers." Em inhaled one of the salmon-colored tulips and smiled. "This is the most gorgeous bouquet I've ever seen. And the card…what you said about being proud of me…it means a lot. Though, after the performance, you might be feeling a bit differently." Em sat on the edge of the table.

"You're right," Nick said. "Because after that performance, I'm even prouder of you." Em could hear the soft smile in his tone. "You are a fucking superstar, Emerie Roberts. I've known you most of my life, and I've never seen you look so confident, so happy, so determined. You shone as brightly as a thousand suns tonight. How could I not be proud of you?"

Em's eyes pricked with tears, and her heart expanded. This was why she adored Nick and was lucky to have him as her best friend. He was her biggest supporter. Even when it didn't align with his interests or ruffled his ego. She needed to do the same. Because no matter how everything else played out between them, he would always be her best friend.

"Thanks, Nick. I'm really proud of you, too," she said, rather than addressing the elephant in the room—the message behind her performance. "Dex tells me that you're in popular demand. I think he's afraid he's going to lose you to corporate," she added playfully, hoping he'd deny it.

He didn't.

The few moments of silence seemed to echo off the walls of the dark wood paneling.

"It's been a good challenge for me," Nick said finally. "But my brain is just about fried. So I could use a fun weekend, and I miss you like crazy, Em. You know I can't function in the world for too long without my best friend." He chuckled.

Best friend.

As in…*Message received. Friends is all we'll ever be, and I'm okay with that.*

Em's stomach knotted, and her chest ached.

Tonight, she'd declared that Nick needed to make a choice and stick with it. Either he was her platonic best friend or her soulmate. Friends with benefits wasn't an option.

He'd clearly made that choice, so she needed to respect it.

"You are still coming to New York this weekend, right?" Nick was saying.

"I'm looking forward to it." Em forced a bright smile, hoping it was reflected in her voice. "I'll see you on Friday."

"Great. See you on Friday."

"Nick!"

"Yeah?"

Em opened her mouth to apologize if she'd hurt his feelings. But she thought of Ms. Idelle's words and Sin's. They were both right. Maybe she could've gotten her point across a little less dramatically. But her declaration had been a cold, hard dose of reality they both needed.

She didn't owe anyone an apology for standing up for herself and putting her wants and needs first for a change.

Not even Nick.

"Can I bring you anything?" Em asked instead. "I could stop by your apartment if there's anything you—"

"I'm good, Em. The only thing I need is to spend time with you. See you soon, beautiful."

Em's eyes drifted closed, silent tears streaming down her cheeks. She and Nick were just going to be friends. Eventually, she'd be fine with it. But for now, her heart was broken, and all she wanted to do was curl up in a ball and cry like a baby because it seemed that Nick Washington wasn't her soulmate after all. No matter how badly she wanted him to be.

Chapter Twenty-Three

- • -

Nick stepped out of the shower, dried off, and got dressed after a long, grueling day of meetings and endless debates about the best approach for the marketing campaign to roll out the changes to his company's line of beach resorts.

He loved his job and found the work challenging, but he'd been distracted. Especially since seeing Em's dance performance at The Foxhole a few nights ago. In fact, he'd been off his game at work since the night he and Em had spent together. The night she'd subsequently decided that his dating history was more than she could handle.

Nick tugged a black T-shirt over his head and groaned. The vision of Em moving across The Foxhole dance floor in that sexy little fire-engine-red outfit that showed off her strong arms, toned belly, sleek thighs, and firm bottom was living rent-free in his head. He'd recorded her performance, but he didn't need to see the footage to recall every sway of her hips and the rotation of her waist as she and Carlos danced in sync. Like they were a single being. The dance was sexy and playful, and the chemistry between the two of them could have set the parquet floor on fire.

The way the older man had hugged Em after their

performance and held her hand possessively as they talked to potential dance students... Nick's fists and jaw clenched involuntarily every time he recalled the way Carlos had touched Em during and after their electric performance.

Nick had hoped to talk to Emerie before he'd had to leave for the airport. But she and Carlos had been... preoccupied.

Nick grabbed a glass from the coffee bar in his hotel room and dropped a few cubes of ice in it. He retrieved a can of soda and a bottle of whiskey from the minibar, poured both over the ice, then stirred. He gulped some of his drink and sighed.

How had he fucked up so royally with Em? More importantly, was there still a chance that he could fix things?

Em and Carlos had stared into each other's eyes with so much heat and passion during the romantic moments of the performance. Was that why Em had been pulling away? Were she and that Carlos guy an item now?

Just thinking of Em with that guy made Nick want to scream. But he wasn't mad at Em; he was angry with himself.

He'd been a coward, afraid to tell his best friend how he really felt about her because he'd been so damn terrified that he'd screw things up. But now it seemed so simple. He loved Em and would do anything for her. So they would navigate the challenges of learning to exist as a couple. Because they loved each other and wanted to be together.

Nick rubbed his forehead, his temples throbbing. Em's plane had landed, and she was en route to the hotel. She was going to get settled into her room, and then they were going to meet at the hotel lobby before heading out to catch an early dinner at Melba's Restaurant in Harlem, then get ice cream at the Sugar Hill Creamery. But food was the last thing on Nick's mind.

He'd prefer to spend the evening showing Em just how much he'd missed her during an encore performance of their night together. Then they could order in afterward.

Nick rubbed his chin and sighed. He'd promised himself that he wouldn't do anything that might jeopardize his friendship with Em. So they'd go on with the evening as planned and see where things went from there.

A knock at the door startled Nick. He couldn't help smiling. His best friend was chaos personified. So of course she hadn't stayed with the plan. She'd probably decided she was hungry now and had a taste for something altogether different.

Nick opened the door, surprised to see his friend toting her luggage. "Hey."

"Hey." Em's adorable, goofy smile made his heart go wild.

They exchanged an awkward hug, then he grabbed her carry-on and pulled it inside, closing the door behind her.

"I thought you were checking into your room first."

"It's not ready." Em glanced around his room before meeting his gaze again. "Is it okay if I crash here until we go to dinner?"

"Yeah, sure. Anything you want."

"A shower would be great, actually. I feel a little sticky from the plane."

"Be my guest." Nick gestured toward the bathroom.

Nick sat at the desk and opened his laptop in an attempt to keep his wandering mind occupied while the shower ran. Instead, he found himself reading the same paragraph over and over as the vision of Em's naked body, soaped up beneath that showerhead, robbed him of the ability to function.

Finally, Em emerged from the bathroom smelling like some heavenly combination of coconut and coffee. She wore a sleeveless, navy-blue dress with a white polka-dot pattern.

She shoved her hands into the pockets of the short, flared skirt and spun around, revealing the keyhole back.

"What do you think?" Em asked with an almost bashful smile.

"You look fantastic." Nick got up from his chair and came closer, stopping a couple of feet in front of Em so she was just out of reach. "But then you always look beautiful, Em. No matter what you're wearing. You always have."

"But you never said that to me before I started doing all this…" She lifted the sides of the skirt, revealing more of the smooth, brown skin of her thighs that he'd gotten intimately familiar with.

"Doesn't mean I didn't notice." Nick rubbed his jaw, his eyes scanning her legs, which looked a mile long in the thigh-length dress. "And that's despite working damn hard not to."

Em took a few steps closer, her eyes locked with his. "And why would you try so hard not to notice?"

Nick inhaled quietly, studying her inquisitive dark eyes. This weekend, he was prepared to lay everything on the line and hold nothing back.

"Because that wasn't who we were, Em. We'd always been friends, and I thought the only way I could keep you in my life was to make sure it stayed that way."

"Why didn't you just tell me that on New Year's Eve?" Em folded her arms.

"Because I didn't want to screw up our friendship. But that's exactly what I did by not leveling with you about my feelings and why I was reluctant to get involved. It wasn't just you I wasn't being straight with. I wasn't being honest with myself about how my feelings for you have evolved.

You're not just my best friend, Em. You're the most important person in my life."

He'd barely finished his sentence when Em lunged forward and pressed her mouth to his.

Without hesitation, Nick kissed her back.

Maybe this was a mistake. But hiding his feelings for Em would be an even bigger one.

————

For the past two days, Emerie had been thinking of only one thing: this moment. The moment she knew she would kiss Nick, hoping he'd kiss her back. And as he snaked one arm around her waist, pulling her closer, Em's heart danced with joy. She leaned into the kiss, her hands braced on his hard chest as he cradled her cheek.

Nick tilted her head, his lips gliding over hers as if he'd been anticipating this moment as much as she had. And when she parted her lips, her tongue seeking his, Nick responded in kind.

His mouth tasted like cola and whiskey. The sensation of his tongue gliding against hers only made her hungrier for his kiss and his touch.

Em took a deep breath. Her heart raced, and her hands trembled as she clutched the hem of Nick's black T-shirt and slowly lifted the material.

"Wait…Em, are you sure about this?" Nick cupped her face, his thumb grazing her cheekbone. "As much as I'd love to take you to bed right now, things didn't work out so well last time."

"I know. I saw those text messages, and I overreacted," she admitted. "I'm sorry. But I'm here now because I am sure that I want you, Nick."

Em tugged her dress over her head and tossed it onto a nearby chair. "You weren't wearing anything under that dress." His dark eyes glittered with amusement as he gazed at her longingly. He slipped his strong arms around her bare waist. "Which means you had absolutely no intention of leaving this hotel room."

Em glanced up at him with a playful grin and shrugged. "Seemed like a really good idea at the time."

She captured his open mouth with a slow kiss and tried not to feel conscious about the fact that she was naked and completely vulnerable, asking her best friend to make love to her when she had no idea where they'd stand once this weekend was over. More importantly, in this moment, she didn't care.

She only knew that she wanted to be with Nick. That she wanted to feel his hands and those incredible lips on her skin again. That she craved the euphoric sensation of Nick being inside her once more. They'd figure everything else out later.

Nick swept her up in his arms and carried her the few short steps to his bed.

Em climbed beneath the covers as Nick shed his clothing, then rummaged in his luggage for a condom. He put it on and climbed into bed with her, kissing her with a hunger and intensity that matched her own.

Em's hand glided down Nick's back, the muscles tense as he inched inside her until he was fully seated, their bodies flush.

Em inhaled deeply, her body adjusting to the delicious sensation of Nick filling her so completely.

"Fuck, that feels amazing." Nick kissed her again, threading their fingers as he lifted her arms over her head, his hips moving slowly as first. "Being with you is amazing, Em."

Em's eyes filled with tears, despite promising herself she wouldn't get emotional this time. But there was something in his tone, in his words, in the way his gaze met hers, that captured her heart.

Nick freed one hand, lifting her leg over his hip and shifting the angle of entry.

"Oh! Yes!" Em's eyes drifted closed, the pleasure building as they moved together, his hand still on her hip. The sensation of Nick hitting just the right spot, combined with the grinding of his pelvis against her sensitive clit, drove her higher and higher until he'd taken her over the edge, his name on her lips, and her tears wetting the pillow beneath her.

Nick kissed her hard and shifted his position, his hips moving harder and faster until he reached his peak.

His body stiffened, and his back arched as he called her name, and it was the most beautiful sound she'd ever heard.

Nick hovered over her, their chests heaving as their eyes met. He traced her cheekbone with his thumb, then kissed her.

"I need to take care of this. But you have to promise me that by the time I come out of the bathroom—"

"I won't be packing up your stuff and waiting for you at the door?" Em giggled.

"Well…this is my room," Nick reminded her. "So that'd be kind of weird."

Good point.

"I just need to know that no matter what, you will always be my best friend, Em. I want you in my bed. But I *need* you in my life. I don't ever want to lose *us*." There was sincerity in Nick's voice and pain in his dark eyes. "Even if it means…" Nick's voice trailed off and he sucked in a deep breath as if he couldn't bear to say the words.

She understood exactly how he felt.

"We'll talk when you get back, and everything will be fine." Em kissed him. "Promise."

Nick nodded reluctantly, then made his way to the bathroom.

Em slipped on Nick's discarded black T-shirt, then climbed back into bed. She pulled her knees to her chest, her back pressed against the headboard.

She was glad that she and Nick were on the same page about their friendship being the most important thing. Even if they couldn't find a way to fit a relationship into the mix. Still, the possibility that whatever happened between them that weekend might be the extent of their short-lived affair made her heart ache.

"Okay. Let's talk." Nick tugged his boxers on and slid into bed beside her. He opened his palm, and she slid her hand inside it. "You first."

The eloquent words she'd penned on the plane and practiced in her head seemed to disintegrate. All that remained was the unvarnished truth.

"Nick, I don't know how *not* to be in love with you." Fat tears spilled down her cheeks the moment she admitted the truth to him and to herself.

Nick flashed a watery smile that made her belly do flips. He stroked her cheek and leaned in to kiss her again. "Good. Because I love you, too."

Em's heart danced, and her face was wet with tears. She honestly didn't think she would ever tire of hearing her best friend utter those words. But her desire to start building a life was unchanged.

Was that what Nick wanted, too?

Chapter Twenty-Four

* ◆ *

You love me?" A soft smile lit Em's eyes.

"More than anything in the world. Deep down, I guess I've always known that. But I was afraid of ruining what we had. Worried that our friendship wouldn't necessarily translate into a romantic relationship. Afraid to risk it because you're not just a friend. You're family, Em. I have always loved you, and I always will."

"I've waited so long to hear those words from you." Em's dark brown eyes welled with tears. "But my expectations for a relationship haven't changed. I'm not looking for a friends-with-benefits arrangement. So if you're not interested in anything serious, Nick, I'll understand. Just please be honest with me and with yourself about it. Because that's the level of commitment I need at this stage in my life."

Nick was so damn proud of Em for standing up for herself and demanding what she needed. For prompting him to set aside his fears and go for the one thing he really wanted.

"All I want is you. Just you, Em. Now and always. I was just so afraid I'd lose you."

Em's expression softened. She slid her arms around his neck. "Why would you think you'd lose me?"

Nick laughed bitterly. "Have you ever known me to have a *successful* long-term relationship?"

"Yes. With me." She tightened her grip around his neck. "Been your ride or die since day one, and you've been mine."

"True." Nick stroked her cheek. "But it's not exactly the same thing, Em."

"Maybe not. But we are the same people. We've loved and gone to battle for each other most of our lives. Why would this be any different?"

"The stakes are so much higher when hearts are on the line. I kept thinking, what if I screw this up the way I've blown every other relationship? I couldn't bear the thought of my life without you in it, Em. These past few weeks... they've been hell for me."

"Me, too. I think my family was five seconds away from disowning my temperamental ass," she joked.

"They would never do that," Nick said. "But losing my relationship with your family and our friends was a *genuine* concern for me. They were amazing and supportive the night of your dance exhibition, and I appreciate that. But if they were ever forced to choose a side...it would shatter my relationship with each of them."

"I hadn't considered why the stakes felt so much higher for you. That you had so much more to lose. I wished you'd told me sooner," Em said.

"The night we made love, I was literally in the bathroom mirror practicing how I was going to tell you that I loved you. When I came out, you were pissed, and you wanted me to leave. Didn't seem like the right time."

"You were going to tell me that night?" Em's eyes widened with shock. "Babe, I'm so sorry. I freaked when I saw those messages about you hooking up with someone else."

"Listen to me, Em. I did *not* have plans with anyone else that night. I swear." Nick stroked her cheek, his eyes locked with hers. "I've been so damn preoccupied with this Soulmate Project of yours—worrying that you'd find someone else—I honestly can't recall the last time I've been out on a date. So I promise you, there was only one thing on my mind then and now. That's being with you."

"I believe you, Nick. But I was on this incredible high, and then I saw those messages. It was so devastating."

"Why? I was there with *you*. Because it's *you* I want. Not anyone else."

She furrowed her brows. "I guess I was feeling a little self-conscious. Seeing the glamorous, voluptuous women who are clearly your type...I couldn't imagine that you'd pick me over one of them."

Nick shifted Em onto his lap, his gaze locked with hers. He needed her to know that he meant every word he was about to say.

"*You* are the most beautiful woman in the world to me, Emerie. And it didn't take a new hairdo or expensive new clothes to convince me of that." He brushed her soft, sweet lips with his own before planting a slow, lingering kiss on the lips whose taste he craved. "Don't *ever* compare yourself to anyone else. There is *no one* in the world like you."

"Is that a compliment?" Em asked in a playful, singsong voice. "'Cause I've heard it used both ways."

Nick chuckled, thinking of all the times they'd teased each other about being *extra*.

"Definitely a compliment." He grinned. "You're the only person in the world I could imagine building a life with."

"You want to build a life with me?" Em's expressive brown eyes welled with tears. "As in—"

"As in I don't *just* want to be your best friend anymore,

Emerie Roberts." Nick's heart beat faster, and his pulse raced as he finally made his own *Brown Sugar* declaration. "I want to be your best friend *and* your man. The one who will gladly worship every inch of that banging body. The man who would do anything to protect your heart. The one who will *always* be there for you...no matter what. For forever and a day and then for a week after that."

Em grinned, her eyes filled with happy tears, and her face practically glowing.

"I don't know, Nick. That's an awfully long time," she teased. "You sure you can deal with me that long?"

For two decades, Emerie's bright smile and perpetual optimism had lit up his life and warmed his heart like the midday sun. He trusted her more than anyone in the world. Because she was both his best friend and the love of his life. Something his heart had realized long before his brain had gotten on board. Em was the reason he hadn't been able to give his heart to anyone else. Deep down, a part of him had always known that it belonged to her.

"I love you, Em. And there is nothing in this world that would make me happier than spending the rest of my life with you." Nick kissed Em, tasting her salty tears. "You have always been my soulmate. I was just too oblivious to realize it."

Nick's eyes stung, and all the other words he wanted to say caught in his throat. But he could show Em how he felt, how much she meant to him.

"That night at your place, when you asked me to leave, I went back to my car and saw those text messages. That's when I realized I had to do something to show you that I'm serious about not wanting anyone but you. So I got this..." Nick reached for a small bag on his nightstand and handed it to her.

"What is it?" Em tucked her hair behind her ear and peeked inside. She pulled out the box for the latest phone. Her brows furrowed with confusion. "This is really sweet, Nick. But I already have this phone. I upgraded a few months ago, remember?"

"It isn't for you. It's for me." He took the phone out of the box, pulled up her contact, and dialed.

"That isn't your number." Em looked up from her watch.

"It is now." Nick slid his arm around her waist and pulled her closer.

"But you loved your old number," she said. "You've had it since before college."

"True. But I love you too much to let my past or nostalgia over an old phone number ruin our future." Nick brushed Em's hair from her face and tucked a few strands behind her ear. "So I've changed my number and wiped all of my contacts except for family, friends, local businesses, and work contacts. I don't *ever* want you to feel the way you did that night."

It had been gut-wrenching for Nick to see how hurt Em had been after she'd seen those text messages. He understood her pain. It had been torturous watching Em go out with other guys in hopes of finding the one with whom she could build a life.

"You can't protect me from every one of your exes." Em's eyes glistened, a soft smile lighting them, despite the tears that threatened to fall. "We're bound to run into one or two of them on the island."

"I'm not the only one with exes," Nick reminded her with a raised brow. "But this isn't about them. It's about us. I don't want anyone but you. No one from my past matters, Em, because you are my future."

"I believe you, and I trust you." Em pressed a kiss to

his lips, followed by another and another. "And I've always known you loved me. I just needed you to figure that out, too."

Em slipped Nick's black T-shirt over her head and tossed it onto the floor, exposing her bare breasts. The firm, brown nipples were begging for his attention, and he fully intended to oblige. When he met her gaze again, the sexy, confident smile that greeted him made him hard and eager to pick up where they'd left off.

"Don't worry, sweetheart. I might've been a little slow on the uptake, but I'm pretty fucking clear about it now." Nick flipped Em onto her back, and she squealed with surprise, then laughed.

Nick hovered above her, taking in her gorgeous features: her playful, expressive eyes and contagious smile. Em was his best friend. His confidant. The woman he'd go to hell and back for. And the one person he couldn't imagine not having in his life. He was grateful they'd finally arrived at this place. That they were ready to dive into the deep end together.

"I love you, Em," Nick whispered.

Her warm smile filled his heart, making it expand until it felt as if his chest could barely contain it.

"I love you, too, Nick." Her soft palms glided up his low back, sending waves of need down his spine. He'd never wanted anyone the way he wanted and needed Em now.

Their lips and tongues met in a clash of hunger and craving. Every kiss, every stroke of his skin sent him higher and stoked a desperate sense of need for the woman lying beneath him.

This was what he'd been missing. What he needed. What they had was so much more than sex. Em was his best friend. She was the one person in the world who understood him better than he knew himself. Even in the moments when they were at odds, he never, ever doubted that she loved him and wanted what was best for him. He felt the same about her.

Em truly got him. She knew how to make him laugh. She didn't pull punches when he needed to hear the truth. And she drove him wild, setting his heart and his body afire.

Emerie Roberts was his soulmate. And he was incredibly grateful to have her in his life.

Chapter Twenty-Five

· — · · · — ·

Em grabbed two glasses, then strutted back toward the bed. She was wearing Nick's black T-shirt and her most scandalous pair of panties: a crotchless number Sinclair had sent her as a gift with a note that said, "Guaranteed to snag that boneheaded man of yours." Emerie chuckled to herself and shook her head.

She hadn't needed the underwear to snag Nick. He was already hers. She just hadn't realized it. Still, it had been nice seeing his reaction to them…and to the toy she'd packed in her luggage.

"What's so funny?" Nick tilted his head as he assessed her.

"Nothing. It's just something Sinclair said." Em shrugged, being careful not to jostle their makeshift picnic in bed as she climbed onto it and folded her legs. She picked up a catfish strip, dipped it into the chipotle sauce, then took a bite.

She murmured quietly. The food from Melba's Restaurant in Harlem was as good as advertised. Thank goodness they were able to have their meal delivered because neither of them had wanted to leave the bed they'd been sharing all evening.

"Sinclair, huh?" One side of Nick's sensual mouth curved in a smirk that made her tummy flutter. He picked up one of the dry rub wings and nibbled on it, his mischievous, dark eyes never leaving hers. "Do I even want to know?"

"Probably not." Em grinned, finishing the last of her catfish strip. "But from here on out, I want us to be open and honest with each other about everything. So I should probably tell you that the reason my room wasn't ready is because I canceled it."

"Oh, really?" Nick laughed. "And what exactly was your plan?"

"To tell you how I felt and hope you felt the same way."

Nick's expression was a mixture of pride and amusement. "And what if I hadn't?"

"I planned to have the most amazing fuck buddy weekend of my life. Then we'd figure out how to go back to being friends."

"Well, it's a good thing we don't have to choose. We get to do both." Nick captured her mouth in a kiss before pulling away. His expression was suddenly somber. "But there's something I need to tell you."

"Okay." Uneasiness lodged in the pit of Em's stomach like a boulder. "What is it?"

"I've been offered a promotion in the company."

"Nick, that's great." Em hugged him, trying not to disturb their dwindling buffet. But when she studied Nick's face, he seemed perturbed. She already anticipated what he'd say next.

"The position is based out of the corporate office here in New York."

It felt as if someone had sucked every ounce of air from the room.

"Congratulations, Nick." Emerie forced a smile, despite the tightness in her chest. She was terrified of what the promotion would mean for their new relationship status. But she would always be his best friend and would cheer him on first and foremost. "I guess Dex was right to worry that he'd lose you to corporate."

"It's a great opportunity and a challenge I think I'd enjoy. But you and I have finally figured out that we should be together, Em. There's no way I'm picking up and leaving without you." He kissed her again. "I meant it when I said I want to build a life with you. Whether it's here in New York or back on Holly Grove Island...that's up to you. Because now that we've finally got it right, I'm not walking away. I'll do whatever it takes to make this work—even if it means saying no to this opportunity. It's not like others won't come along."

Emerie's heart was racing, and everything felt like a blur.

She was thrilled about her friend's career accomplishment. Devastated by the thought of losing him again. Overjoyed that he'd made her a central part of his decision-making. Overwhelmed by the idea of uprooting and leaving her friends and family behind to move to New York.

"What is it that you want, Nick?" Em tightened her grip on his hand. "Do you *want* to move to New York?"

"I love New York."

"I know." Em's gut tightened in a knot.

"But there was a reason I returned to Holly Grove Island. I missed you, but I also missed being home. Missed the Salt Life and the slower pace. The calm and peace of the island." Nick's gaze was on their joined hands.

"Then maybe you don't have to choose," Em said.

"What do you mean?" Nick's brows furrowed.

"Why can't you take on this new job while still based at the resort on Holly Grove Island? I remember Dex mentioning a few of the execs he's dealt with are based at their original resort sites rather than at the corporate office." She shrugged. "Why can't you propose the same thing? And whenever it is truly necessary to be here in person, you can hop on a plane."

The idea had come to Em suddenly. But now that it had, it felt like the perfect compromise.

"The guy I'd be reporting to is old school. He isn't a huge fan of remote work." Nick rubbed his chin, but she could see the wheels turning in his head.

"You wouldn't be working remotely," Em reminded him. "You'd just be based at a different location. Besides, didn't you say that he brought you onto the team because he wanted people who had their fingers on the pulse of the changing needs of resort guests? Well, beach resort guests' needs are dynamic and constantly shifting. You'll lose that edge if you move to some glass tower at the corporate office."

"True." Nick nodded. "I wonder if Jeff would go for it."

"There's only one way to find out." Em grinned broadly. "Give me an hour, and I can put together an impressive PowerPoint presentation that you can present to him on Monday."

"Thanks." Nick grabbed her hand before she could climb out of bed. "But the PowerPoint won't be necessary. Besides, I can think of much better ways for us to spend the weekend." He pulled her onto his lap and kissed her.

In that moment, nothing else mattered. Because whether they stayed on Holly Grove Island or moved to New York together, Nick would always be her best friend and her soulmate. And she would be his.

Chapter Twenty-Six

— • • • —

Nick parked in the parking lot of The Foxhole and hopped out of his car. He smoothed down his tie and straightened his light jacket before opening the passenger door and extending his hand.

Em placed her hand in Nick's and let him pull her to her feet, clad in a pair of Mary Janes with platform heels. Her short, white top revealed a hint of her toned abs and the peekaboo cutouts showed off her strong shoulders. Her yoga-inspired, wide-leg, black dress pants hugged her firm bottom. The look was topped off by a menswear-inspired jacket and a woven black pearl statement necklace shaped like a man's tie.

She looked beautiful, but the style was very much her own. Classic Em with an edge. A little sexier and a little more polished but still the sporty, tomboy style she'd always felt most comfortable in.

"You look fantastic." Nick grinned.

Em's smile widened. She leaned in and pressed a hand to his chest. Her slow, sweet kiss managed to undo him every single time. Em seemed to be well aware of her power over him, and she was enjoying it.

"Remind me to thank my stylist properly when we get back home." She wiped her sparkly lip gloss from his mouth with her thumb.

"As much as I'd like to take credit for this look, I don't really think taking you to a couple of stores, holding your bags, and saying yes or no while you model clothing qualifies me as a stylist." Nick chuckled.

"You found a lot of these pieces," Em reminded him. "You have an eye for—"

"*You.*" Nick pulled Em into his arms for another kiss. He didn't give a damn about the lip gloss or about who might see them in the parking lot. He only knew that he would never be able to get enough of Em's kisses. Of holding her in his arms each night. Or making love to her.

And the fact that she'd just said *when we get back home* had made his heart leap in his chest.

They'd only gotten back from New York yesterday evening, but they'd gone back to her place and spent the night there.

He'd spent the last few days going to bed with Em in his arms and then waking up to her. At the hotel, they'd gotten up and gone to breakfast each morning or had it delivered to their room. That morning, they'd made breakfast together, and it had felt so...right. It was something he wanted to do every day.

Nick pulled back and lifted her chin, studying the eyes he'd spent the past few days drowning in. "Look, I know this is going to seem rash given the journey that it took to get us to this point...but I've been thinking about this since we checked out of the hotel yesterday..."

"Okay." Em tilted her head as she studied his face. There was a hint of worry in her dark eyes. "What is it?"

"I was thinking that you should move in with me." His

mouth curved in a soft grin at the look of surprise on Em's face.

"Wait... you're serious? After having to share a bed with me and waking up to me for the past few days, you actually want to do it on purpose?" she teased.

Em was a wild sleeper, and he'd caught a stray elbow or two. Then there was her early morning routine which involved her waking up at 5:30 in the morning to "Get On Up" by Jodeci and dancing to the entire song, followed by a morning workout.

That last morning, she'd teased that he was probably going to be glad to get back to his own Jodeci-free routine each morning. But when they'd returned to Holly Grove Island and he'd gotten her settled into her apartment, the last thing he'd wanted to do was to leave. He'd been thinking about that all day.

"Yes, Em, I do." Nick dropped another kiss on her lips, his arms wrapped around her waist as he tugged her lower body closer. "But what do you want?"

"I loved sharing a space with you these past few days," Em admitted. She tightened his tie. "But I'm afraid we're still on this kind of honeymoon high where everything feels perfect and beautiful right now. In a few days or weeks, you might get tired of my disorganization or catching elbows in your sleep. And maybe I'll be annoyed with your snoring—"

"Whoa... whoa." Nick held up a hand. "I do *not* snore."

Em flashed a "bless your lil' heart" smile and patted his chest. "You totally do, babe. But no worries. It's super cute and rhythmic. It actually helps me fall asleep."

Em burst out laughing at his expression of mock outrage. Did he really snore? Right now, that wasn't the issue.

"This is definitely what I want. I know it took me a while

to realize that. But now that I have, I don't want to waste any more time apart."

Em grinned, her eyes misty and twinkling in the late afternoon sunlight as if he'd given just the right answer.

"Okay." She nodded. "But since we're running late for Sinclair and Rett's big dinner, maybe we should put a pin in this for now and come back to it later, huh?"

"Of course." Nick kissed her again. He bumped the car door closed with his hip, then took her hand as they strolled inside.

"There you are! For a minute, I was worried that you two might've gotten..." Sinclair covered her mouth mid-sentence, her eyes wide. She bounced up and down, gesturing between him and Em.

"Praise the Lord above!" Sin waved praise hands and glanced up to the sky with the shake of her head, her ombré curls bouncing. "These two done finally figured it out."

"Oh my gosh." Dakota, who had little Olivia on her hip, walked toward them. "Look at you two." She hugged Em, then Nick. "You look so happy."

"He doesn't," Nick whispered so that only he, Em, and Dakota could hear as he tipped his head in Dex's direction.

They all looked at Dexter who wore a frown.

"Don't worry about him. He's just surprised, that's all." Dakota waved a hand, then walked back toward her husband. She put a hand beneath his jaw and lifted it, shutting his open mouth. They exchanged a look, then Dexter seemed to come out of his daze. He cleared his throat and rose to his feet.

"Nick, Em. Good to have you both back." Dexter hugged his sister, then shook Nick's hand. "You two look good together. I hope this means Em's soulmate search is over."

Nick shifted his gaze to Emerie's, both of them smiling. He slipped a hand around her waist and pulled her closer.

"Definitely." Em smiled up at him with so much love in her eyes. His heart felt full. "There is no one in the world who gets me like Nick. No one I'd rather be with. I've always known that. Now he does, too. So the Soulmate Project was a success."

"Here, here." Garrett raised his glass. He kissed Sinclair, who'd settled onto his lap. "We are all very happy for you."

"My babies!" Em's mother approached. She hugged them both. "I'm so happy that you're back, and I'm thrilled to finally see you together. And, Emerie, my goodness, sweetheart." Marilyn sized up her daughter's outfit. "Baby Girl, you look absolutely fierce. I love it."

"Thanks, Mom." Em beamed. "I'm glad you like my outfit. It's a little bit of glamour and a whole lot of me."

Nick grinned. It was the perfect description for Em's look.

"You look amazing, Em. Nothing looks as good on a woman as self-confidence and true happiness." Sinclair grinned proudly. "And now that you're all here, Rett and I have a little news. We've picked a date for the wedding. We're getting married next summer so I have plenty of time to plan the wedding of all weddings. And I promise to keep the bridezilla element dialed down as much as possible."

The entire table burst into laughter.

"Okay, y'all are laughing a little too hard about that." Sinclair pointed an accusatory finger at their friends, though she couldn't help laughing, too. "But seriously, we're gonna keep things relatively simple. Here's what we're thinking…"

Sin beamed with excitement as she shared the plans for her and Rett's wedding, which would surely be the event of the summer the following year. And as Nick watched everyone chatting excitedly about Sin & Rett's upcoming nuptials and fawning over little Olivia who was now in her father's arms, Nick couldn't help thinking about his own future with Emerie.

Thoughts of building a life with someone and starting a family...they had always felt so foreign to Nick. He couldn't understand why a man would voluntarily give up his bachelor card and commit to spending the rest of his life with the same woman. But as he watched the loud, joyous, raucous conversation among his friends, then glanced at Emerie, whose smile lit up the room and made his heart skip a beat, he understood.

He'd always heard the phrase *ball and chain* used to refer to a person being tethered to their wife. But he much preferred the term *anchor*. Because that was what Em had been for him. An anchor in the storm of life. The person who kept him from drifting too far from his center. The person who always made him feel like he was safe and home—no matter where he'd been in the world.

And he wanted that now and always.

The idea of settling down with Em didn't feel scary. She was the person he was meant to be with. He was lucky to have spent most of his life with her. And he was excited about the future, now that they'd added love and passion to the mix. Em wasn't just his best friend and partner in crime anymore. She was his soulmate and the love of his life. Now and always.

Epilogue

•—•—•

Eight Months Later

Emerie sat around the bonfire outside of Blaze of Glory on New Year's Eve and rubbed her hands together. The weather had been surprisingly chilly in the Outer Banks for the past few days, but not enough to deter the die-hard town natives from their annual New Year's Eve bonfire. This year's event was bigger than ever. The town had added a music component to the event, and the Holly Grove Island Players were up next.

The faces of her friends, family, and neighbors glowed in the light of the fire and perhaps from the drinks that Blaze had been serving up all night. Everyone looked cheerful. But this time, she didn't envy their contentment. Because she was genuinely happy, too.

It had taken a couple of months for Nick to convince his new boss to accommodate his request to work out of the Holly Grove Island Resort. Once the man agreed, Nick had accepted the promotion. Things had gone fairly smoothly since then, and Dexter was an excellent mentor whenever Nick ran into a stressful challenge.

Their first holiday season together as a couple had been amazing. They'd enjoyed their time with friends and family. But the past couple of days, Nick seemed a little anxious, though he'd assured her that everything was fine.

Nick and Dexter were in an intense conversation as the band prepared to go on. Her brother placed his hands on Nick's shoulders as if he was reassuring him. She couldn't be more grateful that the man she loved was such a seamless part of her life and family.

She and Nick were good together. Not just as best friends but as lovers and life partners.

Em loved the life that she and Nick had been building together. The quiet strolls on the beach hand in hand. Taking dance classes, watching a movie on the sofa, or enjoying a quiet night at home together. Nights out, double dates, evenings with family and friends. And she loved how they supported one another in their careers.

Emerie glanced over at Sinclair who was kissing Garrett, and she smiled. She was grateful to Sin for her directness and for pushing her to admit her feelings to Nick. Because she was happier than she'd ever been.

"I found this guy on the other side sitting by himself. I figured you wouldn't mind if I invited him to join us." Her mother sank onto her beach blanket, placed beside Em and Nick's. She had a broad smile on her face.

"Dad? What are you doing here?" Em jumped up and into her father's arms, inhaling his familiar Old Spice scent. "You never came to the bonfire before you moved to Elizabeth City. I definitely didn't expect to see you tonight."

"I know, Baby Girl. And I'm sorry. Not spending more time with my family...that's something I will always regret." There was pain in her father's voice. "But with whatever time I have left on this earth, I promise to do better. To be there for the moments that count." He kissed the top of her head.

Her father sat on the blanket beside her mother, the two of them sharing a warm smile. Then her mother slipped her arm through her father's as they shifted their attention to where Nick, Dexter, and the rest of the band took the make-shift stage just outside of Blaze of Glory.

Em often acted as an emcee for the band when they performed locally, but it was a pleasant surprise to see Sinclair taking on the role. As always, Sin was fun and sassy. Her Eastern Carolina twang was in full effect as she promised the record crowd that the band had a huge surprise in store to end the night.

The guys played an amazing set of mostly jazz covers of classic R&B songs with a little pop thrown in. They sounded phenomenal, and everyone was enjoying themselves. Several couples had made their own little dance floor in the sand and were swaying to the band's cover of "Good & Plenty" by Alex Isley, Masego, and Jack Dine. Her parents had even joined them, and the vibe between them was very different from when they'd danced together at Dexter and Dakota's wedding a year and a half ago. Her parents had danced together then because they'd been obligated to as part of the wedding festivities. But now...Em couldn't help wondering if the spark between her parents had been reignited.

The only thing that mattered to Em and her brothers was that their parents were both happy. And looking at them now, she held on to the tiniest bit of hope that maybe they could get it right this time.

When the song ended, everyone hooted and applauded, including her.

"All right, Holly Grove Island. Are y'all ready for this?"

Sin had returned to the stage. "Because tonight, for the first time *ever*, the Holly Grove Island Players will be accompanied by a vocalist...my husband-to-be, Garrett Davenport!" Sin clapped and the crowd—who seemed just as shocked by the announcement as Em was—applauded, too.

Since when did her cousin sing?

Garrett got on the stage, kissed Sin before she exited, then adjusted the microphone to accommodate his height.

"I know you're all shocked that I'm up here. Frankly, no one is more surprised that I've agreed to this than me." Rett chuckled, and a wide smile lit her cousin's handsome face as the crowd laughed, too. "But the three things that mean most to me are friendship, family, and love. So it's for those three reasons I couldn't say no when my friend Nick Washington asked me to sing two special songs dedicated to his best friend and the love of his life—my cousin Emerie Roberts." Rett gestured toward her, and everyone else turned their attention to Em, too.

Em's eyes widened, and she pressed a hand to her open mouth—stunned that Nick had arranged something so sweet. She blew him a kiss, then placed a hand to her heart as she mouthed the words "I love you."

When Rett opened his mouth to sing the opening lines of "Yours" by Russell Dickerson, everyone in the crowd except Sinclair looked truly stunned.

Who knew her cousin could sing? And not the kind of singing voice that sounded better in the shower. The man had pipes and could actually *sang*.

Rett's gruff voice was perfectly suited to the deeply romantic, deeply emotional country song about a man grateful to be with the woman whose love brought him to life and made him a better man. Every single lyric of the song felt as if it'd been penned just for them. Because Em felt the same way about being with Nick.

She'd loved being his best friend all these years. But her life felt so much more complete now that their friendship had evolved into a romantic relationship. Nick Washington was, without a doubt, the love of her life. And now she knew that she was his, too. And so did everyone else on Holly Grove Island.

Tears slid down Em's face as Rett belted out the song and Dakota, her parents, Kassie, and so many others in the crowd watched her with tears in their eyes, too. Sin and Dakota gestured for Em to come up to the bandstand, where her parents stood together smiling at her, along with Sin, Dakota, Izzy, Kassie, and Nick's parents.

Em joined them in front of the makeshift stage, her heart thudding in her chest, and her hands shaking. She still couldn't believe that Nick had gone through all the trouble of having her serenaded at the town bonfire on New Year's Eve. And that their friends and family, who'd been so heavily invested in their relationship, were all there to witness it. She'd been so focused on the smiling faces of the people around her that she hadn't noticed that Nick had come down off the stage and was now standing beside her.

Nick gave her a nervous smile as he took both of her trembling hands in his larger, steadier ones. His dark eyes gleamed in the moonlight, and he stared at her like she was the only person in the world. Her heart swelled with love for the man she'd adored since she was ten.

"Emerie Roberts, you have been my best friend since I was twelve years old. Every one of my most cherished childhood memories...you're right there at the center of them. The years we spent apart were some of the toughest years of my life because it felt like a piece of me was missing. I moved back to Holly Grove Island because I missed having you in my life. We picked up right where we left off.

No, that's not true," he said. "We built a stronger friendship than we'd had before." Nick squeezed her hands.

Em nodded, remembering how thrilled she'd been when Nick had returned to the island.

"Our friendship was the most important thing in the world to me, Em. I was so terrified of losing it that I was afraid to admit my feelings for you. Then one year ago, you changed the trajectory of our lives when you told me how you felt about me. I freaked out and almost blew it." Nick laughed, and the crowd did, too. "I was afraid we couldn't maintain the friendship that meant so much to me *and* a relationship. But every day for the past eight months, you've proven to me that we *can* have both, and that our lives are so much better because of it. And now I know beyond a shadow of a doubt that what I want is to be with you *always*, Em. I love you more than anything in the world, and I don't ever want to be without you. So…"

Nick kneeled in the sand on one knee and pulled a black, velvet box from inside his jacket pocket. Inside was the most beautiful princess-cut diamond ring she'd ever seen. The ring wasn't just stunning; it looked as if it had been made specifically for her. The two-tone white and yellow gold ring had a thick, sturdy band enhanced with more diamonds and a scrolling design.

Em pressed a trembling hand to her mouth, her vision clouded by the fat tears that glided down her cheeks as she gazed at the incredible ring and the man who was presenting it to her. The only man in the world she'd ever really been in love with. The only man she could ever imagine spending her life with.

"Emerie Marie Roberts, I have loved you for so long. But now I truly understand what a gift and a privilege it is to have you at the center of my world. I'm thrilled to be your man, Em. But nothing would make me happier than being your husband. So would you please, please do me the honor of becoming my wife?" The corners of Nick's eyes were wet, and his voice wavered.

"I've waited my whole life for you to ask me that." Em's honest response evoked laughter from everyone around them. "Yes, Nick. I'll marry you. I can't wait to be your best friend slash wife."

Nick slid the gorgeous ring onto her finger, then rose to his feet, took her in his arms, and kissed her as the air around them filled with applause. But as his lips glided along hers, for a moment it felt as if there was no one on that stretch of Holly Grove Island Beach but the two of them.

"I love you, baby," Nick whispered in her ear once he'd finally broken their kiss.

Em grinned, stroking wetness from beneath his eyes with her thumbs. "I love you, too."

"Congrats to Nick and Emerie on your engagement. We all love you both so much, and we're so happy for you." Sin's voice wavered as she wiped tears from her cheek. She blew them a kiss. "We've got about ten more minutes before it's time to begin the countdown to the new year. But before we do, here's a song dedicated to Nick and Em. And we invite you to join our newly engaged couple for a final dance of the year."

Rett stepped up to the mic and tapped his chest twice with his open palm as he grinned at the two of them warmly. Then he started to sing "It Would Be You" by Johnny Gill.

Nick slipped his arms around her waist and started to sway as he softly sang the chorus in her ear. " 'If I could have anything, I'd put it on everything, that it would be you.' "

Em's stomach fluttered, and her pulse raced. She'd never

been happier in her life than she was in that moment. But she needed to be sure that Nick was just as happy as she was.

"So you're not still worried that we'll eventually turn into your parents?" Em asked.

Nick stopped singing and glanced over at his parents dancing together, their eyes filled with love and laughter.

"I didn't know nearly as much about my parents' relationship as I thought," he admitted. "Now that I do, I realize we'd be really lucky to end up like them...together nearly forty years, still friends, and very much in love."

Em grinned so hard her cheeks hurt. Her heart expanded in her chest, and her eyes stung with fresh tears when Nick's parents, as if on cue, waved, and his mother blew a kiss at them. Em blew a kiss back, then looked up at Nick. The raging bonfire reflected in his dark eyes burned as hot and bright as the overwhelming love and desire she had for him. "I think so, too."

She kissed her best friend—something she'd never tire of. Then she pressed her cheek to his chest as they rocked slowly to the swoony lyrics Rett belted out. They were surrounded by their friends and family on the beautiful beach that had always been home. The place where they had so many amazing memories. In the town where they planned to one day start a family and raise their children.

Nick couldn't have picked a more perfect place or a more perfect moment to ask her to marry him.

One year ago, she'd stood on this very beach, determined to find the love of her life. But along the way, she'd found so much more.

Em's confidence and sense of self had grown by leaps and bounds over the past year. She'd expanded her business, discovered an unexpected passion for dance and travel, finally identified her true sense of style, and grown exponentially as a person.

Nick had been right to turn her down when she'd first expressed her interest in him. He hadn't been ready for this then, and neither had she.

Friendships didn't always translate into great love matches. But this one had, and she was thankful for it.

Nick wrapped an arm around her waist when the count-down began. They counted down together to the new year ahead. A year filled with possibilities and the life they were planning together. They both shouted, "Happy New Year!" Then Nick pulled her into a lingering kiss as fireworks that rivaled those exploding in her chest burst into the sky over the Atlantic Ocean.

THE END

Don't miss any of the Holly Grove Island series!

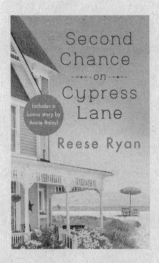 

Join Reese's newsletter list for future adventures in Holly Grove Island: https://bit.ly/VIPReaderList

About the Author

VIVIAN Award–winning author Reese Ryan writes sexy, emotional, "grown folks" romantic fiction set in small Southern towns. Her characters find love while navigating career crises and family drama. The two-time recipient of the Donna Hill Breakout Author Award is an advocate for the romance genre and diversity in fiction. Reese is the host of *The Story Behind the Story*—an interactive YouTube show where readers and authors connect. Her books have been featured in *Entertainment Weekly*, BuzzFeed, and BookRiot.

You can learn more at: ReeseRyan.com
X @ReeseRyanWrites
Instagram.com/ReeseRyanWrites
Facebook.com/ReeseRyanWrites
Tiktok.com/@reeseryanwrites
Pinterest.com/ReeseRyanWrites

Book your next trip to a charming small town—and fall in love—with one of these swoony Forever contemporary romances!

THE SOULMATE PROJECT
by Reese Ryan

Emerie Roberts is tired of waiting for her best friend, Nick, to notice her. When she confesses her feelings at the town's annual New Year's Eve bonfire and he doesn't feel the same, she resolves to stop pining for him and move on. She hatches a seven-step plan to meet her love match and enlists her family and friends—including Nick—to help. So why does he seem hell-bent on sabotaging all her efforts?

HOME ON HOLLYHOCK LANE
by Heather McGovern

Though Dustin Long has been searching for a sense of home since childhood, that's not why he bought Hollyhock. He plans to flip the old miner's cottage and use the money to launch his construction business. And while every reno project comes with unexpected developments, CeCe Shipley beats them all—she's as headstrong as she is gorgeous. But as they collaborate to restore the cottage to its former glory, he realizes they're also building something new together. Could CeCe be the home Dustin's always wanted?

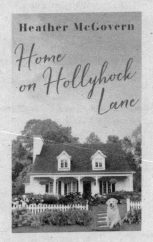

Connect with us at Facebook.com/ReadForeverPub

Discover bonus content and more on
read-forever.com

REUNION IN SUGAR LAKE
by Marina Adair

Pediatrician Charlotte Holden knows better than anyone that love leads only to heartbreak. Then sexy Jace McGraw blows back into her small town of Sugar, Georgia, and utters those three words every woman dreads: *We're still married.* The annulment went through years ago—or so she thought. But now Jace offers Charlotte a deal: He'll grant a discreet divorce in exchange for thirty days and nights of marriage. Easy as peach pie. Except this time, he isn't going to let her go without a fight.

FLIRTING WITH ALASKA
by Belle Calhoune

Caleb Stone isn't ready to give up his Hollywood dreams. But after a disastrous run on a reality dating show paints him as an unapologetic player, Caleb needs a little time and space to regroup. Luckily, his hometown of Moose Falls, Alaska, has both, plus a job helping his brothers run Yukon Cider. Even dialed down, Caleb's flirtatious vibes are a hit at work, except for one woman who seems completely, totally, frustratingly immune to his charms—the gorgeous new photographer for Yukon Cider's upcoming ad campaign.

Meet your next favorite book with @ReadForeverPub on TikTok

SUNFLOWER COTTAGE ON HEART LAKE
by Sarah Robinson

Interior designer Amanda Riverswood is thirty-two years old and has never had a boyfriend. So this summer, she's going on a bunch of blind dates. Pro baseball pitcher Dominic Gage was on top of the world—until an injury sent him into retirement. Now, in the small town of Heart Lake, his plan is to sit on his dock not talking to anyone, especially not the cute girl next door. But when they begin to bond over late-night laughter about Amanda's failed dating attempts, will they see that there's more than friendship between them?

SNOWED IN FOR CHRISTMAS
by Jaqueline Snowe

Sorority mom Becca Fairfield has everything she needs to survive the blizzard: hot cocoa, plenty of books…and the memory of a steamy kiss. Only Becca's seriously underestimated this snow-pocalypse. So when Harrison Cooper—next-door neighbor, football coach, and the guy who acted mega-awkward after said kiss—offers her shelter, it only makes sense to accept. They'll just hang out, stay safe, and maybe indulge in a little R-rated cuddling. But are they keeping warm…or playing with fire?

AN AMISH CHRISTMAS MATCH
by Winnie Griggs

Phoebe Kropf knows everyone thinks she's accident-prone rather than an independent Amish woman. So she's determined to prove she's more than her shortcomings when she's asked to provide temporary Christmas help in nearby Sweetbrier Creek. Widower Seth Beiler is in over his head caring for his five motherless *brieder*. But he wasn't expecting a new housekeeper as unconventional—or lovely—as Phoebe. When the holiday season is at an end, will Seth convince her to stay…as part of their *familye*?

CHRISTMAS IN HARMONY HARBOR
by Debbie Mason

Instead of wrapping presents and decking the halls, Evangeline Christmas is worrying about saving her year-round holiday shop from powerful real estate developer Caine Elliot. She's risking everything on an unusual proposition she hopes the wickedly handsome CEO can't refuse. How hard can it be to fulfill three wishes from the Angel Tree in Evie's shop? Caine's certain he'll win and the property will be his by Christmas Eve. But a secret from Caine's childhood is about to threaten their merrily-ever-after.